COME LIKE SHADOWS

Also by SIMON RAVEN

Novels

The Feathers of Death
Brother Cain
Doctors Wear Scarlet
Close of Play

Alms for Oblivion Sequence

The Rich Pay Late
Friends in Low Places
The Sabre Squadron
Fielding Gray
The Judas Boy
Places Where They Sing
Sound the Retreat

Essays

The English Gentleman
Boys will be Boys

Plays

Royal Foundation and other Plays

COME LIKE SHADOWS

The eighth novel in the
Alms for Oblivion *sequence*

SIMON RAVEN

First published in Great Britain 1972 by Blond & Briggs Ltd, 56 Doughty Street, London, WC1. © Copyright 1972 Simon Raven. Printed by The Anchor Press Ltd., and bound by Wm. Brendon & Son Ltd., both of Tiptree, Essex.

SBN 85634 003 0

Ulysses: Time hath, my lord, a wallet at his back,
Wherein he puts alms for oblivion . . .

SHAKESPEARE: *Troilus and Cressida*
Act III, Scene iii

Contents

Witches: Show his eyes, and grieve his heart;
Come like shadows, so depart!

SHAKESPEARE: *Macbeth*
Act IV, Scene i

PART ONE

THE LAND OF THE PHAEACIANS

Therein grow trees, high and luxuriant, pears and pome-granates and apple-trees with their coloured fruit, and sweet figs and teeming olives. Of these the fruit fails not nor fades in winter or in summer, but stays throughout the year; and ever does the west wind, as it blows, quicken to life some fruits and bring to ripeness others; pear upon pear, apple upon apple, cluster upon cluster, and fig upon fig.

Homer : *The Odyssey*; Book VII

"A thousand pounds a week," said Tom Llewyllyn. "Are you interested?"

"I could be," said Fielding Gray.

"Don't be blasé."

"I'm not. But with that sort of money there's always a great, big snag. To say nothing, in this year of the proles 1970, of great, big taxes."

"They'd do their best for you about those. They'd pay you a lot of your money in hard cash as legitimate expenses, and if you asked nicely they might bank the rest for you in Zurich."

"I thought you socialists disapproved of all that."

"Tax," said Tom, "is a matter of law, not morals. There are legal methods of doing this kind of thing, and these people understand them."

"Did they bank your money in Zurich?"

"No, because I needed it here. Here and now. Patricia's being difficult about her money . . . says she's saving it all for Baby . . . and insists that we use mine for everything."

"Silly bitch."

"Don't call my wife a silly bitch," Tom said equably.

"By making you bring your money back here, she's made you lose half of it to the Revenue."

"More than half. But that isn't your worry. They'd fix something for *you* all right . . . Zurich or Bermuda or the Virgin Islands . . . *provided,* Fielding, that you asked them nicely, like I said."

"Fielding could always talk nicely," Tessie Buttock put in.

Fielding Gray and Tom Llewyllyn were having tea in their old haunt, Buttock's Hotel, where they both still lodged when in

London. Although Tessie had been offered a huge sum, years since, for the site in Cromwell Road, she had refused out of hand. Her lease was good for another twenty years, she said, and so with luck was she, and they could bleeding well wait to put up their squitty new tower of tin and matchwood until she was in her box. So Buttock's had survived into the seventies as furtive and cosy as ever . . . and a good deal less filthy since Tessie's incontinent terrier, Albert Edward, had gone to his ancestors five years before.

"I remember how Fielding used to talk so nice to poor Albert Edward," Tessie now said, and dropped a tear into her saucer.

"Did I?" said Fielding, who neither remembered nor cared. "That's not saying I want to talk nice to all these bloody Jew-boys of Tom's."

"How do you know they're Jews?" Tom said.

"I told you. With this sort of money there's always a snag, and as a rule it's called Moishe or Isaac. Real Jewy Jews, I mean. Not like Daniel or Gregory."

"Oh, come off it, love," Tessie said. "You can't turn down a thousand a week just because it's a shonk signs the cheque."

"I don't mind 'em signing cheques," Fielding said. "It's what they want in return. Muck for the millions, delivered with an air of unction. Turds wrapped in tinsel. They won't even let you be honest about it and call a turd a turd. You've got to quiver with arty enthusiasm, pretend each fart's a divine afflatus of inspiration, so that they can ease their squalid little consciences by babbling about being creative."

"Like that, is it?" said Tessie. "I can't say I'm surprised. I remember from the Bible they always did go in for hocus-pocus. But anyway," she said, "you haven't answered Tom's question : how do you know this lot *are* Jews?"

"Tom is talking about films," said Fielding, "and the film world is heaving with them."

"Look," said Tom : "do you, or do you not, want to hear what I have to say about this rather spectacular offer? If you do, stop talking like Himmler and listen for a minute."

"That's right, Fielding dear," said Tessie, settling comfortably. "You just park your tongue and let Tom tell us all about it. I'm interested in film biz, shonks and all. I get a film book called *Titty Bits* every week, but there's nothing like hearing it personal."

"All right," said Fielding, and turned his one eye morosely to Tom. "Let's hear it personal. I hope it's up to *Titty Bits'* standard."

"Early in July," Tom began, "I was approached by Pandarus . . ."

". . . How very apt . . ."

". . . Which is a London film company," said Tom rather wearily, "and itself a subsidiary of Clytemnestra Films of New York."

"How on earth had such people ever heard of *you*?"

"If you'll just keep quiet," said Tom, flushing slightly, "you'll find out by and by. Now Pandarus, with the support of Clytemnestra, is mounting a new production of *The Odyssey*. Much of the finance, as they call it, is coming from a thing called the Oglander-Finckelstein Trust . . ."

". . . You *must* be joking . . ."

". . . An American fund, administered by Montana University, which hands out slabs of money for cultural and creative projects such as it has somehow been persuaded this version of *The Odyssey* is going to be."

"And is it?"

"It is going to be a valid cinematic equivalent," said Tom carefully, "with the emphasis on the action rather than the poetry. The Oglander-Finckelstein Trust would probably prefer it the other way round . . . in fact definitely wants it the other way round . . . and since the trustees have so far punted in only two million dollars of the eight million they have promised, the producer is having to tread warily. He commissioned a very serious and poetic script for Og-Finck's approval, and further to assure everyone of his artistic integrity he announced that he was going to employ a high-powered academic adviser, none less than the Regius Professor of Greek at Oxford University. This gentleman, as you may know, is called Hugh Lloyd-Jones;

but through some grotesque misinterpretation of *Who's Who*
the post was in fact offered to our old chum, Somerset Lloyd-
James. . . ."

And he, it appeared, had not bothered to clear up the mistake, though well aware of what must have happened. Being
too busy to take up the job himself, since he had just become
front man in the House of Commons for the Marquis of
Canteloupe (Minister of Commerce in the new Conservative
Government), Lloyd-James had politely declined the Pandarus/
Clytemnestra offer, but at the same time had recommended 'a
very learned and versatile Fellow of Lancaster College, Cambridge, Mr. Tom Llewyllyn'.

"He's done me so many bad turns in his time," said Tom,
"that I suppose he thought I was due a good one. Old Somerset
can be quite a brick . . . when he's nothing to lose by it."

However *that* might be, Foxe J. Galahead, the producer, had
weighed the name of Tom Llewyllyn, had confused it with that
of the famous novelist (Richard), had decided that this was just
what he wanted (a novelist *and* don must surely impress the
pundits of Og-Finck), and had descended on Lancaster College
in the depth of the Long Vacation to clinch the matter. But
Tom, at first, had not much wanted to be clinched.

'*The Odyssey*'s not my period,' Tom had said. 'I'm a modern
historian, Mr. Galahead. I know nothing about the Mycenean
Age.'

'Is that when it happened?'

'Roughly. The epic was written, or collated from oral tradi-
tions, around 650 B.C. It purported to be about events which
happened 500 years before, in the so-called Heroic Age, which
was a kind of epilogue to the Mycenean Age, which itself was
a kind of epilogue to the Bronze—'

'. . . Just hold it there, baby,' said Foxe ('call me Foxy') J.
Galahead. 'You seem to know enough about it to me.'

'Everyone knows that much.'

'You English, you're so modest you crucify me. But sorry,
Mr. Llewyllyn . . . I guess you're Welsh.'

'English by habit and dwelling. And preference.'

'But that book you wrote about Welsh miners...'

'...What book about Welsh miners?'

'Christ's balls, Tom, if I'd written that book ... they made a movie of it, I remember ... *How Green Was My Valley* ... if I'd written that marvellous, marvellous book, I'd go about like I had two pricks. But I guess this English modesty ... I mean Welsh modesty ... I mean ...'

At which moment Patricia Llewyllyn had arrived in Tom's college rooms with their ten-year-old daughter, Baby, just in time to stop Foxy Galahead from remembering that *How Green Was My Valley* had in fact been published in 1939 and filmed soon afterwards, and that Tom, though now over forty, must have been in knickers at the time. Not that this would have made much difference, because Foxy had taken to Tom and been very impressed by his impromptu exegesis on the date of *The Odyssey,* particularly by his use of the word 'purported'. This was the guy to show Og-Finck, and no smegma. So as far as Foxy was concerned, Tom was Foxy's man all right; and as far as Patricia was concerned, Tom was Foxy's man all right, since the job carried an enormous screw; and as far as Tom himself was concerned ... well, he had always wanted to go to Corfu, where the film was being shot, and here was Foxy waving a first-class air ticket to the place right under his nose.

"Did Patricia and Baby go too, dear?" Tessie now said.

No, answered Tom. Pandarus didn't like wives and children round the place and would have made him pay their fare, which Patricia, in line with her ever-mounting passion for economy, refused to let him do. She and Baby would be quite content at home in Grantchester, she had told him, and though Baby nearly blew the roof off ('Baby wants to go to Corfooo-ooo-ooo') and was then sick in malignant mauve all over her Levis, it had been settled that Tom should go alone. So there he was, back in July, newly appointed Academic, Historical and Literary Adviser to the Pandarus/Clytemnestra production of Homer's *Odyssey,* at £800 a week, with a bloody great suite in the Corfu Palace Hotel.

"Corfu," said Fielding, "Greece. Greece, Colonels. Colonels, Fascism. You didn't mind all that?"

"It had nothing to do with *The Odyssey*. Or with Pandarus Films."

"But Pandarus Films had to do with *it*. By bringing money into Greek territory, Pandarus Films gave comfort and even recognition of a kind to an oppressive régime of the right."

"A fat lot you care," Tessie said.

"I'll bet somebody cared," said Fielding; "the unions for a start. Some time ago there was a gloating bit in the *Guardian* which said that most unions connected with films and television had forbidden their members to assist in productions anywhere in Greece or its islands."

"That's quite true," Tom told him. "In order to spite the Colonels the union leaders would have been quite happy to shit on their own members . . . to say nothing of the ordinary Greeks who stood to benefit. But in this case there was an odd twist. You see, Pandarus is going to need four million more than the eight million dollars offered by Og-Finck, and Foxy could only raise the extra if he promised to shoot in Corfu."

"How was that?"

"The money was put up by two old gambling associates of Foxy's. Max de Freville . . ."

". . . I've met him . . ."

". . . And a Greek chum of Max's called Lykiadopoulos. They own extensive tourist installations in Corfu, and some sort of share in the casino."

"The last I saw of Max, it was Cyprus he was interested in."

"So it was. But that was no good when the rows there started up again, so they muscled in on the Corfu boom, right at the beginning. And boom it's been ever since. They could find four million for Foxy all right, and were happy to do so . . . on the absolute condition that he made the film on Corfu."

"To the great benefit, every possible way round, of their own tourist enterprises?"

"Right. But that was no skin off Foxy's nose, and he definitely needed the extra money, so in the end he put it to the unions flat : either the film would be shot on Corfu or it could not be shot at all."

Whereupon the union leaders had sneered and shrugged their shoulders; but not so the rank and file, who were sick of being out of work and watching their industry totter into its tomb. They wanted to make films, they said; their leaders had already botched up three big productions in a row by excessive demands and infantile quibbling; and if the twelve million dollar *Odyssey* was now to be cancelled just because a few grubby students disapproved of the Government in Athens, that was the last straw. In no time at all quite a rebellion had flared up; and the union leaders, seeing that they had badly misjudged this particular situation, were looking for a face-saver to enable them to back down with dignity. It was Foxy, or rather his shrewd director, Jules Jacobson, who had found a formula for them. This film, the union leaders were told, would be of great cultural and educational value (witness the backing from Og-Finck), and it was a film which, for essential artistic reasons, must be made on Corfu. For Corfu (the Homeric Scheria or Island of the Phaeacians) was where much of the story had actually happened. Not only were the territory and the coast line ideal, but immortal scenes could be shot in their exact historical locations, thus gaining both in spirit and verisimilitude (etcetera, etcetera). This did the trick : a pompous document was issued, from the headquarters of the unions concerned, announcing that a special exception to the embargo on Greece would be made in favour of the producers of *The Odyssey* because of their unique endeavours in the cause of creative international enlightenment (etcetera, etcetera). And so although a number of trendy bishops and otherwise unoccupied dons continued to snarl and screech about 'this betrayal of the Greek people', the director and his two units had taken wing on 1 July for Corfu, where they had been joined by the newly recruited Tom some seven days later.

"It's all balls," Fielding now said, "about historical locations. The whole thing's a legend . . . where it's not a fairy tale."

"I made out a very good geographical case," said Tom prim-

B

ly, "for positing that Odysseus was washed ashore on the beach at Ermones and then taken to what is now Palaeocastritsa."

"You had to do something for your eight hundred quid a week. Your director could have found that theory, for what it's worth, in any ten drachma guide book."

"Maybe," said Tom. "But it was the sort of thing which kept the unions happy. 'Topographico-historical fidelity,' we called it. And the director thinks the same tactic will pay off with Montana University and the Og-Finck Trust. 'Topographico-historical fidelity' might be good evidence of Foxy's *bona fides* . . . when he starts asking for the rest of the money."

"They'll never be taken in," said Fielding, his eye flickering in irritation. "American scholars are grindingly accurate about that sort of thing."

"Never mind all this book-talk," snapped Tessie all of a sudden. "What I want to know is, what happened to Tom when he got out there?"

"The first thing," Tom said, "was that I had dinner with the director, Jules Jacobson, who filled me in about the whole set-up."

"Jacobson. A shonk?"

"A very special one, Tessie. East End boy who finished the war with a commission and a Military Cross, and started in the film business in 1946 as cameraman for his uncle's blue movies. He'd come a long way since then, and hadn't forgotten an inch of it. . . ."

'The first rule here,' Jules Jacobson had told Tom in the restaurant of the Corfu Palace, 'is that I give the orders. I *direct.* Foxy Galahead *produces,* which means that he comes up with the cash and is entitled to common civility. But no more. If he tells you to do anything, you listen politely, and then go away and don't do it.'

Jules Jacobson was a lean, dark man with close and narrow green eyes. He wore a silk shirt, the tie of a superior though now defunct regiment of Fusiliers, no coat, and very tight trousers. He looked absolutely cool in the sticky July evening, while Tom was dripping with sweat so copiously that he would normally have felt quite embarrassed. But not with Jacobson : for Jacobson had that kind of sophisticated courtesy that refrains from noticing (and thereby increasing) discomfiture which it cannot alleviate. He also had authority of the same subtle order : for while his words (though succinct) were not especially remarkable, his manner, one of self-assured indifference, made them law, as absolutely as if they had been engraven on stone tablets.

'So just remember that,' Jacobson had said. 'Listen to Foxy, if you have to, smile if you can raise the energy, but whatever he wants, don't do it. Unless you know I want it too.'

'I suppose that could be awkward. After all, he is my employer.'

'And mine. He pays me to direct . . . among other things, to direct you. You'll find that a film company is a very hierarchical affair; there's a strict chain of command and everyone has his own clearly defined function. There's a pretence of equality . . . Christian names from top to bottom . . . but every man jack out on location has his own duties, his own status and his own privileges, and woe betide him if he tries to step outside them.'

Tom wiped his brow.

'A chain of command, you said?'

'Right.'

'Well, surely Mr. Galahead is at the head of that chain.'

'Administratively, yes. Not as regards technical or creative processes.' Jacobson used the phrase quite seriously, Tom had noted with regret. 'The staging, the acting, the shooting, the lighting, the dialogue . . . everything to do with the film as such is up to me. I've got it in my contract. It follows that you're here to advise *me;* to find the answers to the questions which *I* shall ask. So don't let Foxy send you off on wild goose chases. He's got his own ideas about this film . . . which aren't mine.'

'So he's paying his money for you to make your film?'

'Wrong. The money isn't his . . . he raises it. And I certainly can't make the film I'd like to. You've heard of the Oglander-Finckelstein Trust?'

'Mr. Galahead said something about it when he came to see me in Cambridge.'

'Just call him Foxy. As I told you, we keep up an illusion of equality; it's traditional in the trade.'

'Foxy to his face?'

'Yes. Everyone does, even the prop men. Everyone except for myself and the two top stars. We can call him "Foxy baby" if we want . . . our privilege.'

'Written into your contract, I suppose?'

Jacobson grinned.

'That's the spirit,' he said, 'Now then: the Oglander-Finkelstein Trust. . . .'

And he had begun to explain the situation, which at that time was still largely unknown to Tom. The Oglander-Finckelstein Trust, it appeared, had provided two million dollars at once, with a promise of six million to be paid later, on condition of 'satisfactory progress'. Since the initial two million had been spent on 'getting the picture off the ground' and transporting the company to Corfu, the production was now being currently financed by the four million which Max de Freville and Stratis Lykiadopoulos had paid over. Now that the company was firmly installed on its location, money would not be used so fast; but, even so, present resources would be exhausted by the end of October, and it was very important that Og-Finck should come up with its next contribution by 1 November at latest.

'Which means,' said Tom, 'that you must show proof of "satisfactory progress"?'

'What they mean by "satisfactory progress",' Jules Jacobson had emended.

And here was the rub. Proof of progress must take the form of rough-cut sequences edited out of such film as could be shot during the next three months. Apart from that, it was quite possible that representatives of Og-Finck would turn up in Corfu to inspect the company in action, and if so it would be important to create an impression of industry and dedication; but far more important, indeed essential to the whole enterprise, was that the syndics of the Trust should be pleased by 'what was already in the can'. Now, what they wanted was what was promised by the existing script: a faithful version of Homer's masterpiece, which would include much of the bard's original dialogue and even of his narrative and descriptive passages, these latter to be recited over the visual scenes as a running poetic commentary.

'And all that,' Jules had said, 'is just too much. The conception is too literary. It won't work as cinema. And yet I shall have to go as far as I can to meet them, or no more lolly.'

'And what does Mr. Gala . . . what does Foxy say?'

'He goes to the other extreme from Og-Finck. He wants to cash in on the film when it's finished, which as he sees it means filling the thing with fighting and fucking, and not a speech longer than "crap".' Jules clicked his teeth savagely and then went on : 'I suppose he thinks he can con Og-Finck along till it's too late for them to back down. *Caveat emptor*. But if he wants an Errol Flynn extravaganza, he's chosen the wrong director. I'm going to make a quality movie, Tom, and I only hope Foxy baby won't squeal too loud when he finds out.'

'But surely your contract covers you there. You said just now that you're empowered to take decisions on all the artistic questions.'

'That's certainly true, and it's also true that I can do most of the shooting when Foxy isn't here. But when he is he hangs over my neck all day yelling for blood, cunt and hurricanoes, and that, believe me, is no help at all.'

Jules, in fact, had two sets of demands to meet, each irreconcilable with the other and each hyperbolic in itself. He had a producer who wanted the crudest kind of box-office and financial sponsors who wanted the purest form of art.

'But the point is,' said Jules, 'that it wouldn't *be* art. That Homeric dialogue, for example. Hulking great five-minute speeches, marvellous pieces to read or declaim, but guaranteed to kill any film stone dead. And I don't just mean that they'd empty the cinema, which is what bugs Foxy about them, I mean that artistically and dramatically they could not work on the screen. That's what I'm concerned with, Tom : the screen.'

And so what, Tom had enquired, did Jules propose to do about it all? Well, as far as Foxy was concerned, Jules proposed

to keep him happy by really going to town on the more famous
Homeric spectaculars (which were packed with blood and hurricanoes if a little short on cunt), and at the same time to defend
the 'culture' scenes by telling Foxy that they could always omit
them from the final version but would definitely need them, in
the short run, to show to Og-Finck and secure the next lot of
money. Thus Foxy would receive the impression that Jules was
a faithful ally in the conning of Og-Finck. . . .

'. . . And that should keep him off my back for the time being.
With people like Foxy Galahead the time being is all one can
worry about.'

'So we've got blood and thunder to keep Foxy happy, and
"culture" scenes for the Oglander-Finckelstein Trust. But what
about these culture scenes, Jules? Will they satisfy Og-Finck?'

'I hope so. They'll be authentically set up for one thing . . .
that's where you come in . . . and they'll carry a full load of
Homer's dialogue and so on to please the egg-heads. I can
always strip that down in the cutting room later on.'

'After the money's all paid and it's too late for Og-Finck to
turn awkward?'

'You're learning fast. Cognac?'

'Please. I've certainly learnt more than I'd expected to in one
evening. Tell me, Jules : why are you letting a stranger into the
skeleton cupboard?'

'I like your face and I'm going to need your help. I've read
your books . . . some of them . . . and I fancy we're going to get
on.'

As indeed they had, so much so that Tom had soon become a
confidential assistant rather than a mere academic adviser.
Officially he was there to give Jules the benefit of his antiquarian
knowledge and his literary taste; he was required to explain
precisely what such and such a phrase or passage would have
signified in its Homeric context. But after he had explained, he
was increasingly often invited by Jules to join him in consider-
ing whether one or other of the actors had the capacity to render
a valid interpretation, and if not, what should be done about it.
This in turn led to long discussions of the idiosyncrasies, careers

and case histories of the entire cast, and of the best tactics Jules could use to elicit good performances or soothe wounded vanities.

'That stupid bitch,' Jules would say, of, for example, the actress who played Penelope. 'She says she's not got enough big scenes in the first half.'

'The story doesn't need them. Homer doesn't provide them.'

'So Homer doesn't provide them. So she wants them written in.'

'Then write them in. Shoot them . . . and lose them.'

'Too expensive . . . in time and money both.'

'Then say so.'

'She'll say nothing's too expensive for the star.'

'She isn't the star.'

'She thinks she is. And God help us if she ever stops.'

'Tell her it's a part of quality rather than length.'

'She wouldn't understand, Tom. She's over forty, she's been a household name for twenty years, and she's made her career in a world in which the star is all-important and has the longest and juiciest part.'

'So he does—Odysseus. She can't think she's as important as he is.'

'Not quite that. But she thinks she's the only woman in the piece that counts.'

'Then she must be potty. There's Circe, Calypso, Nausicaa . . .'

'. . . She won't know about them, Tom. She'll only have read her own scenes, and all she knows is there's not enough of them.'

'Only have read her own scenes?'

'You don't know these people. They're barely literate, some of them—they're moronic. Morons who have the right kind of faces and a gift of mimicry, which on a good day they can pass off as acting. Compared with a lot of 'em this Penelope of ours is a queen. At least she learns her lines . . .'

'. . . And doesn't get drunk by ten in the morning, like Odysseus.'

'Let's leave him out for now. Today's problem is Penelope.

She wants more scenes, she can't have them, and she's going to piss all over everybody if she doesn't get them. Just what does a man do?'

'Start pissing on her first,' Tom said. 'Tell her it'll be time to think about new scenes when she gets her present ones right.'

'But she is getting them right . . . as right as she ever will. No good wrecking her confidence by crabbing decent work.'

'Then find her a lover to keep her quiet.'

'She likes police-women. *London* police-women.'

'So dig up some brawny dyke and tell her it's a London police-woman on holiday here in Corfu.'

'She prefers them in uniform.'

'Sweet Jesus Christ, Jules. . . .'

But eventually the problem had been settled simply by extending Penelope's speeches in her existing scenes to their maximum Homeric length. In this way the wretched woman was given so much homework that she had no time left for further complaint; and although, as Jules observed, it would mean another massive job in the cutting room, that worry could wait.

Comparable problems, of which there were many, were solved by comparable devices. The most serious and persistent difficulty was the inebriety of Odysseus, a grizzled and internationally loved survivor of wartime naval romances, who gave of his best only when he had drunk two-thirds of a bottle of whisky but gave out altogether when he had emptied the whole. The amounts of liquor involved were constant and exact, nor was there ever any variation by so much as the tenth of a gill : at one-third of a bottle the star became passable, at two-thirds (dead on the line) he became brilliant, and at three-thirds he was a goner . . . to the drop. Fortunately the very precision of these mathematics made Jules's job just possible : a specially graded decanter was procured which served the function of a clock, the whole of the day's shooting being governed, not by the passing of the hours, but by the sinking level of Odysseus's bourbon. On days when the level was sinking too fast, and that meant most days, Jules had to work desperately to keep the hero on set and finish the take before the final and fatal measure went down the red lane and Odysseus slumped into unbreachable coma; but at least, as Jules told Tom, a quick glance at the scale on the decanter would always tell him exactly where he was with Odysseus and exactly what quality of acting he could expect, which made it a lot easier than working with most of the booze-artists he'd known.

And so, since Jules and Tom between them found some sort of formula to control everything from Odysseus's dipsomania to the home-sickness of the clapper-boy (who was allowed one free telephone call a week to his mother in Islington), the film had begun, as Jules expressed it, to build. Throughout July and August, while the Second Unit busied itself with stunts for the spectaculars, Jules had divided his time between the early scenes in the absent Odysseus's palace and the amorous and knock-about escapades on Circe's island. During the former he had been able to make much therapeutic and exhausting work for the exigent Penelope; and by his speedy completion of the latter he had happily made possible the early departure for England of the actress cast as Circe, a venomous little witch who had only got the part 'by doing a blow-job on Foxy' and was upsetting the entire company by the airs she put on in celebration of this achievement.

With Circe gone and Foxy, for one reason or another seldom present, Jules had good cause to be pleased with himself. The work (even Circe's) had been excellent; the company's morale stood high; progress went on well up to schedule; expenses were not quite as savage as they might have been. But there was one ugly fly buzzing in the ointment, one anxiety which inexorably mounted : the quality of the script.

"Lawks," Tessie Buttock almost shouted. "More bloody book-talk. What I want to hear about is that Circe . . . her and those blow-jobs."

"You've heard all I know about that," said Tom, "and by this time Circe was gone."

"Didn't give you a turn before she went then?"

"No, Tessie. I'm a married man . . ."

". . . Phooey . . ."

". . . And whether you like it or not I was much too busy with this script. Whatever *Titty Bits* may imply, it's scripts and not blow-jobs that get pictures made."

And the script from which they were working in Corfu had started to present more snags with every hour that passed. It was, as it had to be, the same script as had been shown to the Oglander-Finckelstein Trust, specially prepared by a well briefed and corrupt screen-writer to keep the trustees sweet, short of action, long on poetry and talk. But despite this Jules was confident, as he had explained to Tom, that he could expand the action as he went along and strip away any excess of talk (with or without the approval of Og-Finck) when the film was finally edited. The immediate problem for both of them was something else again : not the length of the dialogue but its language. For the author had totally failed to find an English idiom which in any way answered their needs. In the heavier and bloodier scenes he had merely used, *verbatim,* the pastiche-biblical language of the translation by Butcher and Lang; while for social or domestic events he had switched straight over, ignoring the stylistic contrast, to the demotic version by Rieu, occasionally and fortuitously inserting a chunk of T. E. Lawrence.

In all fairness, the result, though heterogeneous, read rather well; but it was deadly difficult in the acting. For a start, none of the three translations came at all trippingly off the tongue, or not off the tongues which had been hired by Pandarus; and then the juxtaposition of different styles (heroic in one scene, folksy in the next) imposed far too great a strain on the talents of Odysseus and Penelope. Although both could manage not implausibly a wide range of facial expressions, neither was capable of frequent and radical shifts in verbal usage, for after all, as Jules remarked, they weren't 'bloody Gielgud and Evans'.

All this being so, what was needed was new dialogue throughout. The poet's narrative, Jules conceded, such of it as he would retain, might possibly be left, as it was cast at present, in antique English; for this would give the thing a certain 'background', and Jules had a very good man (an unfrocked priest) who could do the unseen Homer's 'voice over' in tones appropriately bardic; but when it came to the speeches of the characters themselves, Jules said, these must all be rewritten in one style, and that a modern one, which should be uniform enough to suit the limited elocutive powers of the actors, yet flexible enough to compass all the passions with which the poet had endowed his *personae*. The new version, Jules had enthused, must have Lang's dignity without his archaism, Rieu's fluidity without his commonplace, and Lawrence's subtle insight without his preciosity : it must also breathe the aristocratic spirit of the legend without being in any way offensive to egalitarian nostrils.

'Rather a strong order,' as Tom had observed. 'Whom shall you get to do it?'

'You and me between us. We've done a good bit already.'

'We've done a bit of tinkering where we could. What you're talking about now is a complete rebore.'

'We'll take it piece by piece as it comes.'

'We can't do it, Jules. It's a job for an expert.'

'Look, Tom. What we want are speeches which make sense of the story and which our crumby actors can enunciate without swallowing their false teeth. On these actors we *are* experts.'

'But not on translating Homer.'

'It doesn't have to be too exact. We just get the gist of what they've got to say and give 'em words in which to say it as naturally as possible. You've written a novel . . .'

'. . . One novel, years ago . . .'

'. . . So you can knock out natural dialogue.'

'But this isn't natural dialogue, Jules. It's governed by all sorts of conventions. These people are gods and kings and heroes and ghosts, and they talk in a special way.'

'Then find an equivalent of that special way, in clear, sharp English which the Odeon audience will understand.'

'Odeon Leicester Square, or Odeon Leyton Orient?'

'Both. Straight, simple stuff, but with an air about it. Like Robert Bolt writes.'

'Like Robert Bolt gets paid for.'

'So you want more money?'

'No,' said Tom the socialist. 'I'm already paid far too much.'

'Then earn it by writing me this dialogue.'

'I can try, I suppose.'

'That's my boy,' Jules had said. 'Start with that bit where Telemachus calls on Nestor.'

'Oh, Jesus Christ, Jules, have a heart. The old sod talks for pages. . . .'

But Tom had sat down and done his laborious best, the more laborious in that Jules, who would normally have helped him, was suddenly preoccupied with an absurd local crisis.

This had its origin in the tactless social behaviour of the company's ten starlets. These girls, who were there to play hand-maidens and the like, had a habit of sitting in the Arcade outside the Corfu Bar through the long hot evenings and soliciting the attentions of any Greek youth who was not still in knickers. The authorities were long since inured to the immodest costume and predatory custom of tourists of all sexes, but the starlets' goings-on went beyond all previous limits. There were violent scenes of exploratory passion on the cricket ground just over the road from the bar; and on two occasions liaisons had been con-summated on the pitch itself, to the applause of hysterical schoolboys, who packed the close field. Fearing lest such perfor-mances should become fashionable, the Corfiot police had at last asked Jules to give the young ladies a warning. He had done so and been (for once) flouted : their private lives, the girls said, were their own. Not, said Jules, if they were carried on in public. Even in easy-going Corfu, he told them, the Greeks had a strain of puritanism which was to be respected. But all to no avail. Two nights later the youngest and juiciest starlet had been apprehended by the police while wailing like a banshee in the extreme throes of orgasm, which had been induced by a waiter from a neighbouring restaurant in an open car parked on the boundary line. She had been led off with her lover to the lock-up, still spasmodically jerking, amid cries of 'Filthy Fascists' from her colleagues at the tables in the Arcade, who had been narrowly restrained by a senior cameraman from active inter-vention.

So it was now Jules's job to get the wretched girl out from behind bars and save her from criminal prosecution under about ninety-nine different headings.

'What was the man like,' Tom had asked Jules, 'this waiter?'

'An absolute beast. Youngish, but with a face like a hog. All snout and jowl.'

'Then try saying she was raped.'

'They'll know that's not true,' said Jules. 'Girls from outside Greece actually *prefer* men like that. There's plenty of nice English and American boys about this summer, but all the women from nine to ninety are hot for black bristly Greeks.'

'Well, why?'

'Novelty. They think the Greeks want it much more and bang it in much harder.'

'Exactly,' Tom insisted. 'They're as good as getting themselves raped. Every woman's dream, I'm told . . . to be tied to the bed and shagged by a gorilla. Nasty, brutish and quick.'

'Maybe. But Elena wasn't tied and she wasn't forced. And it certainly wasn't quick. They were both bawling away for a good ten minutes. That's why the police came.'

'Bawling?'

'With pleasure, Tom. Quite unmistakably, I'm told. Whatever you say, we cannot get this thing up to look like rape. So what are we to do?'

'Push it all on to Foxy's plate.'

'He won't be here for at least a week. Max de Freville or his pal Lykiadopoulos might have been able to cope, but they're both in Athens.'

'Look,' said Tom. 'As far as I can make out there's nothing these people won't do to bring tourists in . . . except let them use hash. They're ravaging the whole coast with their obscene package hotels, they're killing half the trees on the island to widen the roads for charabancs, and they wouldn't at all mind turning the whole place into one huge air strip. Now, we're not exactly tourists but we're all the things which go with tourism . . . foreign money, advertisement, mass entertainment . . . we're the whole modern world rolled into one, and they're keen as Beelzebub to have us. So don't you tell me that a few crisp bank notes won't get that little girl out of quod before you can say *efcharisto.*'

'A few years ago, perhaps. But the new régime likes to boast about not being corrupt or coercible. They don't like arresting foreigners, but when they have to they show no fear or favour. It's all to do with what they call the new Hellenic sovereignty.'

'But in the case of a major film company . . . which they're jolly lucky to have here at all. . . .'

'In such a case,' said Jules, 'they draw the line very low on the page. Very low indeed. But where they do draw it, Tom, they draw it very firmly. You mentioned hash just now. They could easily take a soft attitude on that, at any rate for foreigners, but they just won't do it; it's below their line and there's a score of young Americans in their prisons with five-year sentences to prove it.'

'And Elena's fallen below the line too, you reckon?'

'I know damn well she has. A public fuck on the cricket ground . . .'

'. . . On the boundary . . .'

'. . . Within fifty yards of the Arcade, Tom, making a racket-like the entire London Zoo in rut, *and* after due warning about such behaviour had been very civilly given. Of course it's below any possible line, and no amount of crisp bank notes can change that.'

'Then what will? We need her out to start getting her ready for the Nausicaa sequence.'

The two of them had paused in their walk along the Peripatos and stared across the bay towards the fortress.

'What makes it worse,' Jules had said, sitting heavily down on the balustrade, 'is all that yelling about Fascists when she was arrested. She joined in, you see.'

'Resisted arrest, in fact?'

'They could say so.'

'Face,' said Tom : 'that's the key to it all. I'm sure they'd let her out if they could do it without losing face. What does the Greek lawyer say?'

'Shrugs his shoulders and pouts.'

'And the Vice-Consul?'

'Doesn't want to know about it.'

'Impasse.'

'It certainly seems so.'

And the bay darkened as the sun went down behind the western hills. But two days later Elena had reappeared, as juicy as ever and quite unrepentant, for a preliminary fitting of the costumes for the Nausicaa scenes; and Jules, whom Tom had hardly seen since their conversation on the Peripatos, had arrived in the dressing room to supervise, grinning like a monkey. 'How did you do it?' Tom said during the first break.

'A graceful compliment from Pandarus Films to the Administration. I went round to the Nomarch and two or three other big-wigs and offered 'em walking-on parts as Phaeacian nobles . . . for the palace scenes and the games. An appropriate way of memorializing all the kindness and cooperation we had received from them, I said—oh, and just one little problem : if we didn't have Elena for the Princess Nausicaa's handmaid we couldn't do the Phaeacian scenes at all. She was out within the hour.'

'Very neat.'

'It was your remark about face that made me think of it. Concern for face is a symptom of unsatisfied vanity, and that's what's the matter with all these ridiculous Greeks. Excessive vanity with nothing whatsoever to be vain about. So if only, I thought, one could find some pabulum for their hungry egos, they could afford to relax and make themselves amenable about Elena. And hey-presto, my dear, I was right.'

'It may not be much fun . . . trying to direct a bevy of screen-struck bureaucrats.'

'Only three or four of them. And when they find out how boring and exhausting it is to be on set all day doing the same thing fifty times over, they'll probably back out. Meanwhile, we've got little Elena back, and now we can really buckle down to the Nausicaa bits. I want you to drop everything else and start re-scripting the scene where they discover Odysseus on the beach.'

'You agree it should be done at Ermones?'

'If that's where you think it really happened. The Nausicaa sequence is going to be our big thing to show Og-Finck, and we want every mark for culture we can get.'

'I'm going to have torture with the script, Jules. The girl Nausicaa is one of the most touching figures in literature.'

'So why is that torture?'

'It's all so delicate. Her speeches are some of the subtlest and most beautiful in *The Odyssey* . . . and you want them re-written for your Odeon audience. Can't you conceive how hideously hard that will be? It's one thing to do Odysseus being brave or Penelope being faithful: but Nausicaa . . . she'll shrivel at a touch.'

'So it's difficult,' said Jules. 'So don't stand here talking. Go back to your expensive suite in the Corfu Palace and get to work. I'll look in on you this evening. Now I've fixed this bother about Elena I'll have more time free to help you again.'

So Tom had gone back to the Corfu Palace Hotel, and sat down at his desk, and gazed out towards Epirus over the wine-dark sea; and then he had opened his *Odyssey* at the beginning of Book VI. . . .

. . . "Look," said Tessie in Buttock's Hotel. "What I want to know is, where does Fielding come in on all this?"

"Very soon now, Tessie. You'll see."

"I mean, that's what it's all leading up to? Fielding getting a job?"

"His being offered a job, Tessie. We don't yet know if he'll take it."

"Get on with the story," Fielding said. "There you were, sitting in your plush hotel. . . ."

. . . And reading Book VI of *The Odyssey,* for about the nine-tieth time. Odysseus, newly washed ashore on the island of the Phaeacians, was huddled beneath the brushwood near a river-mouth, 'overcome with weariness and sleep'; and meanwhile the goddess Athene had gone up into the city to rouse the little princess Nausicaa and send her to find and succour the naked voyager. . . .

'. . . Ἡ δ'α'νέμου ὡς πνοιή . . . *Like a breath of air the goddess sped to the couch of the maiden, and stood above her head, and spoke to her, taking the form of the daughter of Dymas, a girl of like age with Nausicaa and dear to her heart:*

' *"Nausicaa, how comes it that thy mother bore thee so heedless? Thy bright garments are lying uncared for; yet thy marriage is near at hand, when thou thyself shalt be clad in fair raiment and must give other such to the companions of thy train . . . Nay, come, let us go out early in the day to wash thy robes . . . for thou shalt not long remain a maid unwed. Even now thou hast wooers in the land, the noblest of all the Phaeacians."* '

So Nausicaa rose with the dawn, persuaded the king her father to lend her mules and a waggon for the day, and set out with her handmaidens and the dirty laundry, which latter she proposed to wash near the sea-shore, 'in the fair streams of the river, where were the washing tanks that never failed'.

At this stage, Tom reached for the script. The original script-writer had handled all this by cutting straight from the beach, on which the waves had just deposited the exhausted Odysseus, to the Palace yard, where Nausicaa and her handmaids were loading the laundry on to the waggon while her kindly mother brought out provisions for a picnic. This method satisfactorily dispensed with Athene's divine interference (a recurrent embarrassment), but it did not give a proper idea (Tom thought) of the family's role and importance. However, this was easily rectified. Tom scribbled a note in the margin, recommending that a regal Alcinous and several attendant noblemen (a good scene for the Nomarch and his chums) should make an imposing appearance to wave the princess off. So far, then, no real difficulties.

Tom now went back to Homer. Nausicaa and her handmaidens (including Dymas's daughter, the pick of the bunch, who was to be played by the juicy and delinquent Elena) arrived at the river, did the washing, put it out to dry on the beach, had a bathe, ate their picnic, and then 'put off their headgear and

C

began to play at ball, and white-armed Nausicaa was leader of
their song.'

No difficulty here, Tom thought. The script followed the
Homeric text in giving a full account of the girls' activities,
which Jules would stage as he thought fit. But what about this
song they were singing as they played with their ball? Had anyone thought of that? Not that Tom knew of. And yet a song was
surely essential to this enchanting scene, a song of the dreams
of maidenhood, a modest epithalamium in anticipation of the
wedding days they all longed for. 'SONG,' Tom wrote in the
margin : 'suggest it be based on VI 11. 30 to 40 (thoughts of
marriage) which do not otherwise appear in script.' And who
would write it? Not his worry, for God's sake.

His worries really began (and how) with Homer's next
incident.

Just before it was time to load up the waggon and start for
home . . . 'the princess tossed the ball towards one of her handmaids, and threw it wide of her, and cast it into a deep eddy,
and thereat they all cried out aloud' . . . and woke up Odysseus,
who was still sleeping off his marine exertions under some nearby bushes. 'Thus he spoke in his heart : "O woe is me, to what
land of men am I now come?" ', and got up to go and find out.
'Forth he came like a mountain lion', having only a branch of
leaves to shield his nakedness, and at once the girls panicked
and ran off to hide . . . all except Nausicaa, who, being a princess, stood her ground. All *that* was all right : what was very
much not all right was the exchange of speeches which now
followed.

Odysseus flattered the princess and asked for help; the princess fell for Odysseus's caddish weather-beaten charm and
promised to take him to her royal parents. That was the essence
of it; but of course the situation was far too delicate, and the
nuances beneath the exchange were far too subtle, for the whole
thing to be settled just like that. The speeches, in consequence,
were canny, sensitive, elaborate, highly stylised and exceedingly
long. As literature they worked superbly, but on the screen they
just could not work, no matter how one translated them. How

the devil, Tom asked himself desperately, was the thing to be done?

The existing script simply gave the speeches straight out of Homer, in Rieu's translation. Sound stuff but flat. Tom himself had been reading from the Greek, as far as he could manage, and otherwise from a standard translation of the 'biblical' school : this, he knew, was quite adequate but far too heavy and mannered for the screen. As Jules had said, a new idiom was required. But what idiom could possibly achieve what was needed? How could a modern audience ever be made to sit through Odysseus's speech of rococo flattery and accept it as plausible, accept that it would do the trick? And what on earth was one to do with the passage later on about the joys of marriage? 'For nothing is stronger or better than this, that a man and his wife dwell in their home of one accord, a great grief to their enemies and a joy to their friends; but best of all do they know it themselves.' A beautiful and moving passage in itself, but the very last thing one wanted tacked on to this already voluminous supplication. Of course these lines could be cut out . . . but oh the pity if they were. And of course they could be kept in . . . but then what about the sheer unreality which would result?

"Well, what about it?" said Fielding Gray in Buttock's Hotel. "It's part of the Homeric convention?"

"But the conventions of Homer and those of the modern cinema just cannot be reconciled. Or not by me. I sat there all the rest of the morning. I had no lunch . . ."

". . . That was silly, dear . . ."

". . . And I sat there half the afternoon, sweating and striving, willing myself to do it. And still I was no nearer even beginning to find the sort of language Jules wanted."

"I wonder you weren't ill, dear."

"Oh, I was. Sick at the heart, Tessie. So in desperation I rang down for a company car and I drove out to the beach at Ermones. Hoping for . . . inspiration . . . comfort . . . God knows what. Peace and quiet at any rate, for it's a lonely little place. They're putting a hotel there, of course, but it won't be up till next year; and for the time being there's just an arc of sand, a hundred yards or so, with rocks and then sheer cliffs at either end, a few olive trees on the bare slopes above it, and this stream, which still flows right down across the beach and into the sea. And when I got there . . . Tessie . . . Fielding . . . I could see it. The girls doing the washing in the stream, a little way up in the tanks, and then bathing and eating their picnic on the beach, and playing with their ball and singing . . . until suddenly the ball goes into the water, and everyone starts squealing and giggling . . . and out of the scrub comes the old rotter himself, covered with salt brine and goat-shit, and only the princess has the guts to stand still and listen to him. A ravishing scene, Fielding, Tessie, and so bloody right . . . right for the screen too, if only it hadn't been for those speeches. And here was I, being given the chance to make them right too, to do the one thing still needed to put this miraculous scene on film . . . and I just couldn't do it. I knew I couldn't do it. I tell you, I sat there and wept . . . the driver thought I was potty . . . till the sun started to go down, just about the time Nausicaa and her party would have been setting off home after they'd cleaned up Odysseus. So I watched them starting from the beach and up along the river, Odysseus walking with the handmaids behind the waggon; and then I made the driver take me to where I could see them all turning away across the fields, towards Palaeo-castritsa as it's called now, getting smaller and smaller as I waved to them over the new golf course; and then I cried a bit more; and then at last I drove back to Corfu and went straight to Jules Jacobson and told him that I'd failed."

'You haven't had time to try,' Jules had said.

'I can't do it, Jules. And that's final.'

'You've done all right up till now.'

'You haven't asked for much up till now. Just a bit of fiddling with the dialogue. But now that you want it . . . transformed . . .'

'You're damn right I do. *And* for the scenes we've already shot, Tom. I've been thinking about them and they won't do now. We've got to go back and shoot them again . . . the bits with dialogue, that is . . . so that there'll be the same sort of language all through.'

'I wonder,' Tom had said, 'that any films ever get made, if this is the way you all go on. We've been here since July, Jules, two solid months, and *now* you decide to begin again from scratch. You really mean you're going to scrap all you've done?'

'Only the dialogue. The action can stand.'

'That still means a hell of a lot of work . . . and money . . . just thrown into the gutter. What'll Foxy say?'

'That's my business. I shall tell him my decision . . . or a version of it . . . when he arrives tomorrow. What we've done hasn't been wasted, Tom. You could say that we've been experimenting with different styles.'

'And still haven't found the right one.'

'I was relying on you to do that.'

The voice had been neutral, not reproachful, and all the more hurting for that.

'You were asking too much. I'm sorry, Jules, but I'm not a magician. And even if I were, I haven't time. Three weeks at most, and I must be back in Cambridge.'

'You could postpone that.'

But Tom could not postpone that. Until recently he had been only a supernumerary fellow of Lancaster, more or less free to come and go as he pleased, but the previous spring he had been elected to a full college fellowship and appointed a Tutor in Modern History. Besides, he had a book to see through the University Press. By 5 October at latest he must be back for the new academic year; back, he now told himself, in the real world, having quitted these realms of fantasy for good. Not that he hadn't enjoyed his time on Nausicaa's island; but the dream was beginning to turn into a nightmare, and he was very glad to have an ungainsayable reason to be gone.

And Jules had understood. With the versatility of his kind, he immediately abandoned a plan which could no longer hold and felt up into the air for a new one.

'Right,' he said; 'so here's what I'll tell Foxy. Tom's done all he can for us, I'll say, and he's set us well on the right lines. The only thing is, there's a bit of a hang-up over the dialogue ... which we must get right, if only for the sake of Og-Finck. So, I'll say to Foxy, what we do is this : we go ahead shooting action scenes only, and meanwhile we get a good man to rewrite the talk from A to Z. A man who knows Greek, who has a taste for this kind of story, a man who can handle character and conversation, a man ...'

'. . . Fielding Gray,' Tom had said without really thinking.

'And who might he be ?'

'A novelist who is well thought of for his dialogue and has a knowledge of Greek Literature.'

'Any scripts ?'

'Not that I know of. So you'll get him cheap . . . by your standards.'

'Shall I like him ?'

'Probably . . . if you like me.'

And that had been enough. The next day Jules had put it to Foxy in Tom's presence. Tom (he learned to his own surprise) had been one of the most clear-sighted and creative advisers with whom it had ever been a director's good fortune to work; but now he had fulfilled his task and must return to his college. The only thing which Tom and Jules hadn't *quite* settled between them, Jules said, was the final cast of the dialogue, and Tom had recommended a friend who would come out and deal with that.

'A lovely friend of Tom's ?' mused Foxy. 'And what might he be called ?'

'Fielding Gray.'

'Man who wrote *Tom Jones* ?'

'Pretty much in the same class,' said Jules, without moving a muscle. 'He's won all the best prizes, Foxy, and Tom reckons he'll understand our problem.'

'Well, I dunno, Jules. Any friend of Tom's, but I dunno.'

'Look, Foxy. While you've been away, little Elena's been in the Greek pokey.'

'*Elena?* However did little El . . .'

'. . . And the only reason she's out again now, and sitting in her room this minute waiting to wrap her boobies round your prick, is because Tom thought up a way to spring her.'

'Gee, Tom baby, I sure am . . .'

'. . . So if Tom recommends someone to do a job, Foxy, then we trust him, baby boy, because Tom Llewyllyn knows what he's at.'

'Well, I'll have to take a little time . . .'

'. . . We've no time to take, Foxy. So just say the word . . . and then you can run off to Elena.'

'Okay, okay. So we'll have this Fielding guy. Any friend of Tom's, like I said. . . .'

'Why did you press it so hard?' said Tom when Foxy had gone panting off.

'Because I want someone . . . different from all these . . . to talk to. Someone like you. Of course, Foxy will want something in return.'

'Like what?'

'When the new dialogue's ready, we'll have to re-shoot the scenes on Circe's island. Ten to one he'll want Circe's part for Elena . . . or whoever's chewing him by then.'

'You'll agree to that?'

'No. I'll get the original Circe back here from England. She's a crabby little bitch but she can act.'

'What'll you give Foxy then?'

'I'll see when the time comes. We'll think of something.'

'We?'

'Me and this Fielding Gray. He'll help me over things like that?'

'I dare say. But watch him, Jules. He's had a few shocks in his life and he can get some funny ideas.'

'Now you tell me. But I'll chance that if he's everything else you say. You'd better be off, Tom. Since you're going, go fast. Go fast, and send me Fielding Gray.'

"So they've got a contract ready for you," said Tom to Fielding in Buttock's Hotel. "A thousand a week for two weeks on probation. If Jules likes your work, and if he likes you, they'll sign you up for three months further. Fourteen thousand pounds, my dear : go there and get it."

"How do I know they'll like my work? What they want is impossible."

"But what is not impossible," Tom said, "is to make them think that they're getting it. They're short of time, Fielding; anything that reads straight and clear will pass for genius."

"Then why didn't you serve it up?"

"Because I'd have known I was giving short measure, and I didn't want to do that either to Homer or to Jules Jacobson. Your conscience, I fancy, is less delicate. You can settle quite happily for second best."

"That's what we all do in the end." Fielding narrowed his eye at Tom. "Don't be so damned smug."

"Sorry. But one thing more, Fielding. Don't let Jules down. Don't cheat him."

"You've as good as said I've got to. You've told me that this dialogue he wants can't ever really be written . . . you've admitted that he'll have to be fobbed off."

"I'm not talking about the dialogue now. As to that, do the best you can and there an end of it. I meant in other ways, Fielding. Don't do what you did to me over that BBC business in Athens. *Don't desert.*"

"There were special circumstances."

"There always are for men like you."

"If you feel like that, I wonder you've recommended me this time."

"Off the top of my head. But come to think of it, it's time you got off your arse and went somewhere."

"I don't yet know that I shall."

"Oh, don't be a drag, dear," said Tessie. "Think of all them girls . . . waiting to wrap their boobies round your prick. I must say, Tom seems to have wasted his time . . . just talking to that dreary shonk Jacobson."

"From the sound of it," said Fielding, "that's just what I'll be expected to do."

"You'll like him, Fielding. And you'll get plenty of chances to amuse yourself . . . if you want to."

"Of course he'll want to," Tessie said. "And perhaps he'll have something worth telling at the end of it. Not all this crap about maidens dancing on beaches."

"Be quiet, you wretched old bag," said Fielding. And to Tom, "When does he expect to hear?"

"There's a ticket waiting for you at Pandarus' London office in Curzon Street. Just book a flight and wire your time of arrival."

"I see. But I'm still not sure, mind you. I'll have to discuss it with Harriet."

Harriet Ongley was Fielding's mistress, with whom he had lived on the Norfolk coast for the last eight years. He had also to some extent lived off her, and still did. For although his novels were reputable and even, as novels go, quite profitable, his income was seldom more than £3000 a year; and had it not been for the very comfortable number of dollars which the widow Ongley had inherited ten years before from her husband, Fielding would have lacked for many of his favourite refinements, to say nothing of the large and pleasant villa in which they lived at Broughton Staithe. This looked out over the end of the golf course and on to the salt-marshes, where Fielding and Harriet were now walking in the early evening after his return from London. Harriet, her round face glowing with sea-side health and her round legs (not bad for fifty) bare and brown above her sandals, was trying to make a brisk pace, since she took a puritanical view of walks; but Fielding, who did not, only lagged behind her every time she put on pressure, and after a minute at most she had to turn and wait while he sauntered over the gap.

"You'll never take off weight this way," she said.

"I don't want to. A certain solidity is becoming in a middle-aged man."

"And leads to coronary thrombosis. What did Dr. La Soeur have to say?"

It was to visit the doctor that Fielding had been in London.

"Dr. La Soeur is a man of the world. He is tolerant of middle-aged solidity."

"He can't think that you're fit."

"We didn't discuss that," Fielding said. "He talked about my face."

Harriet, who had been just about to race ahead again, slackened her step.

"There's nothing wrong?"

"No more than there has been for the last twelve years. The fittings are sound. The Cyclops' eye will continue to see."

"Oh," said Harriet, relieved. "I thought there might be an infection or something."

"No. The Army surgeons did a good job . . . by the standards of 1958. But it seems there are people who could do a much better job now . . . aesthetically, I mean. For a high price, of course."

"We can pay it."

"You can, perhaps. But I told him 'no'."

"Oh Fielding, sweet. Why?"

"I'm only just getting used to this face. I don't want to spend the next ten years getting used to another."

This was true; but it was also true that Fielding did not wish to become further beholden to Harriet Ongley than he already was. To owe her for his very face would be too much.

"Besides," Fielding went on, "a handsome artificial face . . . if it *were* handsome . . . would be even more obscene than a hideous one. And think of the embarrassment when one's friends didn't recognise one. 'I'm Fielding Gray,' I'd have to say. 'Oh no, you're not,' they'd say. 'Fielding's got a face like a marzipan pig.' I'd probably have to get my prick out to prove it, and not *all* my friends would recognise me by that."

This was the sort of remark which Harriet hated more than anything, as Fielding well knew. Now, as so often lately, he was very keen to annoy Harriet, in order to prove to himself, and to her, that he could risk her anger, that she hadn't bought him, that he was still, at bottom, independent. But Harriet knew this particular game as well as he did; she stopped to examine a marsh shrub, picked off a small spray which she tucked into the top of her skirt, and then said, in a reasonable and slightly bored tone of voice :

"If you don't intend to have it done, why mention it in the first place?"

"To show you that I no longer care about it. Any more than I care about getting fat. And let me tell you, I've got nowhere near so fat as Tom Llewyllyn."

"You've seen him?" said Harriet, without much pleasure. I'll soon get her bate going now, Fielding thought.

"Yes," he said. "He'd just got back from Corfu and was spending the night at Tessie's. Now, Tom had something *really* interesting to say."

Harriet, playing at the game with some skill, showed no desire to hear it, but Fielding told her, even making the effort to keep up with her in her brisker spurts of walking, so that she shouldn't miss a word. He was not trying to tell her good news; he was spitefully (as he thought, subtly) demonstrating that after all he was famous, that he could be rich, that he could do without Harriet Ongley. But Harriet, still playing cleverly, merely turned her face away, whenever she thought it might show how much he was hurting, and pretended to gaze at the distant dunes.

"Of course you must go," she said when he had finished.

She wasn't meant to say this. She was meant to say that he would be prostituting himself and his art, she was meant to beg him to stay there in Broughton, so that he could round on her and accuse her of bossing and possessing and managing, of stifling and maiming his whole life.

"Ongley had a cousin," she went on blandly and carefully, "whose brother-in-law was something to do with the Oglander-Finckelstein Trust. It's a very fine organisation, Fielding. You're lucky to work for it."

"I'm not working for it," he grated through his twisted mouth : "I'll be working . . . if I do work . . . for Pandarus Films.

And the whole point of what I've been telling you is that Pandarus Films are taking Og-Finck for a ride."

"I don't know. From what you say Tom said, this director . . . Jacobson . . . is going to do a serious job."

"But not quite the job that Og-Finck wants him to do."

"He's going some way to meet them. They'll come to terms, you see. That's the best anyone can hope for in this world . . . to come to terms."

"You really are very naïve, Harriet. With a man like Foxe J. Galahead producing, the whole affair will turn into a tit-show."

"But Tom said that the director has the first and last word on how the film's actually made."

"And Galahead has a great many words in between. Half the girls have been hired to lick his cock."

That would surely do the trick : both Harriet the feminist and Harriet the maternal protectress would hate and fear this crude vision of the seraglio. As indeed Harriet did; but far greater than her distaste for such a vision was her sorrow over the unkindness and ingratitude which had made Fielding conjure it. He had accepted her in the role of mother as well as mistress from the very beginning, when she had first picked him out of the dirt, both literally and figuratively, eight years ago in Greece. Now, as she knew, he was rejecting her in the mother-role, so she had tried to slough it; yet here he was scheming to push her back into it, so that he might have the better target to resent and to violate. Well, she would not be caught that way.

"It's no good telling me all this," she said. "You must decide for yourself : either you take the job or you don't. If I were you I'd take it. It'll do you good, and your work good, to get a change of air. And it'll be nice for us both if you can make a bit of money."

All of which was exactly what Fielding thought. But it was not what Harriet was meant to think. He, Fielding, might know that he needed a change of air—that for the last three years he had been growing slacker and slower both in body and mind, that he had been self-satisfied and perfunctory in his work, that he was, in every sense, running to fat, and needed brisk and prolonged movement, in almost any direction, to sweat him out. Oh yes, he himself might know this, but Harriet was not meant to know it, far less to say it; Harriet was meant to think him perfect as and where he was and to plead with him to stay there, so that he, with his supreme understanding of himself, could upbraid and defy the silly, whining cow in the cause of his own good. Or again, as to money, he, Fielding, might acknowledge that up to a point he . . . well . . . found her contributions convenient; but *she* was definitely not required even to hint at such a thing. I'll pay you back, he thought, for that. I'll teach you to bray about money. I'll go away and make so much that I'll never need to think of you again. And then you can just sit here by these salt-marshes and rot. But that would be the end of the match; meanwhile he must win this first round.

"Oh, I shall go to Corfu," he told her, "if only for a good laugh and some new material. But I'm afraid that you can't come."

"Oh?" she said, and turned round, slowly and casually, to indicate that it was time to make for home.

"They won't pay your fare or your hotel," he said as he turned too, "only mine."

"I dare say I could pay my own. If I wanted to come."

"Of course you could. But I wouldn't if I were you. The director's not keen on having wives . . . and so on . . . about the place. He thinks that they disrupt things. That they pester. That they're always wanting treats or patent medicines or love . . . irrelevant things like that. The director wants a working company on Corfu, not a miniature welfare state. Or so Tom said."

"No one could stop me going."

"You'd just be ignored. Totally."

Although Fielding had already said a lot of nasty things to Harriet that evening, this was the first time he had expressed naked contempt. Hitherto his utterance, however harsh in meaning, had been softened by some pretence of wit or irony, so that it had been just possible to think of the conversation as a civilised contest between two intelligent people who were working off a mild disagreement; but this last threat was so brutal and direct a statement of antipathy that he might just as well, Harriet felt, have struck her. Her knees sagged slightly, her eyes pricked and blinked, she put both hands to her stomach.

"Would you ignore me, Fielding?" she said.

Ah, he thought; an appeal for mercy. She's had enough for now; the moment I stopped playing about and let her have it straight, she caved in, just like that. And yet he felt no relish in his victory, now it was won. As he looked at the tears springing in her big round eyes and the plump fingers entwined and twisting over her belly, he felt, first of all, disgust with himself that he could have been so violent, and then boredom with Harriet, that she should have buckled so quickly just when things were really warming up.

"Would you ignore me, Fielding?" she said for the second time.

Careful now, he thought. For it was essential, he knew, to his own inner comfort that he should rid himself of the guilt which always followed on his acts of violence; and this he could never do by self-justification, even when he had reason whereby to justify himself, but only by expressing tenderness, however counterfeit, to his victim. He looked at the crumbling gun-sites which were still left among the dunes from the war, and remembered how the blood had welled up from his mother's mouth, here in Broughton twenty-five years ago. . . .

'Mama, I'm sorry, so sorry. *Please,* mama. I didn't mean . . .'

'. . . Nasty little pansy,' she had lisped through the streaming blood; 'nasty, vicious little pig.'

"Would you ignore me, Fielding?" said Harriet yet once more.

Blackmailing sow, he thought; just like my mother. But the guilt will torture me unless I can soothe her into forgiveness. And besides, she's still paying for my wine and my whisky, for my lobster and even for my house. I'm not independent of her yet, and I may never be. Salve your guilt, Fielding Gray : salve your guilt and look to your meal-ticket. A few pleasant words are not a high price to pay for such ample insurance.

"I'm sorry, sweet," he said. "I'm rather on edge about it all.

I only meant that making a film is a very busy, expensive and complicated affair. People get very tired, Tom says . . . tired and wrought-up both at once, and they are always short of time."

"So I'd be in the way." Already slightly mollified. "I'd amuse myself, you know."

"But for the time being . . . until I've found my feet . . . and had a chance to arrange things, to spy out the land . . . best stay here, sweet. Really."

With his left hand he lifted her two hands from her belly, which he massaged gently with his right.

"Piglet pie," he said.

"Don't wheedle, Fielding. I know what it is. You don't want to share this with me."

"But I do, Harry. Only I want to find out what I'm getting into first. And after all, Tom says that this hotel the film people stay in . . . the one I'll be staying in . . . is packed out by Pandarus. So I'll have to enquire where else we could go when you came."

"You'll have a suite. Suites always have double bedrooms."

"For the first two weeks I'm on probation. I've got to work very hard and do everything to please them. If I move you into my suite, and if this man Jacobson doesn't like wives there any-way . . . You must see it, Harry."

"I'm not sure you should go at all. There's something . . . corrupt about it. Something rotten. That producer and those girls. . . ."

"He's not there very much. Harry, you said yourself I need a change."

"A change of *air*."

"That's all it'll be. You know that. Piglet."

She clasped her hands over his and pressed them to her belly very tightly.

"When shall you go?" she said at last.

"No time to be lost. Tomorrow, if I can make London in time for a 'plane."

"That's right, of course. If they need someone so badly. When can I come, Fielding?"

"I'll let you know after the first fortnight. If they take me on permanently, I'll arrange it as soon as possible after that."

"Yes. That's sensible, I suppose."

"You know it is, Harry."

And now, he thought, as he took a last look back at the gun-sites among the dunes, I suppose she'll want to be fucked three times because it's my last night.

PART TWO

NAUSICAA

". . . So the way I see it," said Foxy J. Galahead in the bar at Corfu Airport, "we get that little Nausicaa laid right there on the beach."

Fielding looked at Jules Jacobson, who said nothing and waited patiently for Foxy to continue. Since Fielding had only flown in ten minutes before, he was not at his best. Since Foxy was about to fly out, and was always excited at the prospect of a journey, he was at his worst.

"Out comes Odysseus, raw as a carrot," Foxy was saying, "and there's Nausicaa standing there dazed, because she's never seen a pair of balls till now, and she knows that this is it, and an electric message flashes between them, and he screws her right there on the beach . . . POW."

"While the handmaids stand round them fingering each other?" said Jules Jacobson, poker-faced.

"No," said Foxy. "We don't want any perversions in this picture. Good straight sex and plenty of it : bom, bom, bom and no filth. Got that?" he blared at Fielding.

"The handmaids," said Fielding slowly, "would be bound to know what was going on. Are they peeping out through the bushes? Or do they just hide their faces?"

"No peeping; that's filth. Voyeurism. But no shutting their eyes to it, because that makes out it's disgusting. And it's not," said Foxy, flinging his arms wide, "it's beautiful. It's this little girl's first fuck, and it's the sun and the moon and the stars . . . so what those handmaids do, they stand up above the beach, looking out over the sea, and they sing a love song about wandering mariners and how they all hope there'll be one for them too before very long."

"Like 'One day my Prince will come'?" Jules Jacobson said.

"Yeah, Jules, yeah. Something like that, I guess."

"And who shall we get to write it?"

"Fielding here can start with the words. That's what we pay him for, words. Like to write a song, Fielding?"

"All right with me, Foxy," said Fielding for the sake of peace.

"That's my baby. I like a guy that don't raise difficulties. And that reminds me, Jules : Elena."

"What about her, Foxy? Raising difficulties, is she?"

"She's not the old Elena. She won't play the old games like she used to. Maybe she's hung up on that Greek waiter who stuffed her?"

"Bom, bom, bom and no filth," Jules said. "I don't think Elena has hang-ups, Foxy. She's not the type. Anyway, what can I do about it?"

"Let Gretel have her part as Nausicaa's chief handmaid. Gretel . . . why that face, and those eyes, and that mouth . . . that lovely, lovely mouth . . ."

". . . She can't sing out of it, Foxy. She's tone-deaf."

"So she can't sing. So what the hell?"

"The handmaids have got to sing this great song, remember? While Odysseus pops the weasel with Nausicaa."

"Dub the song."

Foxy's flight to Athens was announced.

"Too late to change now, Foxy. Elena's been dressed and rehearsed in the part . . ."

". . . But it's a different part, now Odysseus is going to lay Nausicaa."

"Different for Nausicaa. Not for the handmaids."

"Yeah, different for them too. Now they've got this love song."

"Which Gretel can't sing."

"Which we're going to have dubbed. Just you listen to me, Jules. That Gretel . . . she's an artist."

"So she's an artist. But she's not Nausicaa's chief handmaid. That's for little Elena . . . even if she won't play the old games like she used to."

"Jules baby, you make me sore as an arsehole. All I'm ask . . ."

". . . Go on now, Foxy baby, or you'll miss your 'plane. I'll do something for Gretel, don't you worry, but it's Elena for Nausicaa's chief handmaid."

As Foxy waddled huffily off, two henchmen moved up to escort him.

"I'm sorry to subject you to that the minute you get here," Jules said, "but he wanted to meet you before he left and tell you his ideas. You heard 'em : now forget 'em."

Foxy turned at the gate and gave them a gleeful, almost childish wave of farewell, his grievance already, it seemed, forgotten.

"Who's Gretel?" Fielding said as they waved back.

"Swedish slut with an underlip like a shovel. Means she can scoop his balls in too, I suppose."

"*Not* a handmaid by the sound of it."

"No. I had her in mind for a cannibal when we get to the Laestrygonians. Which," said Jules, "will be a very long while yet. And meanwhile, Fielding Gray, our business is Nausicaa. Tom told you what's wanted?"

Fielding nodded.

"Well now," said Jules, "I'm going to tell you again, while we go over the ground. I've got a car outside."

"A porter for my luggage?"

Jules shrugged and picked up Fielding's very substantial suitcase. Carrying it without difficulty, he led the way out to the car park, where he stopped by a small Renault and slung Fielding's case up on to the roof-rack. Fielding, who was only carrying his typewriter and a small grip, was a good fifteen seconds behind Jules and collapsed into the co-driver's seat panting.

"You notice I haven't brought a driver," said Jules. "They're not only damned bad, Greek drivers, but they think they have a democratic right to muscle in on their employers' conversations. And this afternoon," he said, as he turned fast but very smoothly on to the main road, "I want your undivided attention. Because on Nausicaa and the Phaeacians depends our next lot of cash from the Oglander-Finckelstein Trust."

"Which you'll want by early November. So we've got to finish shooting the scenes well before then . . . so that you can cut together all the best takes?"

"Right. I want four days' shooting in the palace and ten on the beach at Ermones. Two weeks. So I'll need the new lines for those scenes just as soon as you can have them ready."

"And I'm to forget all Foxy's blah? No fucking and no singing."

"No fucking, certainly. But there *is* to be singing . . . just where Homer says there is, while the girls are playing with their ball. Tom said that would be right, and I agree."

"But I don't suppose either of you wrote the song?"

"No," said Jules with a pleasant smile. "What I want is a kind of refrain. I want one simple, four-line stanza from you, Fielding, two couplets of rhymed iambic pentameters. Subject: the happy marriages they all hope to make."

"And the music?"

"I'll find that."

"You'd be better off with a proper poet to compose the verse. I don't really write poetry."

"For a thousand a week you write everything. You're getting twenty-five per cent up on Tom because you're bound to turn out all the words I want. Tom was only an adviser; I couldn't *make* him write. But I'll make you write what I want, Fielding Gray, or I'll break your sodding neck."

Fielding found this speech rather exciting. It was fun to work for a man who was in earnest . . . though surely he needn't have driven quite so fast over these pot-holes. Thankfully, Fielding saw that they were now approaching a golf course, flat and green on the left of the road, lightly flecked with young trees.

"Surely . . . Ermones is left and just over the course?" Fielding said, remembering Tom's description of the environment.

"Well done. But we're going to the Palace first. We're using the monastery at Palaeocastritsa for that. With a bit of faking it'll pass quite well."

Jules hooted at an oncoming lorry which was taking up the entire road. Just in time the lorry gave way, but the driver shook his fist from the window as they passed.

"Road-works vehicle," said Jules. "Public employees here like to think they take precedence over the public." Then, noticing that Fielding had gone white, "Am I driving too fast for you?"

"These days," said Fielding with a great effort, "all menials put on the airs of officials, just like that driver. It gives them an illusion of status and a chance to get their own back for the tedium of their existence. The usherettes in English cinemas bully one around like drill sergeants."

"Very good," said Jules, "very good. You were scared to shit by that lorry but you thought of an answer."

"The least I can do for a thousand a week. And I want to be clear from the start exactly what else I do for the money. I rewrite the speeches in that script but nothing else. Right?"

"Right. The sequence of action and movement will stay as it is, and neither you nor Foxy nor God Himself can change it. However," said Jules, "I myself just might. We're coming to the first of the bays by Palaeocastritsa. . . ."

And for the next three hours Fielding was taken over every inch of the ground. The Palace/monastery courtyard, probable places for shots of Nausicaa and her girls while *en route,* the point at which they would meet the river, the approaches, along the river and through the low rocky hills near the sea, to the washing tanks, the tiny estuary and the beach; Odysseus's distressful bed in the scrub, the shady nook for the girls' picnic, the sand banks on which they would spread the washing to dry, the flat space near the estuary on which they would play at ball and sing, the hiding places to which all but the Princess would scatter as the hero emerged. . . .

"Can you see it?" said Jules at last.

"Yes . . . but so could Tom."

"Never mind Tom. Make them talk for me, Fielding; please make them talk."

"I must see the actors first. See and hear."

"Quite right," said Jules, with evident approval which over-laid a slight and puzzling reluctance. "I've got them coming to dinner. Odysseus if he's not too drunk . . . and Nausicaa." Again the hint of reluctance. Why, Fielding wondered.

"I've also asked someone else," said Jules, visibly brightening. "The chief handmaid . . . the daughter of Dymas, as Homer calls her."

"Otherwise little Elena . . . who refused to play games any longer with Foxy?"

"Rather impressive that," said Jules. "The rest of 'em would have gone on doing whatever Foxy told 'em, however disgust-ing, and purring all over him. But not, it seems, Elena. Good, honest girl, Elena; says what she means and stands by it."

"I think," said Elena to Fielding, "that your face is not as bad as I was warned."

For of course everyone had been warned, Jules and Foxy by Tom, then the whole company by Jules, which was why no one had shown any surprise.

"Rather *plastic,*" Elena went on, "but I quite like your one eye. Isn't there a character in this film somewhere who only has one eye?"

"Polyphemus," said Fielding, "otherwise known as the Cyclops. Not an attractive fellow. He eats some of Odysseus's sailors."

"My, my. I hope you're not going to eat any of us."

"I shall very soon feel like it . . . if we don't go into dinner."

Jules's dinner party was assembled in the bar of the Corfu Palace, with the unexpected addition of Penelope, who had invited herself at the last minute 'to say hallo to the new writer', and with the exception of Odysseus, for whom they would wait, Jules now said, for five more minutes. Penelope, whose real name was Margaret Lichfield, heaved a long sigh at the announcement and went to work with her lipstick.

"Trouble with these old pissers," Penelope said, "they've got no consideration."

"It's an illness," said Nausicaa, a delicious red-head, of small yet gangling build, who had been introduced as Sasha Grimes. "I do feel so sorry for him."

"It's easy to be understanding at your age, darling. But at mine one's ulcers start barking if they're not fed."

"Poor Margaret," said Nausicaa, in a voice creamy with pity for the whole suffering world. "Have one of these olives."

"And lose my appetite? My intestinal juices, Sasha dear, are very precariously balanced."

"That's what comes of having to rush. Because you weren't really expecting . . . were you, Margaret darling? . . . to be asked out this evening at all."

"The young red vixen has sharp teeth," Elena murmured to Fielding, "but the old black crow has very strong wings. After all, they've carried her all the way from a gutter in Bermondsey to a pinnacle in this profession."

"But she's still afraid," suggested Fielding, "that the young red vixen will creep up behind her and chase her off it?"

"All old-timers are afraid of something like that. But in fact," said Elena, "Sasha Grimes will never be in the same class as old Margaret. Margaret's a star; Sasha's just a very good actress. She got the Oglander-Finckelstein Award at nineteen . . . that's one reason why she's here now . . . she's had some marvellous parts at the Old Vic and so on, but she'll never make it as a star, or not in the sense that Margaret has. Margaret Lichfield is to Sasha Grimes as Greer Garson to Jane Asher."

"If you get much sharper, Sasha darling," Margaret Lichfield was saying, "you're going to cut your own pretty little throat without knowing it. If you want to know why I've made such an effort to get to this dinner," she said, clamping her martini into her fist and marching across to Fielding, "it's because I was anxious to meet Mr. Thingummy here. Now, what are you going to do about my speeches, Mr. Thingummy darling? That's what I want to know. They're as chewy as a hunk of rubber."

"We'll discuss your speeches later on, Margaret," said Jules rather coolly.

"Yes, Margaret darling, later on," cooed Nausicaa. "Tonight,

you see, we have to discuss *my* speeches." She simpered like a
mischievous angel. "Or didn't Jules explain when he invited
you?"

Margaret Lichfield drew strongly on her martini.

"First things first, little one," she said. "Penelope is the
lead . . . as even you may know."

"For such an *experienced* person, Margaret, you do say the
oddest things. What has Penelope got to do with my scenes on
the beach? That's what darling Jules is worried about just
now."

"*Worried,* darling, he may well be."

"Dinner, dears," said Jules, with just a hint of despair. "We
won't wait any more for Angus."

Dinner was unexpectedly agreeable, at any rate for Fielding, largely because he was sitting next to Elena. Jules had
honoured Margaret Lichfield, as a senior star, by placing her
on his right but had punished her as a party-crasher by leaving
vacant for Odysseus the seat which was on her own right. To the
right again of the empty chair was Elena, to her right Fielding,
and to his Sasha Grimes, who sat on Jules's left. As long as
Elena had no one to her immediate left, it was Fielding's clear
duty to devote himself to her, and this he was happy to do : for
although Sasha/Nausicaa was by far the more beautiful of his
two neighbours, she was a girl of didactic utterance and anti-
septic disposition, constantly clearing the space about her with
fierce little movements of her fingers, as if to protect herself
from the touch and taint of imaginary intruders. Elena, on the
other hand, was brown, appetising, rather sweaty young flesh,
which she distributed, so to speak, by the handful. She plonked
her thigh firmly against Fielding's from the moment they sat
down and frequently nudged him in the chest with her bare
upper arm, letting it linger beneath his chin as though to say
'have a nice juicy mouthful if you want one'.

But this would have been to insult the admirable dinner which
Jules had ordered. Elena ate hers voraciously (another strong
point in her favour), the Lichfield chomped away with content-
ment, ulcers appeased, and even the delicate Sasha, who survey-

ed her food as if its presence were a gross affront to her sensiti-
vities, took a few patronising mouthfuls. The result was an
immediate improvement in everybody's temper. Jules and Margaret speculated with cheerful malevolence about the future
fate in the film world of the departed Circe; Sasha/Nausicaa
listened with bright, reproving eyes and smugly enjoined them
to charity; while Fielding, reserving half an ear for the professional purpose of recording the genteel accents of Sasha, lent
the other one and a half to the babbling Elena.

"I hope Angus Carnavon doesn't make it to dinner," she
said. "I don't like the way he paws."

"Oh?"

"Or rather, it's not the pawing I mind, it's the pathetic pretence behind it. He wants you to think he's uncontrollably
randy, when all he ever has is a snail between his legs. Drink,
of course. But they say it was always the same even before he hit
the bottle."

"Perhaps that's why he hit the bottle."

"*You* look a bit boozy to me."

"I am a bit boozy."

"Because of all that plastic on your face? It doesn't put me
off, you know."

"I'm glad. But I was boozy before the plastic, as you call it."

"Why? Snail trouble, like Angus?"

"No. Not snail trouble. Mother trouble, you might say."

"You queer?"

"Some of the time. Not much of it, these days."

"Some of them say Angus Carnavon is queer, but I don't
think he fancies anything. Except whisky, of course."

"But can he act?"

"You must have seen him for yourself . . . he's starred in
enough pictures in his time."

"In his time. Can he *still* act?"

"Yes," said Elena with plain and generous admiration. "He's
bloody fine as Odysseus. Or at any rate he twitches that craggy
face of his about with marvellous results. And his voice sends
me. Sometimes dry and sad, sometimes rasping and cruel, some-

times. . . . Here he comes now, not too stoned, I hope." She ran
her fingernails lightly up the inside of Fielding's thigh and let
her hand linger briefly. "No," she said, "no snail trouble for
you. Come to my room . . . 527 . . . when the party's done. I
want another word with you, and now I'll have to talk to this
bladderful of hooch."

After some confusion while Carnavon, not a large man but
very chunky, manoeuvred himself into dock, demanded
scrambled eggs in place of Jules's menu, and then started to paw
Elena, Fielding was addressed by Sasha Grimes, who was now
gazing at him with schoolmarmish reproach.

"One should never allow oneself," she said, "to be distracted
from one's creative responsibilities."

"Indeed not. Especially when one is being well paid."

"Ah," she diagnosed briskly. "The cynical pose of an unfulfilled artistic spirit. I can tell. I have empathy, you see."

"It isn't a pose. One tries to do sound work and hopes to get
good money."

" 'Sound work'," she echoed, shaking her head. "What has
that to do with the ecstasy of creation?"

"I know nothing about the ecstasy of creation."

"But you would like to. That is why you are unfulfilled. And
why you welcome trivial distraction."

She nodded towards Elena, who was glumly trying to fork
food into her mouth without spilling it on to Odysseus's grizzled
head, which was burrowing about in her bosom.

"We all welcome a bit of that," Fielding said.

"Speak for yourself," she said thinly.

"Oh, I do."

"Then wallow like an animal, if you must; I can't stop you.
But don't let yourself be taken in, my friend. Jules won't like
it."

"I don't understand."

"Even if you adopt a professional rather than a creative approach to your task, you must still value your integrity?"

"I suppose so."

"Then don't swerve from it" . . . again she nodded towards Elena . . . "whatever the temptation."

At this stage Fielding began to be curious, and more than curious, about Miss Sasha Grimes, alias Nausicaa. Prim and self-protective she might be, forbidding in her tone and priggish in her sentiments; but it was precisely this governessy aspect which, combined with the loose limbs and the flowing red hair, made her so fascinating. Her sexual appeal was less immediate than Elena's but far more subtle and evocative; somehow she conjured distant memories, which awakened not so much desire as yearning, of a prudish girl cousin who had turned suddenly shameless in the back of the car on the way home from a panto-mime, or of one stern young nanny whose hands had strayed into his pyjamas even as she rebuked his naughtiness. The nanny had left soon afterwards; the cousin, though often approached, had never again been accommodating; but nothing could take away the remembered and magical moments, those moments when something had occurred of such delicious enor-mity that it briefly revealed another world in which all natural routines and processes were confounded or reversed. It was to this world, Fielding thought, that Nausicaa might give one re-admittance : if ever one went to bed with her, the mere fact of its happening at all would be miraculous, against nature; it would be like pleasuring, and being pleasured by, someone absolutely unattainable, the Queen or the Virgin Mary.

Perhaps Sasha Grimes sensed something of what he was thinking. At all events she smiled mysteriously, put one finger nervously on the back of his hand, and said :

"I hope we shall understand one another. I'm very anxious you should get my speeches right."

She then proceeded to talk, with precision and intelligence, about her own merits and limitations as an actress. Her voice was small, she said, but clear and accurate. Although she was quite at home with difficult language, long sentences were apt to leave her breathless, despite all the expensive lessons which she had taken in voice-control. She was more suited to pique than passion, better at demanding than sympathising, which might not help her in the role of Nausicaa; however, she could do the Princess, she promised him, without making her suburban or coy, and she would be excellent as the nubile maiden upon whose innocent heart concupiscence was beginning to obtrude. To get down to more detail, she preferred iambic or trochaic rhythms of speech to dactyllic or anapaestic (though she realised there must be variety) so would dear Mr. Gray, with whom she now saw she was going to agree perfectly in such matters, very kindly remember . . .

". . . BITCH," shouted Odysseus, making the whole dining-room rattle.

Elena had stuck her fork into his hand.

"I'm very sorry," Elena said, "and I'll put up with almost anything for the sake of peace, but I'm not going to have my dugs bitten off . . . even if you do use Steradent."

Carnavon shook his wounded hand, shambled to his feet and started his farewells.

"Cow," he said quite mildly to Margaret; "Yid," he growled at Jules; "Tight-twat," more fiercely to Sasha; "You writer fairies," with a snarl at Fielding; and to Elena once more, "BITCH."

He leant forward, took a single spoonful of his scrambled egg, then reversed sharply into the Maître d'Hôtel, who spun him round cleverly and trotted him out.

"Rotten dinner," said Carnavon to the Maître d'Hôtel as they went. "No taste at all in that slut's teats."

"Ungrateful hound," said Elena to the rest of the party. "He nearly drew blood."

"At least," said Fielding, "I've got a good idea of his vocal range. He seems at his best with monosyllables . . . pity we can't confine him to those."

"He ought to be confined to grunting," Elena said. "Ignorant pig."

"We must all try to help him," said Sasha. "It's a sickness. you see."

"You're too good to be true," said Elena.

"And just you wait," put in Margaret Lichfield, "till you have to smell the stale whisky on his breath right through five hours' shooting."

"We don't know what he may have suffered."

"Or care."

"I only know he's nearly killed me with whisky fumes this last month."

"Poor darling Margaret. I've often wondered what made you look so tired on set."

"And now you're going to find out, Sasha dear, during those wonderful scenes of yours on that beach."

"I shall rise above it, Margaret dear. I shall disengage myself from crude physical sensations and float like a spirit, directing my body from above."

"Shall you, darling? He won't want to act opposite a waxwork, you know, even one as life-like as you."

"No," said Elena. "He likes tits made of flesh and blood."

"He'd never dare forget himself so far with me."

"Perhaps he wouldn't want to. What was it he called you just now? Tight-twat?"

"Shut up, the lot of you," said Jules, firmly but amiably, "and go to bed. Not you, Fielding, I want a word with you."

"And so do I, don't forget," whispered Elena as she rose to leave. "Room 527."

"I must say," said Fielding as the women all trooped out, "they're very obedient."

"They're worn out after a long day, and they've got to be up again by six. We start early, you know."

"They seemed lively enough."

"Keeping up an act. The show must go on . . . even off-stage."

"There's a lot to be said for the precept. Old Margaret Lichfield keeps marching on like a guardsman. You wouldn't think it's twenty years since she starred in *Zenobia*."

"Guardsman is right. She tramples. She had no business at dinner tonight. She knew very well I wanted to discuss the Nausicaa scenes, but as it was I had the devil's own job keeping her quiet so that the rest of you could get on with it. How did you manage?"

"Quite well, thank you. I had a vivid if brief impression of Odysseus's capacities, and an interesting talk with little Nausicaa."

"What did you make of her?"

"Intelligent when she talks about her acting. Otherwise a pretentious and self-righteous little ninny."

"Sasha models herself on Vanessa Redgrave. She picks up all the progressive clichés, and says it would be frivolous and anti-social just to be an actress. She has to be . . . what's that phrase she told me? . . . compassionately and ideologically orientated."

"But anyone can see she's only *acting* all that."

"She's too stupid to see it herself. Just wait till you hear her on politics."

"She told me that the only thing which mattered was creative ecstasy."

"You mustn't expect her to be consistent. She'll parrot any jargon which takes her fancy. An atrocious little ninny, as you say . . . but potentially an admirable Nausicaa."

"And rather beguiling in a way."

"What way?"

"All this *noli me tangere* of hers. Just suppose," said Fielding, "that she did let one touch her, it would be like touching a goddess. It would be to enjoy what was utterly unexpected and utterly forbidden."

"So already you're beginning to covet it?"

"I didn't say so."

"But I saw you thinking so . . . at dinner. Which is why I asked you to stay behind just now, though I'm more than ready for bed. Hands off my Nausicaa, Fielding. I don't want her disturbed or in any sense diverted. I just want her to concentrate on her acting until those vitally important scenes of hers are safely in the tin."

"I was only theorising, Jules. In a poetic sort of way."

"Which means your mind is on the subject. So get your mind off the subject, Fielding, and on to Elena instead . . . even if she is less poetic. That's why I asked *her* tonight. To provide you with any . . . needful amusement."

"You detailed her off, Jules?"

"More or less. She's as tough as tungsten . . . nothing would disturb *her* . . . and she owes me a good turn for getting her out of clink."

"Tell me . . . did you detail anyone off for Tom?"

"No. He didn't seem to need anyone," said Jules with strong retrospective approval. "But he warned me you would."

"Well, I could certainly do with a change of women. How kind of you and Tom to think of it. You'll be glad to know that Elena is at this very moment awaiting me in her room. 527."

Jules nodded rather heavily.

"I saw you getting on well together," he said.

"So did little Sasha. And do you know, Jules, little Sasha gave me a warning against Elena. Veiled, but an unmistakable warning. Now, what would you say was at the bottom of that?"

"Sasha's not jealous, if that's what you're hoping. She probably disapproves of Elena . . . thinks she's cheap or coarse."

"It's more complicated than that, Jules. Sasha implied that Elena was in some way a threat, that she was going to take me in . . . those were Sasha's words . . . and that *you wouldn't like it.* And yet now I find that it was you who arranged it all. So just what could Sasha have meant?"

Jules's face sagged in weary irritation.

"She's trying to be clever and make mysteries," he said. "Take my word for it, Fielding, there's nothing devious or dangerous about Elena. An honest girl who speaks her mind."

"But a whore."

"A whore?"

"You said so yourself. She's entertaining me, you said, in return for favours received from you."

"All right, a whore. But an honest one. She'll give full value."

"I'm delighted to hear it. But whores . . . even honest ones . . . always ask for *more* favours, particularly if they've been paid in advance."

E

"You wouldn't grudge her a small present? Not on a thousand a week."

"Oh no. But I'd still like to know what Sasha meant."

"I told you. She was just trying to seem profound. Part of her act. But if you're worried about any of this, just go straight to your room and forget it. All I require is that you stay clear of Sasha. If you want a girl, Elena's laid on for you; if you don't, that's fine by me."

"Oh, I want Elena all right. She saw to that at dinner. But whatever you say, Jules, there's more to this than meets the eye."

"Then go and find out what it is," said Jules, yawning hugely. "And don't wake me up to tell me."

"Sod you then, you rotten sod," said Elena in Room 527.

"Why am I a rotten sod?" asked Fielding.

"You come in here, and you help yourself to the sweet trolley..."

"... At your invitation..."

"... And then you refuse to write any lines for a girl."

For Sasha Grimes had been right and Jules Jacobson wrong. Elena did have a game of her own to play: she wanted Fielding, as script-writer, to write in some speeches for her. As Sasha had warned, Jules certainly wouldn't like it.

"I haven't refused," said Fielding carefully. "I've simply tried to explain that my job is not to write in new speeches but to rewrite the old ones."

"You could cut one of the old ones in two and give me half of it."

"Look," said Fielding with a slight sigh. "I write ... or rather rewrite ... under the instructions of the director, Jules Jacobson. This afternoon Jules took me through your scenes very carefully, telling me exactly who would do and say what, and showing me exactly where and when they would do and say it. You and the other handmaidens have a lot to do but nothing at all to say. Homer gives you no lines, the present script gives you no lines, Jules doesn't want you to have any lines. If I wrote any for you, Jules would simply cut them out."

Elena gave a twitch of her naked breasts and considered this. Then she put a hand across and started to scratch Fielding, very delicately, at the base of his stomach.

"I see what you mean," she said in a commonsense voice; "but you could always try to persuade him."

"He'd say I was interfering with his direction."

Elena went on scratching. Fielding put one hand over and caressed both her nipples, one with his thumb and the other with his little finger.

"Save that for your typewriter," Elena said. But she didn't try to stop him and she didn't leave off scratching.

"You'd have had a better chance of getting a speaking part," said Fielding, "if you'd gone on being nice to Foxy Galahead."

"I couldn't stand Foxy. He was so damned sentimental. And then he wanted me to shave my bush off and pretend I was only nine."

"What would you have done about these?"

Fielding gave her breasts a wobble.

"He was going to buy me a special kind of high-neck nightie, nursery style. I was going to lie there in this nightie, and Foxy was going to come in and pretend he was Daddy come to say goodnight to his little girl. Then there was to be some routine about how I had a pain in my tummy. I ask you."

"It doesn't sound very exacting."

"I suppose not. And Gretel said he made it rather fun. But me, I like being myself, lover. I like sex every way it comes, straight as a ram-rod or bent as a spring in the mattress, but I want it to be *me* it gets done to, not some fantasy kiddy-wink of Foxy's."

"So you wouldn't play, and now you've lost yourself an ally."

"Lost myself a big fat slob."

Elena stopped scratching Fielding's stomach. She put her hand between his thighs and started pricking lightly with the points of her nails at the bottom of his buttocks. Fielding raised his knees to give her a larger area to work on.

"I suppose," Fielding said, "it's no good your trying to get at Jules yourself?"

"You think I haven't tried?"

The pricking sensation on Fielding's buttocks was really exquisite. Elena now removed Fielding's hand from her breasts, rested her head on his chest, and started sliding it slowly down.

"Elena . . . what shall I do to you?"

No answer. Prick, prick, prick on the buttocks and a warm circling tongue. Whereas Fielding's first dish from the sweet trolley had only been a conventional recipe, this second offering was an individual confection of genius. Prick, prick, prick . . . and a finger straying to find the valve in the cleft, probing softly for entrance.

"Christ, Elena . . . What do you want me to do to you?"

Tongue withdrawn. Exposed flesh dank and chilly.

"Promise to write me some lines, lover. That's what."

"Oh, Elena. I've told you . . ."

". . . Just you promise."

"But Elena. . . ."

Finger withdrawing its charity. Buttocks untouched, unloved.

"Listen, Elena. . . ." Jules would never consent to a speech for her, certainly not at his, Fielding's, suggestion. He'd be accused of meddling, of disregarding his very clear brief, of wasting time and money. He couldn't afford that sort of trouble while still only on probation. But what was it Jules had said about a song to be written? Yes : a refrain for the girls to sing while they played at ball. "Elena. I suppose I *could* write you some lines and just try them on Jules."

Prick, prick.

"I can't promise he'll like them, but I'd do my best."

Finger poised on valve.

"How many lines, lover?"

Two couplets, Jules had said. Two rhymed couplets.

"A few. Four, perhaps."

"All in one speech? Or separate?"

"All of them . . . I think . . . would be together."

"That's a good lover."

The warm tongue soothed away the chill. Prick, prick on the buttocks. Finger easing snugly into place. *Jubilate*.

"I wish," Fielding said, "that I could feel like this for ever."

But of course he couldn't, and the next morning he felt awful.

To begin with, he had promised to write some lines for Elena. By this she understood a speech; whereas he himself knew that all he would ever write for her was what he had been told to write by Jules . . . four lines of a refrain to be sung in chorus with the other handmaids. That she herself had not behaved well, having forced the promise out of him under duress, did not excuse him; and even if it did, she was going to be absolutely furious when she found out how he had misled her.

None of which boded well for his future relations either with Elena or, more important, with Jules. He could just imagine Jules's face if an enraged Elena formed up to him, on set or elsewhere, and demanded the speech that Fielding had promised her. The confrontations, the explanations, the protestations . . . oh, Christ. Yet the fact remained that it had been Jules who had got Fielding into this mess by 'laying Elena on' for him in the first place; and the question now presented itself, why had Jules done it? Surely, if Sasha was able to foresee Elena's embarrassing and demanding behaviour, Jules himself, wise in the ways of starlets, could have done so too . . . especially as Fielding had prompted him by remarking on Sasha's misgivings. But Jules had simply pooh-poohed all that and told Fielding to go ahead or not as he chose. Again, why? Jules's ostensible motive was to protect the delicate Sasha/Nausicaa from Fielding's attentions by channelling them off on to Elena; but could Jules really think that Sasha was so vulnerable and he, Fielding, so uncontrollable, that it was necessary to provide sexual distraction for him on his very first night in Corfu? Whatever warning Tom had given Jules, he could hardly have made Fielding out to be such a monster of incontinence as that.

Altogether, there were some uncomfortable questions here

to which Fielding badly needed the answers. But since the only answers must come from Jules, and since Jules was in some distant corner of the island watching the stunt men of the Second Unit, Fielding would have to wait till the evening. Meanwhile, he told himself firmly, there was one thing he *could* be sure of . . . the necessity to work, and to work well, if he was to secure confirmation of his contract at the end of the first two weeks. He rose from the balcony on which he had been breakfasting and went inside to his desk.

> "So take, while there is time, the gifts that the gods
> have granted :
> Taste ten thousand kisses, you will yet have tasted
> too few. . . ."

Fielding had decided to start by writing the words of the song which Jules wanted. Four lines, Jules had said, two couplets of rhymed iambic pentameters, in praise and hope of marriage. But it was clear to Fielding that iambic pentameters would not do as the basis of a chant which the girls must sing while they played with their ball. It would be a big ball, which they would throw, in the afternoon heat, with long languorous movements; and these would be far better accompanied by a relaxed and lulling rhythm than by the crisp rattle of iambs, which would be more suitable to P.T. instructors slapping a basket ball about in a gym. So Fielding had devised or remembered a spondaeo-dactyllic line which would go most exquisitely, he thought, with the slow curve of the ball through the shimmering sandy heat and the indolent lapping nearby of the calm blue sea. As for what the verses would say, they would celebrate desire rather than marriage (for desire was what these girls were really on about), and the appropriate sentiments were to be found in an Elegy of Propertius which he had once been made to memorise at school. So now he would translate the remembered lines into his chosen measure, and make rhymes, he thought, at alternate rather than proximate line-endings, in order to keep the ear longer expectant and therefore more attentive through the deliberately dragging words.

"So take, while there is time, the gifts that the gods
                                have granted;
Taste ten thousand kisses, you will yet have tasted
                                too few. . . ."

Now, what followed? If you don't do this, Propertius went on, your beauty will decay, like fallen rose-petals, before you and others have been able to enjoy it. Exactly. So :

"For as the leaves fall from the rose which but now
                            hath flaunted. . . ."

'Flaunted' to rhyme with 'granted'? All right, if the other rhyme were made strong. 'Flaunted' used intransitively? Yes, it would pass in a song. 'Leaves' . . . or petals? Leaves for the metre, petals, he supposed, for botanical accuracy. Botanical accuracy not necessary in context, rose-leaves being sound poetic currency. All right; now clinch it :

"So take, while there is time, the gifts that the gods
                                have granted;
Taste ten thousand kisses, you will yet have tasted
                                too few;
For as the leaves fall from the rose which but now
                            hath flaunted,
As the leaves fade and fall, the same it must be
                            with you."

Very pretty, Fielding thought, if I do say it myself.

"Not what I asked for," Jules Jacobson said that evening.

He frowned over the sheet of paper which Fielding had shown him, then read the lines a second time, silently mouthing the words.

"No," he said at last; "not at all what I asked for. But I think it might do rather well. The slow rhythm . . . I can see it and hear it in a slow rhythm."

"So can I," Fielding said.

"You weren't asked to. You were asked for iambs. Now you've done it this way I'll have to hunt around for some other music."

"You already had some music?"

"Handel's setting for 'Where e'r you walk'. Out of copyright, you see. But now you've dispensed with iambic pentameters I'll have to look for something else. Please, Fielding, do not disobey my instructions again." He mouthed the first couplet once more. "But I agree," he said, "it could work. How are you getting on with the actual speeches?"

"Quite well, I think. I'll have a good deal to show you to-morrow."

"Not now?"

"It needs checking very carefully, Jules. Tomorrow, if you don't mind."

"All right. So long as you're not disregarding instructions."

"No," said Fielding, "I'm not. But I very well might have been." He told Jules about Elena's request. "Did you realise," he asked, "that something of the sort might happen?"

"Oh yes," said Jules.

"Then why did you tell me there was nothing to worry about with Elena? Why did you say Sasha was talking nonsense when you knew all the time that she was probably right?"

"I didn't want to put you off."

"Why were you so keen to put me on?"

"I told you. I wanted to be sure you wouldn't pester Sasha. Tom had warned me . . ."

". . . That I liked a bit of flesh. And so I do. But I don't jump in where I'm not wanted, Jules. I learned that lesson long ago."

"I didn't want to take any risk over Sasha."

"Risk? Did you think I was going to rape her or some-thing . . . and kiss good-bye to a thousand a week? A simple request to keep away from her would have been quite enough. I can take a hint, Jules, and even if I couldn't I've no doubt whatever that little Sasha can take care of herself. So why all this fuss? Why did you go to such pains to bundle me into bed with Elena . . . knowing that she might make trouble of her own . . . on my very first night in Corfu?"

Jules considered Fielding carefully. He looked into his one eye and then into the puckered slit where the other should have been. After this he nodded heavily, just as he had nodded on the previous evening when Fielding had told him that he was expected by Elena in her bedroom.

"I wanted to see what you'd do," said Jules at last. "I wanted to see whether you'd really jump into bed with the first girl who touched you up . . . just like a randy little boy."

"Now you know. And much good may it do you."

"Oh, it does," said Jules. "You see, I've got a theory about you, Fielding. After Tom left, I made a few enquiries. I was determined to have you here anyhow, since he'd recommended you . . ."

". . . You must think very highly of his advice . . ."

". . . Oh, I do, and also of his warnings. So I decided, as I say, to make a few enquiries, and I started, on the off chance he'd be able to help me, with Max de Freville."

"The man who knows too much," said Fielding bitterly, remembering his last meeting with Max. "Tom said he was here."

"With a stake in this film, and so most anxious to help me. And what he didn't know, that woman of his did. Mrs. Angela Tuck."

"*Christ*. Is she still with him?"

"Oh yes indeed. You'll appreciate, then, that I've been very fully informed. All that squalid business of yours at school at the end of the war; your Army career; how you got your face smashed in Cyprus; how you started up as a novelist . . . and not least, what happened when you went back to Cyprus on that job for the BBC in 1962 and got taken for a ride . . . in every sense . . . by that cute little Greek. I've got a dossier on you, Fielding Gray, on everything from your sexual pranks over the last twenty-five years down to the fillings in your teeth. And on the strength of all this I formed a theory. Do you want to know what it is?"

"I don't need you to tell me, Jules. All my friends have the same one . . . that early frustrations and traumas have warped my nature, left me in a permanent state of retarded adolescence, and rendered me incapable of any kind of love higher than promiscuous and juvenile sexuality. I've heard it all before."

"Cut away the jargon, and what it comes down to is, you're just a shit. That's my theory, Fielding. Never mind early frustrations and the rest; we all had them to contend with. You're simply on old-fashioned shit who'll ride rough-shod over anything or anybody to get what he wants . . . and who dissolves into floods of self-pity on the rare occasions when he doesn't get it."

"Perhaps those occasions have always been the important ones," said Fielding, shivering slightly. "The few things I didn't get . . . Cambridge, for instance . . . those have been the things which I really . . . Oh, to hell with it," he said. "What's all this got to do with Elena? We were talking about her, remember?"

"I remember very clearly. Elena was a test. I wanted to see whether my theory was right. After all, you've spent eight years living quietly and perhaps even faithfully with a certain Mrs. Ongley, Max says, and that might have changed you for the better. Or so I thought."

"So you laid on Elena, who showed you I was still a retarded adolescent."

"That you're still a howling shit. Still riding rough-shod, still entirely careless of people as people. Elena could have been an animated dummy for all you cared. Which means you're still a danger, whatever you say to the contrary, to girls like Sasha . . . who may be a ninny but doesn't deserve to be treated as a piece of prey. A director of a large company of highly strung actors likes to know these things."

"And now you know. So you're going to send me home tomorrow, I suppose?"

"Of course not," said Jules lightly. "I need to know your personal form . . . which is contemptible . . . in order to control you within my company; but I've hired you, Fielding, as a professional. Which brings us to the second part of the test. Elena asked you, as I thought she might, to write in some lines for her. Now, here we have to do with a professional problem . . . one brought on to yourself by personal indulgence, but still a professional problem in its essence. How did you cope with that?"

"I told her I couldn't oblige her," said Fielding, "because you wouldn't allow it. So then she stopped what she was doing, which was delicious . . and I said I'd try."

"Just what did you mean by that?"

"This song." Fielding tapped the sheet of paper which Jules was still holding. "I promised I'd try to write her up to four lines, and there they are."

"Shit," said Jules equably. "You knew she meant a speech of her own."

"She used the word 'lines'. And so did I, very scrupulously."

"Shit," said Jules again. "But at least you're not shitting on me. From a professional point of view you get full marks. What are you going to do when she finds out?"

"Nothing. Nothing, that is, that might bugger up you or the script. Didn't Max tell you, Jules? Whatever else may be said of me, my professional record is immaculate."

"Except," said Jules, "when you ran out of that assignment in 'sixty-two to go off with the Greek boy."

"That was exceptional."

"Let's hope so. But you quite see I had to make some tests."

"You lied to me in making them."

"I also showed you the easy way out of them. You can always go to your own room, I reminded you, and straight to your own bed."

"All right. But now get this plain, Jules: my loyalty is to that script . . . or to the money I shall get for rewriting it as you want it rewritten. Nothing will get in my way there, least of all a little tart like Elena. So let's have no more lies and no more tests. Agreed?"

"No more lies. But one more test . . . the proper test, Fielding: can you write my speeches?" Jules fluttered the song-paper. "This is well enough in its way . . . if not quite what I asked for. But can you write me speeches that will work?"

"I told you," Fielding said: "I'll have some to show you tomorrow night."

So far, thought Fielding, so good. He's made his tests, found out that I'm just the sort of bounder he thought I was . . . and he don't care one little bit, provided that I shag only the girls he wants me to shag, and that I get on with the work. He is now convinced that professionally I am *serieux,* and he has deduced from the song I knocked up that I probably know what I'm doing.

But what, thought Fielding, am I in truth doing? He placed a flagon of whisky on his desk with a glass and a bottle of mineral water. Then he sat down and looked through the night, over the narrow sea and on to the black mountains of Epirus. I have, he thought, one aim : to do this work in such a way that I shall be taken on for the full fourteen weeks and shall then pull in £14,000. As Tom said, that shouldn't be too hard : they're in a hurry, they'll be desperate to believe that I can find their answers, and anything that reads clearly and with a bit of a ring to it will make them happy. But all the same, he thought, there's a bit more to it than that.

For the one thing which Fielding could not abide was the idea that he might make a fool, so to speak, out of Homer. Homer had always been his favourite poet, ever since the Senior Usher had read aloud the first lines of *The Odyssey,* one morning long ago, when Fielding was just fifteen and newly promoted into the Under Sixth. . . .

Ἄνδρα μοι ἔννεπε, Μοῦσα, πολύτροπον . . . .

Tell me, Muse, of the man of many wiles, who wandered many ways after he had sacked the sacred citadel of Troy. Many were the men whose cities he saw and whose mind he learned, and many the woes he suffered in his heart upon the sea. . . .

The lines had thrilled him then, and they still did. Whenever he had read them, slouched on a bunk in a frowsty Nissen hut in Ranby Camp, or walking up and down outside the little white house which had been his Squadron Headquarters in Santa Kytherea, or sitting in one of Tessie's rooms that smelled of Albert Edward . . . wherever and whenever he had read them, they had promised breezes singing and waves running, they had promised mountains and haunted woods and secret rivers, little bright ports at morning and fires on the beach at evening, strange faces looking down from high windows, lotus, wine and love. And always the poet had kept his promise; for here in *The Odyssey* was the old gods' plenty, that brought to Fielding, whether at fifteen or at forty, blood's quickness and heart's delight.

And so now, as Fielding considered the task before him, he recognised a duty as well as a mere means to money. He must keep faith with Homer and show his gratitude even while supplying his greed. Not only must he please Jules and produce speeches of the kind Jules wanted, he must also ensure that these speeches were worthy of the poet from whom they were derived and that when spoken they would not injure the poet's honour. Cuts, omissions and much editing by Jules there would have to be—this he fully understood—but it was incumbent on him to work in words of such strength and purity that, however much they might be chopped about, they would still convey the spirit of Homer.

Now, Foxy would not give a damn about this spirit; and he could, as Fielding had already learned, bring strong pressures to bear, should he wish to pervert the tone of the film in his commercial interest. As for Jules, he could and would resist Foxy's pressures, for he had the terms of his contract to uphold him and a most evident integrity; but he had his own ideas of how Homer should be interpreted on film, ideas which, though not Foxy's, were not necessarily Fielding's. Faced, therefore, with the prospect of powerful coercion by Foxy or by Jules or by both, Fielding now formulated to himself some preparatory propositions.

In the first place, he reflected, he must avoid any kind of row, any slightest appearance of disaffection, for the two weeks of his probation; only when he had secured a contract for the full period could he exert himself in Homer's interest with real confidence. Secondly, surely it would be better, even when his position were secured, to eschew violent confrontation. If he were to differ from his employers as to the substance or method of what was to be done, let him hide his disagreement and proceed to his own end by stealth, allowing Jules and/or Foxy to think that the end which he sought was theirs. If they wanted something, then let them think they were getting it; in this way he would be left in peace to contrive for them what he himself wanted them to have. As to his ability to cozen them in this way, Fielding was in no doubt whatever : Foxy was an unlettered booby; Jules, while shrewd and in some ways sensitive, had not had the benefit of a classical education. Fielding alone knew the ground properly, and he was therefore free to play his own game on it. *Caveat emptor.*

His immediate task now was to rewrite the speeches for the scenes on the beach. Rather tricky, Fielding thought, for his first exercise. The speeches in question, as Tom had observed, were particularly beautiful and subtle, and to cast them plainly enough to satisfy Jules yet delicately enough not to betray Homer was going to be a difficult matter. Although he had already done some work on them, he had not done as much as he had implied to Jules, and now he had only until the following evening to produce a solid sample. He scowled at the mountains of Epirus, and then transcribed the first speech, both in Greek and in literal English :

Alas for me. To a land of what mortals am I come? Are they savage and wild and unjust? Or do they love strangers and have the fear of the gods in their hearts? . . .

But this, of course, was not really a speech, though printed as such in the text; it was Odysseus's first thoughts on being woken. In any case, none of it either need be or should be spoken aloud; it must be implied by the hero's actions (peering through the bushes at the beach and the squawking maidens) and by the expressions which passed over his face. First doubt, then determination, as he made ready to do the only thing he could . . . go out, naked as he was, and confront Nausicaa.

So Fielding crossed out the speech and scribbled a note ('Face, gestures, etc.') in the margin. He then read the existing directions for Odysseus's appearance out of the brush and the hysterical flight of all the girls save the Princess herself. What he was now left with was the Princess standing there, courageous but astonished, gaping at the masculine limbs 'all befouled with the brine' and plainly requiring immediate explanation, which Odysseus, on any reckoning, must surely supply. There could be no further evasion, no substitution of gestures or expressions : in all the circumstances Odysseus had got to say a mouthful and a good one at that, and Fielding now had to write it for him.

So Fielding transcribed, again both in Greek and in literal English, the first few lines of Odysseus's 'gentle and cunning speech' :

I beseech thee, O queen . . . a goddess are you, or are you mortal? If you are a goddess, one of those who hold wide heaven, to Artemis, daughter of great Zeus, do I liken you most nearly in fairness and in height and in form. . . .

Here was the text : how to make what Jules wanted of *this*? Now he was finally up against it. Have at it then : neck or nothing. He took a deep drink, then a deep breath, and began to write. . . .

". . . So have kindness, lady," said Angus Carnavon, "for I come to you out of the sea after much toil and danger, and of those who live here I know not even one. Show me where is your city, and give me clothes to put about my body; and then may god be kind to you also, and give you all that your heart desires, a husband and a home, when you would have them, and fellowship to bind you, which is the best gift of all."

"Cut," called Jules. "Take fifteen minutes."

Angus/Odysseus tottered away over the beach, sat down under an awning, and applied himself to a gigantic drink which was waiting. Sasha/Nausicaa, seeming taller than usual in a white ankle-length dress, swished up to Jules and Fielding, who were sitting together beside one of the cameras.

"Well?" she said.

"Well enough," said Jules. "You stood there like a picture,

my dear. If you can get your speech off as well as Angus did his . . ."

". . . It's not the speech that worries me. Will Angus still be conscious when I get to the end of it?"

"He's a sixth of his bottle still left, I'm told. He'll be good for the next take, which is all we want of him today. You go and rest, honey. Ready for take 137," he called to those round him, "in ten minutes' time."

Jules rose and beckoned to Fielding. They walked away from the cameras and the groups of hunched technicians towards the sea.

"It seems to be working," said Jules with cautious congratulation. "The rhythm's right and the style's right. When you showed me the first draft ten days ago, I had my doubts. But now . . . I think we shall be all right."

"Then I'd better get back to my desk, Jules. I've got the rest of the book to work on."

"You'd better just wait and hear Sasha say her first piece. If that's all right too, then you can get going with the rest as fast as possible."

"She was all right in rehearsal."

"Not the same thing as a proper take. Don't ask me why, Fielding, but you can only be certain it's all right when the cameras are rolling for real . . . as Foxy would put it. Well, the cameras are now doing just that; and if Sasha's bit goes as well as Angus's, I'll take your stuff as proven, and I'll extend your contract to the full period as soon as I get in tonight."

"Without asking Foxy?"

"He's left that decision with me. So back to the barricades, my dear, and just you pray that little Sasha makes a go of it."

They turned to walk back to their chairs.

"What the devil's this?" Jules said.

'This' was a procession of three people winding down from the rocks above the beach. First, a dapper figure in tropical whites and a wide panama; then a fat little fellow (apparently made up, like the Michelin man, of pneumatic rings) who was

wearing a dark suit and a grey homburg; and finally an enormous, scarlet-faced woman, with heaving torso and legs like
flabby Doric columns.

"Max de Freville in the lead," Fielding said.

"And Lykiadopoulos. Come to watch. It's a nuisance but
they've paid for the privilege."

"Who's the woman?" Fielding asked.

"Max's woman. Angela Tuck."

"CHRIST. She's got grotesque."

"Come and meet 'em. We'll have to settle them down before
we start the take."

As Jules and Fielding went forward to greet the procession,
Fielding saw that Max had hardly changed since their last meeting eight years before. The furrows between his nose and the
two ends of his mouth, always very noticeable, had deepened
and widened a little; but that was all. Angela, on the other
hand, he would not have recognised, if Jules had not warned
him who she was. Eight years ago, although she had un-
doubtedly been coarse to look at, her legs had still been brown
and firm and her face not without a bawdy and suggestive
charm. Now she was just a mass of meat: her face was
smothered under three huge sweaty rolls . . . two cheeks and the
chin . . . which toppled inwards to overlap the corners of her
lips and almost to envelop her nostrils; and the trunk-like legs,
in thick white stockings, wobbled at every step.

"You there, you one-eyed satyr," she called, with all her old
bitchy authority, "long time no see. Come and thrill me with
tales of your sex-life."

In the end, after the more decorous grettings were done, the
colonial Max and the Edwardian (Greek version) Lykiadopoulos were seated one each side of Jules, while Fielding and
Angela were parked together a little way behind. When they
were all comfortable, Jules gave a signal, on which Angus/
Odysseus was trundled by three assistants into his position and
Sasha/Nausicaa strode fiercely forward into hers.

"Interesting build," said Angela; "well honed hussy.
Unusual."

F

"Strict silence during the take, please," said Jules over his shoulder.

"This is very important," Fielding whispered to Angela; "if this goes right I'll get a full-length contract . . . another twelve weeks."

"Here's luck, then," she growled back, and clamped one hand over the inside of his thigh in what he hoped was intended only as moral support. She gave a squeeze that made him wince, then relaxed her grip but did not remove her hold; and he was just wondering whether or not this ogress risen from his past was indeed contemplating a trip with him down Memory Lane, when all thoughts of Angela were temporarily driven from his head by the clack of the clapper that heralded Take 137.

What was to be filmed now was Nausicaa's answer to Odysseus's plea for help. Close-up of Nausicaa, the script ordained, her lips trembling. Close-up of Odysseus, who sank on to one knee and bowed his head. Then pull back slowly to see and hear the Princess as she answered. Now; now she must speak the words which could mean £12,000 to Fielding.

She opened her mouth, seemed to gag slightly, and closed it. Oh Christ, the silly bitch was going to fluff. Fielding trembled all along his body with chagrin and anxiety . . . and was then reminded of Angela, whose hand moved up his thigh in a light caress and settled snugly into his groin, not to excite, it seemed, but to soothe, or rather, to soothe by partly exciting, as an unscrupulous mother might calm a fractious child by mildly pleasuring its innocent body. Nice, thought Fielding, nice, easing his thighs apart to accept the comfort and placing his hand on Angela's to show his gratitude. As he did so, he became aware that Sasha Grimes was now moving splendidly through her speech, was indeed already more than half way through it.

". . . Since it is to this land you have come, you shall lack for nothing. I will show you our city and tell you the name of our people : we are called the Phaeacians, and I myself am the daughter of Alcinous, who is first in power among them."

She stretched out her hand to Odysseus to raise him, and he took it in both of his, turned it over and lowered his lips into the palm, while the Princess went taut with pleasure. First she gave a slight shudder at the male proximity, then she went rigid at the moment of Odysseus's kiss on her palm, her lips just parted and her belly slightly arched towards him, then she closed her eyes, willed her body to subside, and opened her eyes again in time to smile back brilliantly as Odysseus raised his head to smile up at her in his thankfulness. Oh you wonderful, clever little cat, Fielding thought, and without either surprise or warning he felt himself throb with violent release, three, four, five times, under Angela's hand.

"Cut," called Jules. "Bloody marvellous."

Sasha stalked off. Odysseus remained down on one knee, being unable to rise without assistance. Angela very slowly withdrew her hand from Fielding, while he eased his copy of the script over his lap to disguise any damage. Max and Lykiadopoulos nodded pleasantly to each other behind Jules's back. Three henchmen appeared to carry Odysseus back to the awning. Lykiadopoulos winked with almost regal dignity at the clapper-boy, who crossly pouted back. Jules rose and turned to Fielding and Angela.

"That's it, Fielding," he said. "Go and do the rest of the book just like that."

"Bully for you, sweetie," Angela said.

Odysseus fell forward out of his armchair and lay prone under the awning.

"Cart him off home," called Jules : "we're through with him for today. Take 138 in twenty minutes. Nausicaa rounding up the handmaids and organising them to feed and bath Odysseus. What are you waiting for, Fielding? I don't need you here any more. Go and write speeches."

"I'll walk up with you," Angela said.

It seemed that for all Jules's preoccupations Max and Lykiadopoulos wanted a few words with him; at any rate they took one arm each and walked him away from his chair, leaning in towards him, each talking alternatively into one of his ears. So Angela and Fielding were left by themselves to make their progress off the beach, Angela waddling breathily, Fielding stepping carefully in pace with her and clasping his script before him.

"You want that actress girl, don't you?" Angela said.

"Not particularly. What happened was because of the nervous strain. "

"Not very flattering, are you? But I know it wasn't me. It was me at first, warming the works up, but it wasn't me at the end, and it wasn't the nervous strain, it was little Miss Prim Airs going stiff and sticking out her fanny. That's when it really started. One moment you just had a rise, the next you were half an inch longer and beginning to twitch."

"Need you be so analytic, Angela?"

"Yes. It's the only way I get my fun these days. Watching and working out the form. This has been a rare treat for me, I can tell you."

"I'm glad. But you're wrong about Sasha. She's locked, so to speak, into armour. It'd be like lusting after Joan of Arc."

"People did that, I dare say. And if ever the armour came off . . ."

"There'd probably be something very, very wrong underneath it. Not worth the trouble and the risks, Angela. I've got something quite good enough to be going on with . . . over there." He pointed to Elena, who was being carefully arranged under the olive tree from behind which she was to emerge at Nausicaa's summons. "Succulent, as you see, and inventive."

"Muck," said Angela. "A pretty little bit of muck. Now Miss Prim Airs . . . Sasha . . . she's altogether out of the ordinary."

"Perhaps. But even if she's worth the labour of unbolting all that armour, the director has issued an embargo. He won't have her touched, in case she gets put off her acting."

"He needn't worry about that. She's full up to the eyes with ambition and tough as they breed 'em. Anyway, now you've got your contract you don't need to bother so much about the director."

They began to climb a rocky path up from the beach towards a small plateau which had been cleared and levelled for privileged cars. Angela breathed still more heavily. You poor old bag, Fielding thought : when I think of you in that summer of 1945, striding over the turf like an Amazon and flaying the arse off your golf ball . . . twenty-five years ago, so you're still well short of fifty. What on earth's done this to you? Cheap Greek brandy? But Max can afford the best . . . which of course is also the strongest.

"Do you mind," said Angela, "if we rest for a moment?"

She propped her bottom on a convenient rock. Fielding stood facing her, still shielding his crutch with his script.

"You remember when we last met," she said eventually, "and had that rather jolly afternoon together?"

"Very clearly. On Hydra."

"That's right. 1962 it must have been, just before Max and I went to Cyprus. Well, as you see, I've changed a bit since then. No more jolly afternoons in the hay for me."

"You're still . . . an impressive woman," said Fielding dutifully.

"As impressive . . . and as bedworthy . . . as a female gorilla. Max, you understand, has never wanted me in that way . . . not even at the beginning. As for other men," she said equably, "I suppose I could pay. I've done that before. But in fact there are very good reasons why I should leave it alone from now on . . . just leave it alone."

She looked at Fielding as if expecting him to ask what the reasons were. But he scented danger and even horror in this topic, and merely nodded.

"So," she continued, "any pleasure I get these days comes, as I said just now, from watching and weighing the form. Procuring too. I've always had the soul of a bawd." She laughed merrily, raised her bottom from the rock, and started slowly on up the path. "If you like," she said, "I'll help you get that girl . . . Sasha. You would like, wouldn't you? It'd be worth it, if only for the experience. Not every man gets to do it with Joan of Arc."

Fielding helped her over a large rock which was embedded in the path.

"What's in it for you?" he asked. "A peep-hole in the bed-room door?"

"Very uncomfortable, and not at all easy to arrange in the Corfu Palace Hotel. Now, back at Max's and my place there's a room with a fake mirror in the wall. . . ."

"Fair enough. It might be rather exciting . . . knowing that you were watching behind a fake mirror. But first things first, Angela. First you have to help me to her bed. Now, little Sasha shows no sign at all of wanting anybody. She's a serious girl, dedicated to social causes. Why should she want to put out the honey pot for a cynical old wreck like me?"

"Just because you are a cynical old wreck." Angela led the way across the little car park to a maroon Rolls-Royce. "A serious girl with a sense of duty might respond to an appeal. 'I'm so unhappy,' you might say : 'I'm so ugly and horrid, and you're so beautiful and pure.' So then she thinks of you as deprived; she thinks she owes you something to repair the inequity."

"She'll hardly think she owes me her maidenhood."

"Why not . . . if it *is* her maidenhood? It would show her sacrifice was really sincere. But if she still holds out, you go a stage further. You pretend to be guilty and wretched because you're prostituting your literary art to the movie moguls and thereby raking in more money every day than twenty Indian peasants in a year. Really pile on the agony. Little girls like Sasha won't do anything for fun; but if you spread enough sheer misery around, down come their knickers at the last, because misery's their substitute for romance."

She opened the rear door of the Rolls.

"End of lesson one," she said. "Pile on the agony and see what happens. If it works, I'll invite you both to Max's place so that I can collect my fee in kind. If not, we must think again."

Very suddenly the high colour drained from her face.

"Angela . . . are you all right?"

"Go now."

She scrabbled her way into the car and sprawled along the back seat.

"Angela . . ."

". . . Go away, damn you. No. Turn on the air cooler first. Yellow knob on the dashboard. . . . Thanks."

"I'll stay till Max comes."

"Just you bugger off," she croaked, "and write your pretty speeches."

When Fielding arrived back at the Corfu Palace, he ordered a bottle of champagne to be sent up to his room, though it was not his custom, these days, to drink in the afternoon. I've got the contract, he thought, as he toasted himself in the wall-mirror: whatever disagreements there may be now, over Homer or anything else, I've got myself another twelve thousand quid.

He had also got himself some immediate personal problems. The first was Elena. Since there was a lot of work with Nausicaa and the handmaids still to be done, and since not all of the amended script for these scenes had yet been passed round, Elena still did not know that she hadn't been given the lines which he had promised her. But every day she was becoming more suspicious, every night more perfunctory in her services. Very soon she was going to ask him straight out where and when her lines were coming, and she was not going to be amused when told, 'You've had 'em, duckie . . . I thought you knew . . . that pretty little song you all sang with the ball.'

So Elena would be angry and would be off with Fielding; and even after two weeks of her, he would feel the lack. Which led to an interesting but perturbing question: should he follow Angela's advice and make a set for Sasha instead? This would certainly be intriguing; but leave aside any trouble it might bring with Jules if he found out, Fielding was very uneasy about the possible reactions of Sasha herself. Let him assume that Angela was right, let him assume that a pretence of unhappiness would indeed bring him into Sasha's bed, he must still pause at the question of what he might find when he got there. For as he had told Angela, a man who dared to unbolt armour as impregnable as Sasha's appeared to be might discover something very disconcerting underneath.

To have or not to have? On the whole, and despite his misgivings, he inclined to have, if he could, especially if Elena withdrew her present offices. But whichever way it all worked out, one thing was quite certain : he did not want Harriet Ongley cluttering up the ground. Since he had been in Corfu she had written twice and then, the day before, sent a cable, wanting to know urgently what plans he was making for her to join him. If he ignored her, she would just turn up unbidden; it had happened before. The only way to keep her off was to write . . . to wire . . . that there was delay over the decision on his contract and that he could make no firm plans as yet. He could play it that way for another two weeks, perhaps; then he would have to think of a new lie. What a bore women were, whether wanted or unwanted . . . more boring, on the whole, when wanted, because more powerful to command their own witless way. There were times when he could wish that that bomb in Cyprus had made him a eunuch.

But since it hadn't, he must proceed as a whole man. He rehearsed to himself what he would say to Elena when she accused him of double-crossing her; he drafted a cable to Harriet attributing the delay over settling his contract, and hence his own inability to make arrangements, to the absence of Foxy Galahead; and he wrote a polite little note to Sasha Grimes, praising her performance that afternoon and asking her to dine with him and discuss her remaining scenes on the evening after the next.

Nausicaa watched her maidens as they stowed the last bundle of dry washing on to the waggon, and then strode to the front of it, beckoning to Odysseus, now clean and properly dressed, to follow her. He offered her an arm to help her up into the driving seat, but she shook her head, came close under his shoulder, and began to talk very earnestly.

"Listen, stranger from the sea. Now you are fed and clothed I will bring you to my people, and this is how it must come about. As long as we are passing through the woods and the fields, walk with my handmaids behind the waggon; but when we draw near the city, you will see a harbour set on either side of it, and all along the road you will see the curved ships of the Phaeacians, drawn up in their posts, and many men busied about them in the last of the evening light. It is their mocking speech that I fear, should they see you following my waggon. So do you look about you for a grove of poplar trees that is near to the road. . . ."

Ideal, thought Fielding, as Nausicaa went on, at some length, to tell Odysseus exactly where he must hide, and for how long, and what he must do when it was dark : ideal; they couldn't have come on a better day's schedule.

For there had been an unexpected visitation of enormous importance, and hence Fielding's presence on the beach when he should have been sitting in the Corfu Palace writing speeches for the rest of the film. He was there on set to answer such questions on dialogue or related matters as might be put to him by Dr. Emile Schottgatt or any of his three colleagues on The Creative Authentication Committee of the Oglander-Finckelstein Trust. The Committee had flown in unobserved on the previous afternoon (that on which Max de Freville and his friends had come to the beach) and had emerged from nowhere this morning, all of them wearing calf-length linen shorts and fawn ankle-socks, avid, it seemed, to commence creative authenticating.

'Christ,' Jules had said to their courier, a plump but rather wan P.R.O. from Clytemnestra Films. 'Why didn't you warn us you were bringing this lot ?'

'They like snap visits. I was given just ten minutes' notice by Foxy Galahead to bring 'em over from New York.'

'You could have wired.'

'I did. To the hotel for rooms.'

'You could have wired me.'

'Foxy said not. He said you'd cope much better if it came as a surprise.'

'Why should he think that ?'

'Because you'd just carry on naturally and not get all ballsed up with making special arrangements.'

'A lot of help Foxy is.'

'He's coming over himself tomorrow. Meanwhile, he says have the script-writer do any explaining they want. He thinks the script-writer's a sharp cookie.'

So it was at this stage that Julies had sent for Fielding, to tell him to accompany them out to the beach for the day's shooting.

'This is Burke Lawrence,' Jules had said, introducing the P.R.O.

'We met some years ago.'

'Christ,' said Burke Lawrence; 'so we bloody did.'

'No time to talk over old days now,' Jules had said. 'We've got problems.' And he had rapidly briefed Fielding on the proposed course of the day's shooting, before sending him to join the Inquisition in their minibus and ride out with them to Ermones.

And now Sasha was going great guns in a scene which, Fielding thought, Dr. Schottgatt and his chums must surely approve. For it was faithful to Homer, rather static, definitely poetic and somewhat verbose. A 'culture' scene beyond any possible doubt. What precisely their reactions were, however, Schottgatt & Co. were not letting on just yet. They sat in a little row of canvas chairs, their hands clasped in their laps, their thin, white, hairless legs planted in four prim parallel pairs, their faces spongy and totally impassive. What a crew, thought Fielding : God alone knew what sort of questions he was to expect from a tribunal like that.

"And when you have reached our house," Nausicaa was saying, "and have passed through the court and entered the great hall, walk on swiftly till you come to my mother, who sits by the hearth in the firelight spinning the purple yarn. . . ."

Interesting hint here, thought Fielding, that the Phaeacians had still to some extent preserved matriarchal customs. It was getting in with the Queen that mattered, or so Nausicaa seemed to be saying. But for all the learned gentlemen from Montana University appeared to care, Nausicaa could be reciting her three-times table or repeating an old wives' cure for warts. No poker-table had even known such absolute poker faces. They looked as if they had been sealed silent by the hand of God; and indeed the only words they had spoken to Fielding so far that whole day were 'good morning', which Schottgatt, as their leader, had pinged at him as he entered their minibus. Nothing more had been said on the way to the beach; and when Fielding attempted to interest them in a brief description of the topography, as they were crossing the golf course towards the sea, they had not even troubled to turn their heads in his direction. Americans, think what you might of them, were generally so courteous and pleased when you tried to tell them something; but this lot might just as well have been zombies . . . zombies under the total control of Dr. Schottgatt, at whose nod they had alighted from the minibus, behind whom they had walked in Indian file on to the beach, and at whose nod, once more, they had seated themselves in identical postures which they had then held without moving for the entire morning. How was one to communicate with such a party? Perhaps Burke Lawrence would know? But communication with Lawrence himself was going to offer yet another awkward problem, Fielding thought, in view of the curious circumstances in which they had last met.

"Cast your hands about my mother's knees," Sasha was concluding, "for if you find her favour, then, though you come from the end of the earth, you can hope to see your friends once more and return to your own sweet country."

"Cut," called Jules.

Schottgatt beckoned to Fielding. Now at last the silence was going to be broken, perhaps, now at last the questions and the criticisms would begin.

"Four glasses of water, sir, if you will be so good," Dr. Emile Schottgatt said.

After fetching water for the committee-men, each of whom took his glass in his right hand and rested it carefully on his right knee, and after being thanked by Schottgatt on behalf of all four of them, Fielding felt that however embarrassing it might be, he must now have a word with Burke Lawrence. This seemed to be his only hope of achieving some understanding of the bizarre ensemble which the P.R.O. had brought with him from New York. Having spotted Lawrence slip away with a tin of beer into the labyrinth of rock at the south end of the beach, Fielding now followed him and ran him to ground where he sat hunched into a tiny cave in a low wall of incipient cliff.

"Last time we met," Fielding said, grasping the nettle, "you were beastly drunk and in bad trouble."

"I remember well enough," said Lawrence, and sucked at his beer.

"What happened to you all? You and that Holbrook woman and her ex-husband?"

"We all kept as quiet as little mice, and after a time it was safe to come out of our holes. After all, the big row was in Venice and we were in England."

"But I should have thought the Italian police could have interested Scotland Yard in your activities?"

"We were very peripheral, you know . . . even Jude Holbrook, and he was the most involved of us. Besides," said Lawrence, who seemed amiably or at last equably disposed, "when it came to the point there wasn't any evidence. The wop police thought they had bushels of it, but it crumbled under their noses. Hearsay, conjecture, a lot of Venetian tattle . . . that's all they had. They barely managed to fix three years on Salvadori himself."

"But the writing was on the wall?"

"Oh yes. I cleared out to Canada. Somebody said that the Canadians wanted young film directors . . . which was what I was meant to be. It didn't quite work out as I hoped, but I'm not complaining."

"And the other two?"

"Penelope Holbrook still lives in London on alimony which Jude sends her . . . or did when I last saw her five years ago. The money comes in from Hong Kong. God knows what Jude does there. . . . Why are you asking all these questions?"

"I like tidying things up. And I wanted to know where I stood with you . . . after our last encounter."

"I'm P.R.O. of an outfit which employs you as script-writer. That's where you stand with me."

"Good. But I'm damned if I know where I stand with those four wise men you've brought here. What do you know about them?"

"The Creative Authentication Committee of the Oglander-Finckelstein Trust," said Burk Lawrence, "consists of four senior members of Montana University who are nominated by the Professor of English Literature. At present the four nominees are Dr. Emile Schottgatt, an expert on early Aegean dialects; Dr. Gayland Webb, an archaeologist who made his name investigating Viking settlements in Greenland; Dr. Gabriel Rutter, an anthropologist who specialises in the Australian aborigine; and Dr. Pym K. Zimmerei, a sociologist, who is currently writing a treatise on Post-Menopausal Masturbation in the Affluent Female."

"Christ." Fielding turned away from Lawrence and peered back through the rocks to the beach, where the four magi were still seated in line, clasping their glasses of water. "How do you tell 'em apart?"

"You don't have to. Schottgatt answers for all of them."

"And what do *they* know about being creative?"

"Search me. I dare say they know a bit about being authentic."

"But listen, Lawrence. It appears that the future of this film depends on the report which those four curios turn in when they get home. Now, we were reckoning on quite a tough job when it came to getting the rest of the money, but no one expected to have to deal with four old spiders out of the Sibyl's Cave. Will you, as P.R.O., kindly explain to me just how I'm meant to approach them?"

"You're not. You wait till they approach you."

"That's what Foxy wants?"

"Sure is. So just sit tight, Major Gray, and obey your orders."

"I don't use the rank these days."

"But I shall. I like ranks," said Burke Lawrence. "I get sick of all these damn silly meaningless Christian names. 'I'm Si, meet Syd.' Do me a favour, and let me call you by your proper title."

"I don't see why not."

"Thank you. And now, Major Gray : would you care for a little tip?"

"I always appreciate tips."

"Then steer clear of that red-head, Sasha Grimes. I saw you looking at her just now . . . with that certain look. Forget all that and forget it fast. Sasha Grimes is Calamity Jane . . . in that department at least."

"How can you be sure?"

"P.R.O.s," said Lawrence, "are paid to be sure about these things."

"I've already been warned off by Jules," said Fielding. "He doesn't want her disturbed."

"I bet he doesn't . . . and especially not just now. Sasha Grimes, you see, could be a great help in keeping Og-Finck happy."

"She's certainly acting well enough."

"It's not just her acting. Miss Grimes, Major Gray, has a privileged relationship with the Og-Finck Trust. A year or two back she won the Oglander-Finckelstein Award for Drama . . ."

". . . So I've heard . . ."

". . . And the twelve-month Fellowship at Montana University that goes with it. Youngest person ever to get it, and the first from Britain."

"They must have thought very highly of her."

"They did, Major Gray. And during the year she held the award, she got herself in even better with them. Not only as an actress but as a . . . lovely, sensitive person . . . full of compassion and conscience . . . all that crap. By the end of that year, Sasha Grimes was the apple of Og-Finck's eye, which is why she got this part . . . a condition of their deal with Foxy. And so those old men in knickers will listen breathlessly to anything she has to say . . . on or off the set."

"I see. Handle with care."

"Not to be handled at all, Major Gray. As Jules Jacobson

says, do not disturb. For every possible reason. Leave aside that she's the darling of Og-Finck, just remember that I'm warning you on a purely sexual level as well : it's you too that will be *disturbed,* Major Gray, if you start anything with Sasha Grimes."

"Would she let me start anything?"

Burke Lawrence cocked his head, focused his eyes, and then swivelled them from left to right and back again several times, as though consulting an invisible dossier in the air before him.

"She might," Lawrence said at last. "For your sake I hope she doesn't. Not but what you could get into a big enough mess just by *trying.*"

"I'm meant to be having dinner alone with her tomorrow night. That is, I've sent a note to ask her."

"Then you'd better pray she writes back to say 'no, thank you'," Burke Lawrence said, and tossed his empty beer tin into the never-resting sea.

But as it happened, Sasha Grimes had already written back to say 'yes, please', and Fielding found her note as soon as he returned to the Corfu Palace. That engagement, however, was for the next evening; meanwhile he had to get through this one, which was to be devoted to the entertainment of the Creative Authenticators. Jules was to be host (in Foxy's absence) and he had bidden Fielding to come along and assist him; Sasha, as the favourite of Og-Finck and an ex-member of Montana, would also be in attendance. The scheme was that the three of them should conduct the Committee plus Burke Lawrence on a tour of 'traditional' Corfiot evening amusements, these to consist of eating a dinner of crawfish somewhere on the coast, watching peasant dancing at a rural Taverna called the Persephone, and admiring the Castle of St. Angelo by moonlight.

Since three of the four committee-men did not eat shell-fish, and since the keeper of the Persephone had forgotten to hire any dancers, and since the Greek driver missed the track which would have brought them to the Gorge of St. Angelo, the outing was not a success. Jules had hoped that his guests would give some idea of whether or not they had liked what they had seen on set that day; but the four wise men had eyes and ears for no one but Sasha, and even with her they refused to discuss any subject connected with the film or its making, though she tried hard to elicit their reactions. She gave up this attempt when it was at last clearly hopeless, and switched her conversation to 'compassionate' statements about the miseries of Greek workers, statements which the Committee (though as ignorant of the matter as Sasha was) complacently endorsed by ponderous iteration.

"It's all very well," said Fielding to Burke Lawrence in the putrescent loo of the Taverna Persephone, "but when *are* they going to talk about what they're here for?"

"Remember your orders, Major Gray : just sit quiet until challenged."

Which was sound enough precept; but by now Fielding was starting to jitter. If even the much respected Sasha could not make the Committee talk about the film, there must be something wrong somewhere. Such total silence on the one topic which really concerned everyone present, though an optimist might have attributed it to discretion, seemed to Fielding to be discourteous to the point of malignance. It could not bode well. After he had said good-night to the four doctors, he came away feeling rather as though he had dined with a posse of undertakers on the eve of a mass funeral. The Committee smelt of the graveyard; and if they buried the Odysseus project, there was an end of Fielding's contract; for although Jules had now extended this for the next three months, Fielding's engagement, like everyone else's, was contingent on the funding of the production. All in all he was in a bleak mood as he went up to bed and he was not at all cheered, as he opened the door of his drawing room, to see Elena sitting at his desk.

"Sorry, sweetheart," he said. "My evening's already gone on too long. That Committee . . ."

". . . It won't take you long to hear what I've got to say."

"Drink?" said Fielding, scenting trouble.

"No. Just a straight answer. Where the hell are my lines?" She thumped both fists down among the papers on his desk.

"I've been through your copy of the script, I've been through every scrap of paper on this fucking desk, and nowhere can I see my lines."

Ah, well. It had to come sooner or later.

"You've got a short memory," he said : "don't you recall that song?"

"Song?"

" 'So take, while there is time, the gifts that . . .' "

". . . Like a heap of crap I recall it. What about it?"

"Your lines, sweetheart. And you were jolly lucky to get them. Jules was very doubtful at first."

"But we *all* sang that bloody song. Including bloody Nausicaa."

"Exactly. It might have been *only* Nausicaa. I interested Jules in sharing it out a bit. Why, you had one whole line to yourself."

"Half a line the second time through. You promised me *lines* . . . four lines, you said . . . to myself."

"I said I'd try, and I did try, and that's what came of it. It was always a strong order, most unlikely to get past Jules, and so I said at the time. But I did my best, I positively got a song for you to sing, so now let's have a little gratitude."

"Why didn't you tell me that my lines were that song?"

"I thought you'd realise."

"But we were always going to have a song, even before you came. Jules had been discussing it with Tom Llewyllyn. It's not true what you're saying, lover." Reproachful now rather than angry, he noticed, even though giving him the lie direct. "You never tried to write my lines. You've just been doing me a load of dirt."

"All right," Fielding said. "But you didn't play it very clean yourself. Getting a fellow's balls bubbling and then threatening to stop. What sort of a game is that?"

"Horrid," she admitted, and gave him a sad little grin. "But then I'm just a slut, and I haven't any real talent, so it's the only sort of game I can play if I want to get on in this business. Almost all of them . . . even those who have got talent . . .

started out like that. You ask Margaret Lichfield. It's the only way, lover, at any rate for scrubbers like me."

"But you must know by now that promises extracted in bed are apt to be dishonoured. They always have been, Elena. There's a rule which says they don't count, and it was the gods themselves who made it."

"And of course all the shits in this trade take full advantage of it. But I'll tell you what it was with you, lover. You had just a slight thing about you of being a gentleman. Oh, I knew that most of it had worn off years ago, but it was still possible to see that once upon a time you'd been brought up to open doors for ladies and to be kind to underdogs and to tell the truth. It was in your cut, in your style, in a way it isn't in Jules's or Foxy's or Angus's . . . or even in Max de Freville's . . . though you might find it in that little Greek pal of his, come to think of it now. Anyway, lover, when I saw you, I said to myself, 'Elena, my dear,' I said, 'this here is the remains of an old-fashioned English gent, and he might, he just might, keep his promise to a girl.' Well, it turns out you just didn't. One more in a long line of disappointments, but a bigger one than most, lover, because it was wrapped up in a gentleman's word."

She smiled at Fielding quite kindly, and then left.

The next three days had been set aside by Jules as an interval. The scenes on the beach had now been finished bang on schedule; and since Odysseus, Nausicaa and her maidens would all be working in the scenes next to come (Odysseus's appeal for passage home in the hall of Alcinous, and the Games given for his entertainment), it had seemed to Jules, when he was drawing up the programme, that they would be glad about now of a rest. Furthermore, a three-day respite would give Jules himself the chance to make his final preparations on the new sets to which they would now be shifting, and also—or so he had hoped—the time to rough-edit some clips of the beach scenes for despatch to the Oglander-Finckelstein Trust.

But now these sensible and leisurely plans must be changed. The O/F Trust, instead of biding quietly on its own side of the

Atlantic, had sent scouts and outriders to demand and disrupt, and their leader had made it plain that they would brook neither idleness nor delay. If there was no shooting for them to watch, they would watch rehearsals, and if there was none of these either they would see what film had already been made—every single foot of it, and now. There was no time to prepare special sequences, Jules decided; he would have to make do with the rushes, *mal soignés* as these might be. With some difficulty the Authenticators were induced to take the morning off and were promised, to make up, a bumper afternoon screening of every inch of celluloid that could be found for them. The occasion would be graced by the presence of Foxe J. Galahead, who was flying in at noon.

"Jesus wept, baby," said Foxy to Jules as they drove from the airport. "They can't be as bad as that."

"Worse, Foxy. Why did you let 'em come?"

"Couldn't stop 'em. It was always on the cards that Og-Finck would send someone."

"But why these four scarecrows?"

"How do I know why? Can't Burke Lawrence handle them? Or Fielding Gray?"

"Foxy. Three of them are vegetarian, two are also teetotal, and one is a sociologist. How does anyone handle a crowd like that? They just sit there in a row waiting to be shown things. This afternoon they have to be shown what there is of this film, and you've got to be there helping out."

"Helping out?"

"Laughing and crying and falling about in the right places."

"But I was going to spend the afternoon with Gretel. I cabled ahead to ask her to lunch. Can't this show wait till to-morrow?"

"No, Foxy. They are sitting like vultures on a fence, and they got very impatient when I said that no carcasses would be served this morning. If they don't get something by two-thirty, they'll be on the wing back to Montana. And you know what that means."

"Okay, Jules. How did they like what they've seen so far?"

"They just don't say. They watched the seven last takes out at Ermones yesterday, and not one word did they say to anyone."

"More like mummies than vultures?"

"Like both," sighed Jules.

"All right. So I'll give them lunch," Foxy said, "and strictly no Gretel. Tell Fielding to be there and Burke Lawrence. Where's the screening?"

"In the hotel. The large room they use for their Winter Casino."

"And that gives me an idea. Ring Max de Freville and Lyki, and get them to come. Not that Angela, she'd give J. Christ himself the creeps, just Max and Lyki. And tell 'em I'd like a word with 'em before we join the rest for lunch."

What Jules had to show the Committee was as follows : some high-class stunting, by the men of the Second Unit, which would later be cut into the battles, brawls and storms; a lot of sound work by Penelope and the suitors in Odysseus's palace on Ithaca (a cleverly decked-out Corfiot castle); the sequence on Circe's island, shot on the lush hillsides near Corfu's Benitses; and the scenes in which Nausicaa and her handmaids set out from Alcinous's palace and discovered Odysseus on the beach. It was these latter, the only ones to have been made so far from Fielding's revised script, by which Jules set much the most store and by which alone he would have chosen, had matters been left to him, to have the quality of his achievement assessed.

But matters had not been left to him. The assessors were now on the spot and breathing heavily down his neck; they were insisting on seeing *all* the film available; and it was tolerably clear to everyone, even if it had not been stated in so many words, that on the strength of that afternoon's exhibition the Committee was going to hand down a straight and irreversible verdict as to whether or not the Trust would release the further six million dollars which were needed to complete the production. No doubt about it, thought Fielding as the umpteenth reel unwound in the Winter Casino; the chips were finally down.

At Foxy's luncheon party the committee-men had spoken hardly a word. Max and Fielding had tried to engage the archaeologist in a discussion of the site at Pylos; Burke Lawrence had rallied Zimmerei the sociologist with some choice tales from his early days in advertising; Foxy and Lykiadopoulos had done their best with Rutter and Schottgatt, Lykiadopoulos being particularly fluent about the erosion and inevitable destruction (as he predicted) of Venice : but none of this had drawn more than curt nods and cold smiles from the committee-men… who were now, some three hours later, watching Nausicaa's reception of the naked Odysseus, a passage which they had requested should be put on for them a second time. They alone were paying any attention to it; the rest of the audience had long since been reduced, by weariness and anxiety combined, to a state of stunned hysteria. Even Foxy, who for hours had reacted with vigorous and appropriate noises to every shadow which passed over the screen, had now exhausted his repertoire and was sitting absolutely still with his head hanging almost between his knees.

On the screen Odysseus turned over Nausicaa's hand and kissed the palm; the Princess arched her back, closed her eyes, and opened them to smile down at the battered hero; then the blue and yellow of the beach suddenly flicked to a gleaming blank; and somebody switched the light on.

"That's the lot," Jules said, "except for the scenes you gentlemen saw being shot yesterday."

"Can we not see those on film?"

"They're still being developed."

"Still being developed?"

"They have to go to Athens; it takes thirty-six hours before we can get them back."

"Very well," said Dr. Emile Schottgatt with hatchet face; "and now we should like to ask a few questions of the scriptwriter, Mr. Gray."

"At your service, gentlemen," said Fielding, trying to summon up some strength.

"Mr. Gray . . . would you describe your speeches as natural language?"

"No, sir. As formal language. Simple to speak and easy to understand, but definitely formal."

"And are we to infer, Mr. Gray, that in the late Bronze Age everyone habitually spoke in this formal and stylised manner?"

"Of course not. It is a poetic convention to suit the legend and the kind of people about whom it was written."

"What kind of people was that, Mr. Gray?"

"Gods and goddesses. Kings and queens and heroes."

"No ordinary people? What about Odysseus's sailors?"

"The only ones who matter in the story were his chosen officers and companions. Nobles and heroes like himself."

"I see. So the story excludes all but the pagan gods and the human upper classes?"

"Effectively, yes."

"Then will not the average audience feel itself to be excluded? Will it not understand that the common people, the equivalent of itself, was confined in those days entirely to menial tasks and was unfit even to be mentioned in literature or legend?"

"If the audience understands that," said Fielding, irritated and reckless, "it will be quite correct."

"And so we are to compound the insult which that particular social system inflicted on the people at large by repeating it in this film? And by parading it under the noses of all those who watch the film, thus making them feel, albeit at a historical distance, degraded and inferior?"

"A bit far-fetched, surely?"

"No," said Dr. Zimmerei, speaking for the first and only time. "To portray a hierarchical system in a work which extols the actions of the hierarchical leaders is to condone the methods of hierarchy."

"I thought you gentlemen were here as judges of our artistic authenticity."

"There are more important things in this modern age," said Dr. Schottgatt, "than considerations of pure art. Social questions must be paramount."

"But this whole story is happening in another world."

"Whose values differ totally from the democratic and egalitarian values of our own."

"That is inevitable."

"It is also unacceptable. You see, Mr. Gray, the world of Odysseus has so far been represented in this film as being better and nobler than ours is. Despite its indifference to the plight of the common people, indeed just because of this indifference, Odysseus's world is made out to be beautiful, joyous and heroic. We find that the appeal of your *Odyssey* depends very largely on sheer snobbery and brutal contempt for the labouring classes, who are treated as merely invisible."

"Look," said Foxy, "I don't get it. We went over all *that* stuff when the Trust agreed to back us. The Trustees said that *The Odyssey* was high-class cultural entertainment, just the sort of thing they were meant to subscribe to, and the best of luck to everyone. So why are you fellows making such a fuss?"

"Because we want the tinsel stripped off it," said Schottgatt. "We want Odysseus and his gang seen for the nasty thugs they were, and to this end we want their victims to be shown, and shown as suffering . . . not just neglected altogether."

"You haven't answered Mr. Galahead's question," Jules said. "When this production was first mooted, the instructions of the Trust were that we should stick as close as possible to Homer's text. The original script was prepared and approved on that basis. There was no suggestion whatever that we should superimpose the kind of . . . social realism . . . which you apparently advocate."

"There have been changes since then, Mr. Jacobson. Changes in our University and therefore changes in the administration of the Trust."

"No one warned us of a change of policy about our film."

"That's one reason why we're here now."

"Then would I be right in saying," Jules asked carefully, "that you do not object to our portraying a hierarchical society, *provided* that we give a square deal to those at the bottom of it? What you resent is the Homeric technique of leaving the ploughboy and the scullion right out of it."

"We want it made clear," said Schottgatt, "that the superficial splendour and romance of the world in which Odysseus moved depended to a great extent on the misery and exploitation of the working class as it then existed."

"Should be possible," said Max de Freville languidly. "Dot a few scraggy peasants round the fields, put a few louts to turn the spits at the banquets. . . ."

"The treatment," said Schottgatt, "must be a compassionate study of a forcibly brutalised slave caste."

"If that's what you want," said Jules, "I could use locals. You don't want them to speak?"

"Not necessarily. So long as they are visibly there and are seen to be ill-used. In those scenes in Odysseus's Palace, for example."

"I've explained to you," said Jules, "that I've got to shoot those scenes and several others again, with Mr. Gray's new dialogue. A change in the domestic flavour can be introduced then."

Schottgatt pursed his lips and nodded coldly, conceding this possibility.

"Look here," said Foxy to Schottgatt. "Are you saying that you're going to play ball? That providing we do all this about these peasants and so on, you'll recommend we get our money from the Trust?"

"As to that," said Schottgatt, "my colleagues and I must now retire to decide. You have made your attitudes plain enough, I think. Can I trouble you, Mr. Galahead, to come to my room in an hour's time?"

"Dear me," said little Lykiadopoulos after the Committee had retired, "so now American professors are doctoring the Classics to suit their political ideas?"

"It's an old left-wing trick," said Fielding. "Like the Russians rewriting history."

"Not unheard of on the right wing," said Max de Freville.

"Right wing, schmight wing," Foxy said. "What bugs me is, how do we pay for these damn peasants? The budget's stretched to busting already."

"You'd better just pray, Foxy babe," said Jules, "that we've still got a budget. I don't think Dr. Emile Schottgatt cares about our ethical tone."

"We said he could have his mother-fucking peasants, so what the hell more does he want?"

"Compassion," said Lykiadopoulos, "and he didn't hear much in your voices. Let us hope that when you present yourself in an hour's time you are going to hear more of it in his."

"You must understand," said Schottgatt to Foxy, "that matters are no longer as simple as they were."

Foxy and Schottgatt were alone in Schottgatt's room.

"There have been . . . structural changes in our University," Schottgatt went on, "which have affected our operation of the Oglander-Finckelstein Trust. The provision of money by the Trust must now be ratified, not only by me and my colleagues, but by a select committee of students. Even if we assume that you will abide by our conditions, and that you will do so in the spirit intended, the student committee may reject the whole project as being irrelevant."

"Just who tells who what to do in Montana?" Foxy said.

"As things are at this time," replied Schottgatt, "the students must be allowed to feel that they tell us. However, I think I can guarantee that they will vote you the rest of your money."

"Well thank sweet Jesus for that."

"No," said Schottgatt, "thank me. For the point is that the students will be told by myself and my committee that for political reasons we are compelling you to tear Homer to shreds. They will enjoy the idea of that . . . those of them who have heard of Homer . . . and so they will allow us to continue funding you. Out of spite to an established classic."

"Do I detect a hint, Dr. Schottgatt baby, that you're on our side?"

"Mr. Galahead, the Trust has already invested a large sum

of money in a film which is being directed, we have reason to think, with considerable expertise. It would be folly to withdraw at this stage. While student idealism would of course reject such a calculation, my colleagues and I are more sensible of mundane necessities. So we are prepared to compromise along the lines already discussed."

"Yeah, squads of peasants. But what about this stuff you'll tell the students . . . about tearing Homer to shreds? What we've discussed doesn't add up to that."

"No."

"And so when the kids see the film, and realise that you've been stringing them along? What then?"

"By the time this film is publicly shown, Mr. Galahead, we shall have an entirely new student committee. The great thing to remember about students is that even the most troublesome of them are impermanent."

"I see. But you *do* still want peasants?"

"Insurance, Mr. Galahead."

"In case the kids get nosy while we're still shooting?"

"Correct. What's more, the students will wish to know that they have effective means of exerting control right through to the end of production. In order to induce them to vote the way we wish, I shall have to say that your funds are being paid by instalments, each instalment being conditional on your continued obedience. I suggest instalments of three hundred thousand dollars a week."

"But it was to have been paid all at once."

"Three hundred thousand a week," said Schottgatt very firmly, "over the next twenty weeks. Always provided, as I shall have to tell the student committee, that our representative here continues to send in favourable reports."

"Your representative here?" said Foxy. "Will one of you gentlemen be staying on?"

"No," said Schottgatt. "We propose to appoint someone whom we think will report responsibly to ourselves and the student body. Someone," he went on blandly, "who is in sympathy with progressive political ideals and understands the ideological connotations of a collective enterprise of this kind."

"Look," said Foxy in a moment of rebellion, "you needn't think you're buying the whole show. De Freville and Lykiado-poulos have a one-third investment in this film."

"Then perhaps they would care to invest a further six million dollars . . . in the event of the Trust's withdrawing?"

For once Foxy said nothing.

"Very well," Schottgatt summed up, "the Trust will pay you three hundred thousand dollars a week, for twenty weeks, starting on Monday, 2 November. These payments to be conditional on the good reports, with respect to the future tone of the production, from our representative here in Corfu . . . who, we have decided after deep consultation, shall be that talented and concerned young lady, Miss Sasha Grimes."

"Dr. Schottgatt, baby," said Foxy after a long pause, "you have to be joking."

"Far from it. Look at it this way, Mr. Galahead. If you are to have your money, as you and I both wish, the students must be convinced that they hold an effective watching brief or that someone they can trust is holding it for them."

"Yeah, I get that. But why Sasha Grimes?"

"She was quite a personality in Montana, Mr. Galahead. Most of the students have heard of her, and some of the older ones met her while she was still with us. She is now a well-known actress . . . but not yet so rich and famous as to arouse their disapproval or mistrust. She is modest in her demeanour and manner of living, she eschews lavish social occasions, she is a professed egalitarian with revolutionary sympathies."

Foxy shuddered and Schottgatt grinned.

"That is just why she is so useful to us, Mr. Galahead. Because if *she* says that the progress and management of this production are satisfactorily in line with current left-wing orthodoxies, then the student committee will believe her and let the thing go on. But they must be sure that they have the power to interfere if they should want to. So we set up the young and idealist Miss Grimes as the symbol of that power, and we tell them that her appointment as their representative here will be its guarantee. There is no better way, Mr. Galahead, of securing their necessary consent."

Foxy pondered this.

"Okay," Foxy said. "I agree."

"You have no choice."

"But listen, Dr. Schottgatt baby. What if Sasha starts to go overboard about all these peasants and things? Peasants we gotta have, I know this, but too much of them could wreck the whole film . . . and you know *that*."

"You and Mr. Jacobson are very experienced men. Let us hope," said Dr. Emile Schottgatt, "that between you you can contain Miss Grimes's enthusiasms."

"Let's hope so, Dr. Schottgatt baby. Let's hope so indeed."

"So what it comes to," said Jules to Fielding later on, "is that they've appointed Sasha as a kind of commissar. There was nothing, Foxy says, that he could do to stop it."

"Where's Foxy now?"

"Prostrate with relief and with Gretel."

"Oh. . . . Can you manage Sasha, do you think?"

"I don't know. I've never thought of her in these terms."

"Nor have I. But now that I'm starting to, I think they stink."

"Foxy says we're stuck with the arrangement. I'd as soon have a crate of dynamite under my bed. . . ."

What would Jules have thought, Fielding wondered, if he'd known that Fielding was taking the dynamite out to dine that very evening?

But Jules would have had little time to worry about Fielding's social arrangements even if he had known of them. As soon as he left Fielding he was summoned by Schottgatt, and what Schottgatt had to say sent him post-haste to Foxy, though Foxy, he knew, would still be prostrate with Gretel.

"Aw, piss," said Foxy, after Gretel had been bundled out by Jules, "I hardly got my socks off. What is it now, for Christ's sake?"

"I've just been with Schottgatt."

Foxy got off the bed and put on a dressing gown which was embroidered with sumptuous silk erotica.

"So what's with Schottgatt? He already said his mouthful for today."

"And now he's said another. The Committee's leaving tomorrow, he said . . ."

". . . Thank God for that . . ."

". . . And he just wanted me to know that from now on a copy of our accounts out here is to be sent direct each week to the accountant of the Oglander-Finckelstein Trust. Did you agree to that, Foxy?"

"Yes. No choice, baby. Anyway, they've always been entitled to ask how their money was being spent. They have done once or twice already."

"I know. But they always used to be content with a rough breakdown. Now it looks as if they mean to go through it all with a toothcomb."

"So what? We're not cheating them."

"No," said Jules, "but we are doing things of which they may not approve very much. Your expenses, for example, all those air passages and helicopter rides, have a privileged look about them."

"I have to travel. They know that."

"And they know you could do it cheaper. Or take this arrangement with Margaret Lichfield. Instead of paying her money down for the part, we're going to 'employ her' at £5000 a year for the next ten years, thus saving her as much as twenty thousand in tax. I don't say it's illegal, but I don't think schemes like that will give the new régime at Montana much pleasure."

"Too late to change that now."

"You realise that those students only have to get hold of one little thing they don't like, and they can cut off supplies just like that?"

"Yeah."

"Then what have you done about alternative backing?"

"Jules baby, you are bugging me. Because you know as well

as I know that just now there is no backing to be had in the
whole wide world—except maybe for James quim-cranking
Bond. It did occur to me that our friend Max de Freville might
think of upping his stake if things got really rough for us, which
was why I asked him and Lyki to drop by before lunch. But
no joy there. The best they could do would be half a million."

"Then what happens if O/F cuts us off?"

"They won't, if we do like Schottgatt tells us. He may look
like Oliver Cromwell's arsehole, but it seems he wants this film
finished and he's got it all added up. Which is why he wants
the accounts from now on . . . to stop any trouble he sniffs out
before it can start really stinking."

"Like the Lichfield tax racket?"

"That's a back number, baby, and it's too well hidden. Come
to that, our accountant is probably more than a match for Og-
Finck's any day of the week. But from now on, Jules, we play
it straight, just in case. Until the last of those cheques for three
hundred grand is into the bank and cleared, we keep those
accounts so clean that Schottgatt could eat his nut cutlets off
them. No help with tax dodges, no special currency rates, not
for nobody . . . nothing whatever that could bring the lightest
blush of indignation to the purest student cheek. Get it?"

"No helicopters for Foxy?"

"All right. No helicopters for Foxy," Foxy said.

"We've still got to keep Sasha Grimes sweet."

"Then keep her sweet, if you have to dish out pictures of
Chairman mother-fucking Mao to the whole damn company.
Now for Christ's sake go and find Gretel and get her back here
before my balls drop off."

Fielding had arranged to take Sasha Grimes to the restaurant
out at the Achilleion, where the Summer Casino was. (In the
Casino's system of chronology, summer didn't end till mid-
November.) It would make a nice change, he felt, and then
the Achilleion was far enough from the town to lessen the likeli-
hood of their being discovered by Jules, but not far enough for
Fielding to be accused of deliberate concealment if they were—

quite the contrary, in fact, as it was a resort of some fashion.

Fielding's ostensible reason for asking Sasha to dine, and the one which he would offer to Jules if caught and castigated, was that he wished to discuss her remaining lines. These were very few but very important; for Nausicaa, though appearing prominently in several more scenes, would remain brooding and silent until at last she caught the hero alone to deliver a bitter and poignant farewell.

"The point is," said Fielding, dutifully pursuing this official topic, "that Odysseus isn't actually leaving for some while yet, and they both know it. So what she's really saying is, 'I may as well say good-bye now, because I know you're too important to be having any more time for me. But do just remember, it was me that helped you in the first place'."

"In short," said Sasha, "he's treating her with typical masculine brutality."

"No, dear. He realises, first that it will make scandal if he pays too much attention to her, and second that she's in love with him, which must be stopped for her own good. So although he has to answer her dismissively, the dismissal is as kind as he can make it. 'I'll always remember you,' he says, '*after* I get back safe to my own country.' Or in other words, 'There's nothing in it for either of us here and now' . . . a point which has to be made for everybody's sake. So he makes it, and then goes straight off to join her father before there can be any tears or trouble."

"Yes," she said, "that makes sense. I'll remember it all when we get to the scene. Thank you, Fielding."

This subject now being exhausted, Fielding bethought himself of his second and undeclared reason for dining Sasha, which was to give a try-out to Angela Tuck's formula for arousing her pity and hence her concupiscence. 'Really pile on the agony,' Angela had said, 'misery's their substitute for romance.' Well, yes : but how did one begin? Declarations of agony weren't much in Fielding's line. He could be Stoical, Cynical, Cyrenaic or even Socratic without much trouble, but personal concern or guilt about the woes of the world (woes which in his view it did much to invite by its own sheer folly and greed) he did not find easy to simulate.

"I'm glad," he said rather awkwardly, "that you'll be staying on in this . . . er . . . new capacity. We could do with a voice like yours round here."

"Oh," she said, "do you mean that? I could do with some support."

"In what way?"

"Well, for the next two weeks I'm still under contract and finishing my acting schedule, so I can keep an eye on things without being conspicuous. But after that I shan't be in the company any more, I shall just be employed by the Trust to report. I shall feel . . . alien from you all."

"No need to feel that," Fielding said. "Why don't you just attach yourself to me, as a kind of assistant script-writer? You'll have suggestions to make about how to bring in all these ser-vants and workmen . . ."

". . . Yes, for a compassionate *Odyssey* . . ."

". . . If you like to call it that," he said, suppressing a shud-der. "What more natural than that you should convey your suggestions through the script-writer, who can keep a running record of them?"

"You'd be prepared to help me?"

She fluttered her fingers in the air between them, half as if beckoning him towards her, half as if repelling and exorcising his probably evil intentions.

"It'd make me feel better," he said, trying grimly. "It isn't always comfortable, you know . . . earning all this money and wondering what one's doing for it."

"I shouldn't have thought you were the type to feel sensi-tive about that."

"One can't but notice a certain contrast," he ground out, "between our own lives and that of most Greeks."

"There are many people much worse off than the Greeks," she instructed him. "You should see them in Egypt or India."

For the life of him he couldn't bring himself to mouth any more hypocrisies just yet. Instead he nodded solemnly.

"It's shameful," he said, "it's disgusting . . . that people are coming to this place tonight to gamble with money they don't need. Every penny in their pockets ought to be seized and given to Oxfam."

Will she ever learn, he wondered, that if you stop people starving, they just breed more people to starve? And then aloud : "Unfortunatly there's not much we can do about that. But I suppose we can try to get some things right . . . this film, for instance. I'd like to think I was being of some use to you."

"Should you, Fielding? Well then, let me tell you what I'm planning."

What she was planning was quite hideous. Not content with dragging menials and mechanicals into every scene (*and* sometimes giving them speeches about their deprivations), she wanted to plant a social conscience in Odysseus himself. He would begin by repenting his killing of the Cyclops (an innocent shepherd), he would later be racked with guilt at having exploited Circe and Calypso (instead of helping them to 'fulfilled womanhood and sexual equality'), and when he finally returned to Ithaca he would give away all his lands and money to found a commune in place of his kingdom. The only parts of the film Sasha did not propose to change were those in which she appeared herself : there would be no beachcombers or fishermen around to catch the eye when Miss Grimes was on the screen.

"I see," Fielding said at last. "But I'm not sure that we can manage a programme quite as radical as that."

"Why not?"

"The changes you propose would cost a lot of money. I don't know that the Trust would authorise an increased investment."

"It's a question," she said, "of making proper use of the money which *is* coming. We can move the company out of that expensive hotel for a start."

"No, dear," he said quickly. "There is a pre-paid contract with the hotel for bookings up to March. If we moved out, we'd lose the money altogether." He had no idea whether this was

true, but it sounded plausible. "Once a concern is actually going, it is difficult to change the pattern of expenditure."

"I thought you were going to be on my side."

"I am. But there are certain realities to be faced. What other
economies did you have in mind?"

"I thought . . . that everyone might agree to a cut in their
salary."

Yes, he thought: you'll have finished drawing yours.

"You might have a little trouble with the unions," he said,
trying not to sound ironical.

Although she pouted at this, she took the point. She is not,
thought Fielding, a complete imbecile; just young and ignorant
and, like all left-wingers, rather spiteful; in the end she thinks
more of bringing ruin to Dives than relief to Lazarus.

"It'll be exciting, working on the script together," he said.
"What do you say we go back and make a start tonight?"

"I don't know about tonight."

"It's been so lonely, working on that script in the evenings,"
Fielding said. "But with someone to help, and something worthwhile to aim at. . . ."

"All right," she said, "let's start tonight."

God, Fielding thought, you really are delicious. That long,
luscious red hair, those little breasts, those rather clumsily circling arms; that dedicated, priggish face . . . oh, to see it sweat
and grin with lust.

"Evening, Major Gray," said Burke Lawrence from behind
him. "Going into the gaming rooms?"

"No."

"I am. My last night, you know. I'm taking the Four Stooges
away tomorrow morning."

Sasha frowned. Fielding signalled for his bill.

"Come and have a flutter," said Lawrence, "you and Miss
Grimes. That old regiment of yours . . . Lord Hamilton's
Dragoons—"

"—Earl Hamilton's Light Dragoons," Fielding emended
automatically, "or Hamilton's Horse—"

"—They were great ones for gambling, I heard. Come to the tables and show us."

"Thank you, no. Miss Grimes and I have work."

Burke Lawrence belched audibly and tottered on his way. The bill came. Fielding paid it at once but they had to wait for change.

"What was that 'Major Gray' bit?" Sasha said.

"A long time ago I was in the Army. Everyone was then."

"Not everyone was a Major in Earl Hamilton's Light Dragoons. Rather repulsive, all that."

"Oh, come off it, dear. We had to have soldiers, and someone had to tell them what to do."

Too late, he saw from her face that he had made a grave mistake. His guilt, if it was to convince Sasha, would have to embrace his Army career.

"I mean," he said, "that was how it seemed then. Over the last ten years we've all come to see it differently." God, he thought, why should I be apologising to this stupid slut for one of the few things in my life I'm proud of?

"Then why do you still call yourself 'Major'?"

"I don't. Burke Lawrence does. It's a kind of joke."

"Yes. A joke on the side of Majors. Against all the poor people they order about and kill. I heard it in his voice."

"You're reading too much into it, Sasha. He was drunk. . . . And here's my change. Let's go home and get to work on that script."

"You corrected him when he got the name of your regiment wrong."

"So would you have done if you'd been in the bloody thing twelve years."

"I'd have made myself forget it. . . . I don't think I want to work on the script this evening."

God damn Burke Lawrence.

"All right. But I'll see you home."

"Stay and play roulette with Burke Lawrence."

"I hate roulette and I don't much care for Burke Lawrence. He used to push drugs in the old days."

"Better than being a Major and getting people killed."

How mindless could she get? But he would have to cry *'peccavi'* over the Army or lose Sasha for good.

"Look, Sasha," he said, hating himself for his treachery, not to her, but to his past. "I was forced into joining the Army when I was still very young" . . . that, in a sense was true . . . "and I've had nightmares about it ever since I left it." And so was that true : the hum of cicadas in the afternoon, the bodies being moved from the truck into the ambulance, the sudden shout of warning from the Corporal-Major, and the black grenade curving through the air . . . *despite the agreed truce.* Oh, the swine, the scum; bloody Cypriot scum. Now as often when he thought of it he started to tremble in despair and rage, and only stopped when Sasha placed one hesitant finger on his wrist.

"Peace," she said, "peace."

"Thank you. . . . You'll come and start work on that script?"

"Not tonight. I think you'll still be Major Gray for the rest of tonight. But tomorrow, Fielding, if you're feeling well again. . . ."

The next day Burke Lawrence and the Creative Authentication Committee flew away early in the morning and were followed by Foxy early in the afternoon. Foxy was going to stop in London to consult with Pandarus and in New York to consult with Clytemnestra, and then go on to Montana to make sycophantic noises at the Oglander-Finckelstein Trust.

"Which means," Foxy said to Jules and Fielding at the airport, "that I shall wave my new social conscience at them as big as blown up tits in a nudie show. To make good and sure they get the weekly payments ready. Meanwhile, you two stop that Grimes dame from gumming up the ball-cocks round here."

"Rather a stiff order," Jules said.

"I know, Jules babe, I know. But do your best, huh? Otherwise we'll all be in the crap. Right up to our teeth."

After which Foxy's flight was called, and he went to join his henchmen at the gate. As he went, Fielding noticed, he was perceptibly less jaunty than usual and he didn't turn to wave. When he reached his henchmen, he gave them a polite and apologetic nod and motioned them to go ahead of him. Foxy, it seemed, wished to be alone.

"He'll have to get rid of that retinue from now on," Jules said : "Og-Finck will never stand for a private bodyguard."

"Is that what they are?"

"Not really. Just two actors who flopped, so he employs them for old times' sake. Og-Finck still won't stand for it."

They went out to Jules's car and started to drive towards the little inland valley where Jules was going to stage the games of the Phaeacians. Fielding ought really to have returned to the Corfu Palace to get on with his speeches, but since they were all rather winded after yesterday's events it had been agreed that he take the afternoon off to bear Jules company.

"I've got a request," Fielding said.

"Not a good time for requests, Fielding."

"This one must be made now or never."

"Well?"

"Now that you've taken me on for the next three months, can you send my money to a bank in Switzerland?"

"What have we done so far?"

"My first two weeks' salary is going to my bank in England."

"But you don't fancy paying tax on the rest?" grinned Jules. "There's schools and hospitals rotting into the ground for lack of cash, but Fielding Gray wants all of his for Fielding Gray."

"I need money for my old age, Jules. £12,000, even now, is a useful sum of capital. Cut off the taxes, and it's merely money to piss up the wall."

"That's the intention, boy. They don't want you to collect any capital, because capital makes you independent, and independence is the new dirty word."

"Will you help or not, Jules?"

"No. I sympathise, my dear. I quite understand that you don't want your money used to provide seaside outings for imbeciles or universities for verminous rabble. But you see, little Sasha Grimes thinks otherwise. So if she found out we were helping you dodge your social duties, she might say something very damaging to her friends at Og-Finck."

"She need never know."

"They might find out for themselves. We've got to send in the accounts."

"Saying how much you pay out and to whom. Not where you put it for them."

"Look, Fielding," said Jules. "If I went to the accountant who's here with us, and asked him to do this for you, he could certainly do it. I don't know the details . . . I expect the money would be transferred through a Clytemnestra account in Switzerland . . . but somehow or other he could do it. So normally I'd get him to oblige. But not now. Now we keep our noses clean, Foxy says, and polish up our social ethics. As of now we're taking not the teeniest, weeniest risk. So that's how it is, my dear, and there's an end of that."

They turned off the main road and drove down a track, through trees on either side, until they came to a large meadow. On three sides of this rose a gentle slope scattered with olive trees, while on the fourth, from which Fielding and Jules had approached, was a long wall of poplar mingled with cypress. Although the meadow was square, the slopes which ascended from it formed a rough semi-circle, so that the whole made a natural theatre. Here they would film the games which the Phaeacians held for Odysseus, and here Jules now busied himself with checking areas and angles.

"You know," said Fielding later on, as they sat to rest in the shade of the olives, "I could make it worth your while."

"Make what worth my while?"

"The risk, such as it is, of paying my money in Switzerland."

"Don't go on about it, Fielding. You've had my answer."

"There's something you don't know, Jules." And Fielding, having admitted to his dinner with Sasha the previous evening, proceeded to describe Sasha's ideas for a 'compassionate' *Odyssey*. "But it's possible," he concluded, "since she can't change the script without my help, that I can keep all this within limits. It is also possible, if Sasha likes me as much as I'm beginning to think, that I can influence her reports to Og-Finck."

Jules chewed his lower lip vigorously.

"If you're trying to bed her," he said, "remember what I told you at the start. I don't want her upset."

"Neither do I. I want her purring with pleasure."

"I don't want her mind taken off her acting."

"Jules. She only has two weeks' acting left and only one more really important scene. After that she'll just be here as an informer . . . and an interferer. We need to get her into a pleasant and acquiescent state of mind as soon as possible—even if it should mean taking her mind off her acting."

"And what makes you think that *your* treatment will get her into a pleasant and acquiescent state of mind?"

"She's beginning to believe that I'm a convert to her way of thinking—equality and all that. Women like making converts. And she's also beginning to pity me."

"Beware of pity."

"Indeed . . . if you are the one that pities. It dulls the faculties and stirs up false affections, even false passions. But if this happened to Sasha, it would keep her out of mischief. Sasha engrossed in an object of pity would have less time to meddle with your film."

"Until she snapped out of it, as sooner or later she would. When she saw she'd been conned, she'd tear you apart."

"I'm not deceiving her as much as you think."

"Oh yes, you are. Pretending to be converted to her socialist fads while dreaming of numbered accounts in Zürich."

"About that, I agree; but I'm not conning her altogether. She pities me, Jules, because she's convinced that I was cruelly victimised while I was in the Army. And so I was . . . though not in the way she thinks. When I remember what happened to me in Cyprus, I sometimes get a kind of fit . . . I start shaking with sheer hatred of the Cypriots who destroyed my face. That was how it was with me last night . . . and she pitied me because she thought I was trembling with horror and guilt for all the wicked things I'd been made to do when in uniform."

"So she was conned."

"The fit was genuine."

"But she was conned, because she thought it meant something it didn't mean, and you didn't put her straight. She'll sort it out in time . . . and then God help you."

"But meanwhile . . . if I can keep her from ruining this production?"

"In that cause," said Jules casually, "I don't mind if you kill her."

"That would be overdoing it and might not please Og-Finck. I'll stick to conning her, if it's all the same to you."

"Then make a good job of it."

"And in return . . . you'll tell the accountant to send my salary to Switzerland?"

"It's totally against Foxy's new policy."

"But a very small price to pay for what you'd be getting."

"If we get it." Jules scowled in reluctant agreement. "I'll see how things go this next fortnight," he said. "And then if I'm convinced you've really got your thumb on her, I'll tip off the accountant to fix you up any way you want for the last ten weeks of your contract. Fair enough?"

"Fair enough."

"So be it," said Jules rising. "Now then : where's the best place for the King and Queen to watch these games from? The King and the Queen and of course our dear little Princess. . . ."

It was the dear little Princess who entirely occupied Fielding's thoughts as he bathed, dressed and ate the dinner which he had ordered in his room. For he was to meet Sasha later that evening for their first session together on the script. This was to be a general discussion, in which Sasha would outline her proposed reforms over wide areas and they would then take a preliminary look at possible methods of applying them. This evening, then, no very definite decision would be taken; but Sasha was bound to press for these before long and, it was essential, Fielding considered, that he should get his thumb on her, as Jules had put it, without any further delay. So many things depended on this : the quality of the film and indeed its continued production; his own money and his plans to have it banked in Switzerland; his future prestige and influence with Jules . . . and, it now occurred to him, with Foxy. For if he could bring this off, if he could contain the menace which Sasha now represented, then Foxy would surely, as they said in this world, *owe* him; and it was interesting to speculate on ways in which he might be persuaded to discharge the debt.

But that was for the future. Here and now the problem was how to get his thumb on Sasha. Since she had an eye and an ear for a good scene, he could possibly get her to agree that it would be a shame to spoil too many of Homer's by crowding them out with proletarian extras; she had already made it clear that her own scenes were not to be altered at the dictates of social realism, and she might be induced to extend this indulgence. Again, feigned sympathy with her aims, and feigned co-operation in them, might help him to limit and reduce them. After all, he could tell her, too much misery on the screen would bludgeon the spectator insensible. She could make her political point much more effectively by showing one mutilated stump than by parading a regiment of beggars, because she would have given one clear-cut image which was easily retained in the memory. This was the sort of thing which Sasha instinctively understood. 'Yes, you're so right,' he imagined her saying, 'and it would save us money. . . .'

All of which was very well, but Fielding had a strong idea that the kind of hold he needed to gain on Sasha must be, in the end, personal. Aesthetic argument, pretended but qualified agreement, calculated deceit . . . all these might achieve something; but final victory could only be won by making her like him (which she was already disposed to do) and then depend on him. If he was to soften up Sasha to the degree she would have to be softened, he must first make her trust him and hold to him for purely personal reasons. She must do as he said because it was he that said it.

And now came the big question : with a view to bringing this about, would her seduction be a help or a hindrance? If he made a good thing of it, it would clearly be a great help. As he had already told himself and others, however, seducing Sasha would be one hell of a job and might lead to horrors and complications beyond imagining. (What had Burke Lawrence called her? A sexual Calamity Jane, something like that.) On balance then, Fielding concluded, he would be wise to keep out of Sasha's bed even if she gave him the most cordial invitation to climb into it. But at the very same time as he formulated this prohibition he knew he would never obey it. For the truth was that Sasha, as a carnal prospect, was so elusive, alluring, perilous and unpredictable, so hedged about with sanctions and tabus, that to Fielding, with his taste for the arcane, she had now become irresistible.

". . . Two good examples of what I mean," Sasha was saying to Fielding: "Nestor and Menelaus. They are both presented as kindly if boring old men. But in fact both were authoritarian princes who trod on everyone near them. As for Menelaus, let's not forget that he had allowed tens of thousands of lives to be lost in a long and brutal war simply so that he could get his unfaithful wife back. All those people butchered just so that one man could keep his property. Because that's how he saw her. . . ."

At least, thought Fielding, she's read it all. I do wish to God that she hadn't. As Sasha went grinding on, he wondered if he could pour himself a whisky. They were, after all, in his sitting room. But Sasha did not approve of stimulants and would consider any suggestion of a pause for refreshment to be disrespectful of her exegesis. But ah, he had it . . .

". . . Sound point, dear," he said, "but if you don't mind I must mix my draught." A quick look at the clock on his desk. "I have to be very punctual about that."

He went to his bedroom, poured himself half a large tumbler of whisky, dripped half an inch of mineral water on top, and rejoined Sasha in the sitting room.

"Draught?" she said. "What for?"

Fielding pointed vaguely at his face. Let her make what she

could of that. But in the event she didn't, apparently, bother to make anything.

"And another point," she droned : "those people down in Hades. Why are they all lords and ladies? Why aren't there any ordinary soldiers and their wives to say what *they* thought of it all?"

"You've got to allow for the convention, Sasha. In the same way as Shakespeare never gave a serious or important part to ordinary men, so Homer, being much earlier, gave them no parts at all."

"What about that soldier of Shakespeare's on the eve of Agincourt? He was serious."

"But very brief. Exceptional in any case."

"Exceptional but there. It's up to us to make a few exceptions in Homer . . . since he didn't do it himself. Now, for this scene in Hades I'm going to suggest. . . ."

Followed a quarter of an hour of suggestions, of which Fielding dutifully scribbled notes. This can't go on, he thought. She must be stopped, or at least brought within reasonable limits. A personal approach is the only way, and of all personal approaches the sexual is the strongest. If it goes wrong, it'll just have to go wrong; if she explodes, then at least my little world here will end with a bang and not a whimper. But there's no point, he thought, in rushing things, in being crude or violent; there is still, for all these intolerable suggestions, a day or two of grace before anything need be done about them. So first try the gradual way; softly softly catchee little red monkey.

"I think," he said, when she next took a split second's pause for breath, "that that's about all I can assimilate in one evening. I'll analyse these ideas of yours and break them down, and tomorrow I'll tell you how we might incorporate them in the script."

This seemed to satisfy her, and she began to make gathering up and going movements.

"Don't go," he said. "I've got something different to discuss with you. Let me send . . . for a glass of lemonade or something?"

"Thank you. Water will do."

"Mineral water?"

"Out of the tap. What all the Greeks drink."

Fielding fetched it from the bathroom.

"I've been thinking," he said, "about when you say good-bye to Odysseus."

"We've already talked about that. I'm sad because I know I'm no more use to him . . . however kind he may be about it."

"I think you're something else as well as sad. I think you're a bit provocative . . . a bit 'come hither' . . . forgive me, Sasha . . . sexy."

"Oh?" Cold eyes, intelligent interest.

"You want him to pay you attention, although you know it's almost hopeless. Your only chance is to tempt him . . . not right into bed, because a Princess doesn't do that, but into feeling a bit randy for you, so that you'll at least have the satisfaction of seeing that look in his eyes. And since you're attracted by him, as you've already shown on the beach, it's easy for you to try to rouse him. You just show him that you've got an itch for him, which is the surest way of giving a man an itch for you. As it happens, Odysseus is far too wary and wily to respond, but that's no reason why you shouldn't try."

"How should I play it, do you think?"

"That must be for Jules to say, if he accepts this line of thought." He came and stood close to where she sat. "But as I see it you've got to be hinting at offering yourself . . . rather like you did on the beach, though then it was almost unconscious and anyhow he didn't see. This time it'll be deliberate, a consciously worked version of what you did without meaning to on the beach." He paused for a moment and brought his mouth close to her ear. "You could do it marvellously, Sasha. Show me how you think it might go."

While Fielding drew back a yard or two to give her room, Sasha sat very quiet, her eyes as cold and dull as iron. Then suddenly a light smile flicked over her face, her eyes dipped and rose again, shining now, and she rippled upright in front of him. She circled one of his wrists with a single finger and brought one thigh almost up to his crutch, making it tremble till it seemed ever closer, till its warmth seemed to flow into his groin.

" 'Farewell,' " she said, " 'stranger from the sea. Perhaps you will remember me hereafter, when you have your wish and come safe home. Then, perhaps, you will remember me, for it was I who first heard you and gave you back your life.' "

"My God," Fielding said, as the warmth came in waves from her trembling thigh. "this is superb. You really understand it."

He put his arms out to bring her to him, but almost before he had moved she was half way to the door.

"As an actress," she said, "I had an intuitive understanding of what you meant." Her eyes were cold again, holding neither desire nor disgust nor reproach, totally neutral. Fielding thought she would leave immediately, but in fact she lingered, looked at him very calmly, and said,

"Tell me, Fielding. How did Burke Lawrence know you'd been a Major and all that?"

"I met him once a long time back. We didn't talk much about it, but he could always have enquired later."

"I keep remembering that when he called you 'Major' last night, you didn't mind."

"Why should I, if it amused him?"

"I keep remembering it. What you said about how it gave you nightmares to think of what you did in the Army . . ."

". . . So it does . . ."

". . . And how ill it suddenly made you. *And yet,* when he first called you 'Major', you didn't at all mind."

"I scarcely heard."

"Perhaps not."

"I was concentrating on you."

"Perhaps."

"Forget it, Sasha. It's all been over too long to bother with."

"I hope so. Good-night, Fielding. And thank you for your ideas about Nausicaa."

Harriet wrote in answer to Fielding's telegram :

Dearest Fielding,

All this is very muddling. If they promised you a decision about your contract after two weeks, then a decision
there should be. We can't go on like this. I want to know
whether I'm to join you or whether you're coming back
home. It's very lonely here without you. Do please, dearest,
make them give you an answer and cable me as soon as you
can. I'm very unhappy and upset.

Then you'll just have to go on being unhappy and upset,
thought Fielding. I've got a very big bank running and I don't
want you out here nagging in my ear-hole. But how to keep you
away. . . . ?

As you will see (Harriet went on) I enclose a letter from
Gregory Stern. I'm afraid I opened it by mistake when it
came . . .

. . . Not half you didn't, you prying bitch . . .

. . . and once having done so I thought I might as well read
it. It seems to me a very good suggestion of Gregory's, and
just the sort of work you ought to be doing. So if those film
people refuse to commit themselves and go on playing about
with you like this, why not show them that you know your
value if they don't and just come on home and start this
book for Gregory?

Why not? I'll show you twelve thousand reasons why not.

Although he says nothing about dates, I don't suppose
his offer will be open indefinitely. It would be nice to have
something settled with him, even if it did mean giving up
part of that film money you're earning.

That's it. You don't care how much money I lose so long
as I'm sitting safe under your beady eyes. And yet when all
this started you said you wanted me to make money. Bloody
bird-brained woman.

But perhaps things have altered since you last cabled.
Perhaps Pandarus has now confirmed the contract. In that
case, of course, you'll have to continue, and we must hope
that Gregory can wait another three months before you make

a start for him. At least I'll be able to join you in Corfu, which will be all the comfort I really need.

All my love, pumpkin,

Harry.

Jesus, Joseph and Judas. Another lie needed for her within twenty-four hours. Should it be a small and temporising lie, which would be easy to devise but would only keep her off for a few days? Or should he risk a real whopper, which might raise the siege for weeks but might equally well bring her down on him, in desperation and disbelief, with her biggest battering ram. Seeking temporary distraction from this problem, he applied himself to the enclosed letter from his publisher, Gregory Stern.

It appeared that Gregory was planning a new series of biographical and critical studies of Modern English Novelists. 'Modern' meant going back, in Gregory's view, as far as Joseph Conrad, who was to be the subject of the inaugural volume. Would Fielding like to undertake this? Gregory's rates (unspecified, needless to say) would take account of time and effort needed for research, and expenses within reason (whose reason?) would also be paid. As Harriet had observed, no dates were mentioned, but Fielding had the impression that Gregory was keen to up-anchor and be off.

It was, no doubt about it, a very promising notion. Notwithstanding his sour reflections just now about Gregory's shifty attitude to payment, Fielding knew of old that Gregory would be as generous as possible within his means, which these days were rapidly increasing. But even so any offer of Gregory's would be peanuts as compared with the princely provision of Pandarus; and the task, particularly the research, would be quite gruelling. But yet again it was good work, the kind that ought to be done, the kind that ought to be done by *him*. For while he had never pretended to be committed or inspired as a writer, he did claim to be a conscientious professional who gave good value; and here was a worthwhile professional job to be done if ever there was one. What was more, there would be no intrigue or backbiting in this assignment, no psychopaths or paranoiacs such as filled the Corfu Palace to the brim, no dirty little schemes about Swiss banks . . . just scholarly peace and quiet, and Harriet bringing in the tea-trays.

And there, of course, was the rub. He could not go back to peace and quiet and Harriet's tea-trays . . . not yet. Corfu, at the moment, smelt of money, sex, excitement, power and popular fame. Although not all of these would be for him, the scent of them, floating in the air about him, was very sweet in his nostrils. Uneasy and ungrateful as he might feel at shilly-shallying over Gregory Stern's most seemly proposal, he could not bring himself to quit the halls of Sybaris until he had penetrated its innermost chambers and gathered up his share of the goodies which were going there.

And after all, he now told himself, there was this to salve his conscience : amid all his other activities, he was using his skill and taste to promote the honour of Homer. All this deceiving and flattering and seducing . . . its chief end was to protect the poet against the abuses of commercial hucksters on the one hand and political fanatics on the other. True, there might be both profit and pleasure in it for Fielding himself; but the poet would surely have been too large-hearted to grudge a man that.

To Gregory he now wrote briefly, expressing his pleasure at being chosen and stating his willingness to devote himself un-swervingly to Conrad as soon as his contract with Pandarus was done, if Gregory would wait that long. He could, he added untruthfully, find the leisure to do a little general research while he was still with Pandarus.

To Harriet he wired that his contract was now fixed (he could hardly disguise this any longer in view of what he had told Gregory) but that she must wait in England until she received the letter which he was posting that very day. The composition of this was a ghastly job; for Fielding had decided on the second method of dealing with Harriet . . . an enormous fib which would keep her away from Corfu for at least a month . . . and adroit through he was in this line, to find and frame a falsehood of the superior quality needed here was almost beyond him. However, he eventually ran up quite a plausible tale to the effect that for a month or more he was to go on tour through Greece and the Aegean in order to spot out possible new locations, as it now appeared that Corfu was in many respects inadequate. He would communicate, he said, from various points *en route,* but he could give no definite schedule of his movements, since these must depend on local information which he could only gather as he went.

He then scribbled four notes of the 'much in haste, just off again' category, on four different kinds of paper and with four different pens. These he dated over the next month at rough intervals of a week; he sealed them, stamped them, addressed them to Harriet, and sent them with covering letters to four trusted and worldly expatriot acquaintances, two of whom lived in the Peloponnese, one on Skyros and one on Mitylene. Each correspondent was adjured, for love of Fielding, to post the enclosed envelope in or near his own district on or near such and such a date. Finally, Fielding made a record, to refresh his memory later, of his supposed peregrination.

Harriet, he reckoned, was just vague enough to believe that a script-writer could be employed as he had told her. If she didn't, if she came to Corfu to check, that particular balloon would go up with a nasty bang; but this was just one more risk he had to take. Meanwhile, were there any loopholes which he could close but hadn't? There was certainly one. After he had posted his packets at the concierge's desk, he had a friendly talk with the concierge, at the end of which it was agreed that any lady who might telephone for him *from England* should be told that the Kyrios Gray had left the hotel and was not expected back for the next four or five weeks. For this service there would be a weekly charge, payable in advance and in cash, of three thousand drachmae, but the concierge proudly guaranteed a faultless professional performance.

The next thing Fielding did was to ring up Angela Tuck, who asked him to a tête-à-tête luncheon at 'Max's place'. This was a restored Venetian palazzo which overlooked a bay some miles north of the town; it had a lawn which sloped down to a private beach, and on either side of this lawn were a number of little arbours, most of which sheltered rather good Hellenistic statues of life-size nymphs or demi-gods. One of them, however, was furnished with benches and a table, and it was here that Angela had arranged for them to have lunch.

"Max is in Athens with Lyki," Angela said, "drumming up more Government support for their bloody tourist hotels."

She pointed across the bay, on the far side of which three hideous erections, looking like Martian forts in a cheap science fiction film, occupied two-thirds of the visible coast line.

"What's the use of having a lovely place like this," said Angela, "if you've got to sit and stare at that?" She was looking better than when Fielding had last seen her, just as massive and flabby but not so high-coloured. Yet now her hatred of the hotels was bringing her rapidly out in a kind of orange sweat, as though her face were smeared with marmalade. "They're going to murder this island," she said. "Look at the way they're destroying the trees. Don't they know what happened on other islands? Once they all looked as green and beautiful as this, but their trees were destroyed and they turned into lumps of rock."

"That was a very long time ago," Fielding said, "and modern Greeks don't know any history. Not that they'd change their ways if they did. Greeks destroy trees—it's almost a natural law. The only reason there are any left here is that the Venetians and the British kept planting them."

"The good old raj, eh? There was a lot to be said for it. But Max and Lyki between them are going to turn Corfu into a desert. Hotels, roads, camping sites . . . there isn't a square inch of the place which they're not going to change into something hideous."

"Tell 'em to stop."

"They just laugh. 'My dear lady,' Lykiadopoulos says, 'you might as well try to stop the flow of time itself. Someone will make money here : why not us?' And Max is just as bad. He's a kind and civilised man is Max, he's been all over Europe *and* looked at what he's seen, so he knows exactly what horrible damage he's doing here; and yet nothing, short of the Last Trump, is going to make him stop. It's not just for money either. He resents nature, Fielding. He resents something which can get on perfectly well, indeed much better, without *him*. So he's out to teach nature a lesson . . . chop it and change it and pull it about until it's quite sure who's master."

She took a huge gulp of vodka and tonic and then wiped the marmalade off her face.

"That's why those hotels are so ugly," she said, "to spite nature."

She clawed the air in the direction of the Martian forts, immediately started to exude more marmalade, dabbed at it rather despairingly, and then sat still.

"I'm not supposed to excite myself," she said, "so to hell with it. Now, duckie: Max has been asking after Harriet Ongley. I must confess I'd forgotten her."

"Why is Max interested?"

"She's a friend from way back. You must have known that."

"She used to talk of him when we first met, but she hasn't mentioned him in years. Even when I told her that Max was out here, she said nothing."

"There's not a lot in it. Just that her late lamented husband sometimes played in the chemmy games which Max used to run in the fifties."

"Tell him Harriet's staying in England." He outlined his plan for keeping her there. "Will Max mind?"

"Not in the least. He just likes to know what's going on. We'll back you up, if Harriet would get in touch with us. Speaking for myself, I'm delighted, because I suppose this means you're going ahead with little Sasha Grimes?"

Two waiters appeared with cold *hors d'œuvres* and wine. Angela, when served, took only a small piece of egg and a mushroom. Fielding, hungry after a long morning, helped himself liberally; he noticed that Angela gave his plate a look of repulsion and then hurriedly turned her face away.

"So what's cooking with little Sasha?" said Angela when the waiters had gone. She kept her face turned from Fielding as he ate, and was visibly compelling herself to eat her own food, forking it to her mouth crumb by crumb. Where does she get all that flesh, he wondered.

"Little Sasha," he said, "has become a very important person." He gave a full account of this, and also of his own sessions alone with Sasha. "I think," he said, "that the sooner I have her the better. It's urgent, Angie. What shall I do?"

Angela pushed her plate away and carried her wine glass up to her bosom, where she held it in both hands.

"You're sure," she said, "that all that business with her thigh was only faked."

"Yes. She was acting Nausicaa. She turned it on and off like a light."

"So that means that the time she really liked you best was when you told her about the Army?"

"I suppose so. I trembled a lot and she put her hand out to calm me. She meant to be kind and she was."

"Well there's your line. You keep it up about the Army, she pities and soothes you . . . and finally you end up in bed."

"It's a tricky area, Angela."

"I don't see why. Just tell her what happened . . . how you were blown up in Cyprus and had your face ripped off . . ."

". . . But that's just what I can't tell her. She thinks I was trembling with *guilt* that evening, for having been a nasty fascist soldier. If I tell her about that grenade, she'll know the real reason . . . that I'd like to kill every Greek in Cyprus and was trembling with rage because I can't. If she knew that, I'd be finished. She's suspicious about the Army anyhow; she keeps going on about how I was a Major in a smart regiment. Best keep away from all that."

"Then we must find something that you really are guilty about."

"That's it. I've got to cry '*mea culpa*' and mean it. That's the only sort of misery to satisfy her."

The two waiters returned with two mullet. Angela accepted hers, took a tiny mouthful, and gagged on it. Fielding was about to commiserate on her lack of appetite but then wisely decided to keep quiet. He watched her swallow a whole glass of wine in one pull and shakily refill from the bottle.

"You've got plenty of things you can work up guilt about," she said when she was recovered. "That time you hit your mother down at Broughton . . . or better still, the way you let down that wretched little boy at your school. Christopher."

He had almost forgotten how much Angela knew of his past. He had seen her so seldom over the years, and thought so little about her, that it was hard to realise quite how deep their relations went. Yet of course she knew all about his mother and all about Christopher too. She had been there in Broughton when it all came to a head, in 1945, and had indeed used it for her own ends at the time. And for her own pleasure later on. 'Show me, Fielding,' she had said that afternoon on Hydra eight years ago, 'show me what you did with Christopher.' Oh yes; she knew it all.

"You could even make her read that novel you wrote about it," Angela now said.

"I haven't got a copy."

"I have. Somewhere up in the house."

"She might not approve. Turning it into a book . . . into money."

"Then pretend you're guilty about that too."

"I am."

"So you'll really be able to wallow in it, won't you? Lust, betrayal, incestuous love-hate, and violent death. Topped off with dollops of tears, because you used it all to make money. She'll think she's hearing a play by Webster."

Funny, thought Fielding. The Angela he used to know would never have referred to Webster, or worried about the trees on Corfu, come to that. She seemed to have picked up a certain literate wisdom during her wanderings with Max . . . while still unmistakably remaining her old coarse and cynical self.

"And when you've finally got up her," this self now remarked, "don't forget the fee for my advice. You remember what that is?"

"Very clearly. I'll bring her out here as soon as I can, so make sure your fake mirror's working properly. If Sasha saw you standing there on the other side she might be rather cross."

"But you've got to get her first," Angela said. "So one last hint. Blame it all on your wicked public school. She'll like that. Tell her you were maimed and perverted by pedagogues and pigs."

"In fact they were extremely nice and understanding men."

"That's not what she wants to hear, duckie. You just get your part straight : I'm guilty, I'm guilty, I'm guilty . . . but so are those public school pigs."

The waiters brought fruit, sweet wine from Samos, and coffee. After a little while Fielding said he must go.

"No," said Angela, slipping her hand between his thighs, "don't go yet. Sit here and let me hold you. For old times' sake."

"Come with me," said Sasha Grimes late that night, and led Fielding towards his bedroom.

"Lie down," she said. "No, don't undress. Just lie down and be still."

While Sasha moved about the bedroom making preparations, Fielding went on muttering and blubbering about pigs of parents and schoolmasters, and what they had all done not only to long dead Christopher but to Fielding too. By now he was no longer sure which parts of this were sincere and which were simulated; but to judge from the results so far, enough of it was genuine to lend conviction to the whole. He was just getting ready to do the bit about his mother again (perhaps two-thirds sincere, this) when something in Sasha's activities stopped him dead. He lay absolutely quiet now, watching her during every second, and with each that passed he became more puzzled. At length, after she had looked carefully round to make sure that everything was ready, she began to walk, still fully clothed (as he was) towards the bed; she turned aside to Fielding's dressing table, from which she took a clean handkerchief and a bottle of Eau de Cologne; then she continued towards the bed, until she was standing right over Fielding. She unscrewed the top of the bottle which she was carrying, poured some Eau de Cologne on to the handkerchief, and began to bathe Fielding's forehead and cheeks. As she did so she whispered.

"Sasha," he said at last, looking up at her rather wildly, "Sasha, are you sure?"

"Just lie still," she said, "and later do exactly as I say."

She put down the bottle and the handkerchief on the bedside table, then lifted her dress up over her thighs and tucked it into the patent leather belt round her waist.

"Filthy bitch, Sasha," she said, "you filthy, filthy bitch."

She started to lower the tights which she was wearing under the dress.

"You like it when he looks at you, Sasha, don't you?" she said. "Poor Fielding, he's suffered so much. So you think that's an excuse to let him look. *You filthy bitch.*"

She went on carefully lowering her tights. Fielding seeing her narrowed eyes and remembering the way she had whispered to him, was strongly minded to get up and send her away before it was too late. But already it was too late . . . her eyes and her parted lips told him that. He had deliberately tried to start this and now he must see it through. Only one thing for it : lie there still, as she said.

"Poor Fielding," she murmured, "so many tears. Will you take this dirty whore to make up? Will you let her comfort you for what you suffered on the cross?"

She raised both hands as high as she could, and as he saw what was next to happen he stiffened violently along the bed.

PART THREE

A MAN OF MANY WILES

"Thank God," said Jules to Fielding, "that we're finally finished with the Phaeacians. That bloody Nomarch and his friends. . . ."

"Were they so awful?"

"Yes, Fielding, they were. Larking about like a lot of school-boys. If I hadn't owed them for getting Elena out of clink, I'd have sent them home after the first morning."

"How do they come out in the rushes?"

"Not too badly, as it happens. We hardly see them during the games, and in Alcinous's palace they look quite sombre and dignified. It was between shots that they were so trying. They'd start feeling up the girls and wouldn't come back on set. So then I'd have to shout, and they got all puffed up and offended, and the girls got right out of hand, and on one occa-sion Elena lost her knickers and came back on with her bush showing under her tunic . . ."

". . . There, there," Fielding said. "It's all over now. On to the next thing. Are you happy with the dialogue for Odysseus and Calypso?"

"Yes, thanks."

"And the scenes in Hades? I had rather a tussle with Sasha about those. She wanted more lower-class ghosts, but I man-aged to keep her down to one."

"Which we can always cut out later. . . . Anyhow, you've done a fine job. Thank you, Fielding."

"We aim to please. What shall I work on now?"

"The scenes after Odysseus's return to Ithaca. And then start rewriting Circe. I'm not sure when I can get that little madam back here, but I want to be ready for her. And now, my dear, my turn to do something for you."

"Oh yes?" said Fielding, pretending that he had forgotten.

"The stipulated two weeks have gone by since we discussed that bargain about Sasha. She seems to be behaving very reasonably, and I'm prepared to give the credit to you . . . though sometimes I wonder how long it can last."

"I'm well into gear. But it has been an effort, Jules."

"I believe you. And now you shall have your reward. If you go and see the accountant, you'll find him cooperative."

"About Switzerland?"

"Anywhere you name. But if I were you," said Jules with a funny glint in his eyes, "I'd ask the accountant's advice."

In order to avoid predators, the Pandarus accountant in Corfu lived in a small hotel some way from the Corfu Palace and operated from a tiny office which had been rented for him at the back of the American Express. Since it was a warm and clear November day, Fielding decided to walk there along the sea.

There was no doubt about it, he thought; things were going very well indeed. To everyone's relief, the Og-Finck money was coming in as promised, three hundred grand weekly and bang on time. Jules was still on schedule with the filming, despite his troubles with the ill-disciplined Nomarch, and was evidently pleased with the script. Sasha had acted out her final scenes beautifully and in other respects, though occasionally intransigent, was being by and large biddable. She had been coaxed out of imposing much change on the script, while the two reports which she had so far sent to Og-Finck and the student committee were known to be quietly favourable.

But of course, Fielding thought, as he breasted a slope and came into sight of the gardens, Sasha would continue volatile. There were few easy moments with her around, and if ever a man had earned his employers' gratitude, it was he. There were times when he woke in the night sweating with anxiety, thankful to God that Sasha was not there beside him (for she hated sharing beds after it was over) but all the more fearful of whatever feverish and guilt-ridden fantasy she might even now be devising against their next encounter. Which of them would crack first, he wondered; how long could it go on? Yet one way or the other it must go on; he must maintain his authority. And certainly (he now comforted himself) that was still unquestioned; for Sasha, unwilling as she had been to accept Angela's invitation to Max's place, had nevertheless done so purely because Fielding said it would please him, and they were to go there for 'dinner and the night' the day after next.

For the time at least, then, that front was holding up. Fielding turned left and skirted the cricket ground, on which a fat little schoolmaster was superintending an autumnal game. In England, Fielding thought, the stumps were put away weeks ago . . . much too early. He had always felt that cricket was at its best late in the year, a dying game in the dying year. Not that he thought the game was dying, or at least he prayed not, but Harriet had once said . . . Ah, he thought, bringing himself sharply back from reverie to current reality: Harriet. Well, here too was cause for satisfaction. Harriet had apparently accepted what he had written about his fictitious tour away from Corfu, and had sent back to wish him a good trip.

'I hope this finds you somewhere,' she had written. '. . . Have you been in touch with Gregory? If you convince him you're really keen on the Conrad proposal, I expect he'll wait till you're ready.'

So there was no need to worry about Harriet . . . though he must remember that the weeks were going on. As for Gregory and Conrad, there was nothing to be done until he heard from Gregory, and meanwhile he had prepared himself to abide, without regret or recrimination, by whatever decision should be made. If Gregory would wait, good; if not, there was an end of it. After all, there were more urgent matters than Conrad . . . such as enjoying, and using, what little was left of his youth. Just now that meant concentrating on Corfu and Sasha (who, however hazardous, was certainly a high-class enjoyment) and, not least, on making money. There would be time enough later for research and biographies, when he had had his fill and made his packet and could settle in comfort to the work. All things being equal, he would like to write about Conrad, but there would doubtless be other subjects and other offers quite as good.

Soothed by this philosophy, and satisfied that his concerns in general were going as right as any rational man could expect, he entered the American Express and made for the accountant's office.

"Hi, man," said the accountant, who was perhaps thirty years old and dressed in an expensive Red Indian outfit with his hair styled to match. "What's with you?"

Fielding explained what was with him.

"Yeah, that checks. Mr. Jacobson warned me," said the accountant, adopting a more official but hardly more respectful manner. "So what are your instructions, sir?" he leered.

"Mr. Jacobson suggested I should ask your advice."

"The two best places for your money are Malta and Switzerland. Don't touch the Carribean; the blacks may start grabbing." The accountant spoke concisely and confidently but also with an air of scepticism, as if he was telling a lucky player how best to make use of a wad of Monopoly money. "Some say Portugal is safe, but you'd never get it out again. Ditto South Africa. There's always Japan, but in my book that's just too far away."

"In mine too. Malta or Switzerland then: which is the better?"

"The Swiss are beginning to get a conscience about all the loot which crooks and politicians stash away there. One day they may fling their accounts wide open . . . say in two hundred years."

"Not a very pressing conscience?"

"Insulated by layers of cream cake. In Malta, on the other hand, you might get interest on your money, which would be much harder to arrange in Switzerland."

"Interest is always nice."

"Then I'd suggest a deposit account in Malta. The only

thing is . . . Malta I don't quite trust. It looks good, it should be good, it will be good, as long as the Church there goes on calling the old tunes. But that may not be for as long as some people think."

"Why not?"

"The Holy Catholic Church," said the accountant, adjusting the Red Indian riband round his forehead, "is getting ready to jump on the liberal juggernaut. Just look at the recent record: no more Noble Guard or papal creations of nobility; duller gear for the Cardinals; Masses in the vernacular instead of Latin. The next step could be giving money away . . . not the Church's money, natch, but somebody else's, for there's nothing your liberal likes better than giving away somebody else's money."

"I hardly see that the Church could give away mine."

"If your money was in Malta; and if Rome told the Church in Malta to stop being anti-socialist; and if the socialists got in as a result: then it might not look so good for your money. And the Church could say, look, everybody, we've stopped supporting privilege: on the most Catholic island of Malta we've just allowed the People to sequester all the wicked tax-evaders' pelf."

"Switzerland then. It's what I always had in mind. I'm sorry to have taken up so much of your time."

"No trouble, man. Just a professional service, for which I shall charge you £50 against your salary. Now then. We get you to open an account with the same bank as Clytemnestra uses in Zürich, and then we work a straight little transfer job."

"How will it appear in the accounts?"

"It'll appear okay. Leave that to me. What concerns you is that £1000 a week . . . less my fifty . . . will go smoothly into your lovely new account in your lovely new Swiss bank."

He passed Fielding some papers to fill in and busied himself with others.

"And I trust I see another satisfied client," he said when they were both finished.

"Indeed you do," said Fielding, and then remembered something in one of the documents he had just signed. "Am I to understand that your fee of £50 is *weekly*?"

"That's right, man." The accountant collected up all the papers. "Perhaps Mr. Jacobson didn't make it quite clear. In specialised cases like this, you are, of course, bound to take advice; and this case is so specialised, if you follow me, that the fee comes rather high."

"I follow you," said Fielding crossly.

"What the hell, man. It's all dream money. Or rather, it would be, if there weren't people like me to help you hang on to it after you've woken up. It's quite a trick, bringing money out of dreams and into the real world, and the man who does it for you deserves his five per cent."

"A very fair point. I'm sorry if I sounded annoyed."

"That's okay, man. They all get annoyed but not all of them apologise like you. So here's a tip for free. Your money will be safe in Switzerland, and you can spend it anywhere on the continent; but dream gold is apt to turn to dross if you carry it across the English Channel."

"The tax man smells it?"

"Yeah. The odd hundred quid's worth now and then . . . that's all right. But don't take it over in sacks."

"Thank you. I'll remember."

"You do that, man. Most of them don't. They forget, you see, where the money first came from, and then they get careless. To keep dream money, Mr. Gray, you've got to stay very wide awake."

When Fielding returned from the accountant's office to his room in the Corfu Palace, he found a letter from Gregory Stern:

> My dear,
>
> I want you and no one else to do the book on Conrad, as I think both your style and your sympathies will suit the subject. You match Conrad in pessimism, and you understand, if you do not share, his belief that some sort of hope is to be found in the discipline and decency of

those few men who have succeeded in clearing and for a while defending small patches in the universal jungle.

I am sorry that we must wait three months before you can make a proper start, but I accept this. We will go into details about the terms when you get back.

Detterling asks me to tell you that he is probably coming to Corfu at Christmas, to stay with his old friend Max de Freville. He hopes to see something of you, and to tell you more of our plans and aspirations for the 'Modern English Novelist' series.

Meanwhile, my dear, take care that you are not eaten alive by the Movie Moguls.

Love as ever (and from Isobel)
Gregory

Excellent, thought Fielding. His day was going very well. A sound arrangement just made with Mammon and now a gratifying letter from (so to speak) God. What was more, it would be nice to see Detterling at Christmas and very convenient; for as Gregory's partner and Fielding's old friend Detterling was always a useful ally in getting Fielding good terms for his books, and this would be a timely chance to raise the topic *re* Conrad . . . even if he did have to endure a lecture on his publishers' 'plans and aspirations' first.

But the important thing, Fielding thought, was that he was now engaged and trusted to undertake a reputable and serious literary task as soon as his allotted days in Corfu were done. Work on Conrad would wipe out the professional indignity of having played the whore in Cockaigne, while the profits of his whoredom would still remain intact. He would be having it both ways : he would be winning esteem as a man of letters and yet still eating caviar when he fancied it. . . .

Or would he? By the time he left Corfu there would be £10,000 (less the accountant's five hundred) safely banked for him in Zürich. But this was money which he had intended as a capital reserve; it was not to be frittered away on caviar, it was not to be spent at all until it was really needed. But then

K

again, if this money was not to be used, he must go back to live in Harriet's house on the Norfolk coast; and one of the pleasures of Cockaigne which he did not at all wish to forgo was independence of Harriet.

The simple truth was, as he had always known, that he needed more, much more, than £10,000 . . . less the accountant's five hundred. Not only did he need enough to live in ease and independence while he was working on Conrad, he also needed a really large sum of capital behind him (even if preserved, ten thou. was merely marbles) in order to alleviate old age and to subsidise future failures. He was, after all, already well over forty; tastes were changing all the time; so that even if his talent did not desert him, his public might.

Dream money. He must drum up more dream money while he was yet in dreamland, and this gave him just ten weeks.

Very well, Fielding asked himself : who mints the dream money?

Foxy Galahead does.

And why should he give any more of it to you, Fielding Gray?

Because he *owes* me for my good offices with Sasha Grimes.

But surely Pandarus has paid that debt already, by helping you to dodge your taxes?

Not so, not so; the Swiss arrangement, however 'specialised', will cost Pandarus nothing, and my services with Sasha are worth a lot more than that.

Perhaps; but will Foxy acknowledge the obligation? And if he does, will he discharge it?

As to that, we shall see. . . .

"Tell me," said Fielding to Max de Freville during dinner at Max's place, "how does Foxy Galahead stand with Pandarus and Clytemnestra? On what terms do they employ him?"

"He is a director of both firms," said Max, "and as such is highly salaried. He also produces films for them and takes a cut of the profits."

"He's just a leech," Sasha said, "sucking money."

"But first," said Lykiadopoulos, "he must find a host to suck it from. He must find means to finance productions beyond the relatively very small sums which Pandarus or Clytemnestra can put up for themselves. These days this is hard to do, but Mr. Galahead is good at doing it . . . thus finding money not only for himself to suck but for you and Mr. Gray and many others."

"A clown like that," said Angela; "I wonder anyone trusts him with a penny."

"He has a name for being a lucky clown," Lykiadopoulos said. "So men with money to invest, who like most powerful men are often superstitious, think maybe he will be lucky for them too."

"And that being a clown," added Max, "he will later be easy to cheat of more than he owes them."

"Is that why you invested in this film?" Sasha enquired.

"No," said Max. "You see, I happen to know he isn't a clown. It just suits him to appear as one."

"Has anyone ever seen him," asked Fielding, "without his motley?"

"Yes," said Max : "wearing a mask and a long black apron at the Board of Clytemnestra. They listen to him there all right, and they don't laugh while he's talking."

This information pleased Fielding. He was beginning to make plans for doing his deal with Foxy, plans which would run a lot smoother if Foxy's writ was respected inside Clytemnestra. But despite what Max had just said he found it hard to conceive of Foxy in the role of authoritarian.

"I must say, I can't quite see it," he now said.

"Let's hope you'll never have to," said Max.

"I can see it," said Sasha. "It was just the same with Hitler. He looked like a clown to Chaplin and everyone outside, but in Germany itself he was an ogre. Underneath it all, Foxe J. Galahead is just another bloody Nazi."

"You are surely too young to remember the Nazis," said Lykiadopoulos with avuncular reproof of such crudeness.

"The German ones, yes," said Sasha, annoyed by Lykiadopoulos's tone, "but there are some good examples here in Greece just now."

There was a brief and embarrassed silence, after which Max began to talk of the guests he was expecting for Christmas. "Detterling you know," he said to Fielding. "He may be bring-ing his cousin, Canteloupe . . ."

". . . Don't just pretend I haven't said it," shouted Sasha challenging the whole table. "I've said it and I meant every word."

"My dear," said Lykiadopoulos, "do not upset yourself. We cannot all see these things alike. Greece is a poor country, and if it is to have the wealth it needs to be truly free, it must first have discipline."

While Lykiadopoulos talked on calmly, despite Sasha's angry interruptions, about the essentially practical nature of the régime, Fielding reflected that if Sasha was still in such a taking at bed-time Angela would have but poor entertainment watch-ing from behind the fake mirror. He was here to pay Angela her 'fee', and he wanted to pay the poor old bag generously; but Sasha in her angry mood would later make for a dismal spectacle at best and possibly for none at all.

"No compassion," Sasha snapped now, "no dignity, no justice. Nothing but talk of tourism and trade. What are your lights, your guiding lights? I know the people have them if their leaders haven't."

"Yes," said Lykiadopoulos, losing patience at last, "our people have a guiding light, and as with any other people it is greed. The régime here caters for that, and so it is accepted by the people. All this talk some of them put out about yearn-ing to return to democracy is simply to save face. You have heard, Miss Grimes, how important is *face* in our country? Φιλοτίμη, as we call it?"

Sasha sniffed a graceless confession of ignorance.

"Then I shall explain to you one good example. So long as the colonels make us richer, we shall bear with them and crawl; but at the same time we shall strike Byronic attitudes about liberty and justice, in order to disguise from the world the fact that we are crawling. That, Miss Grimes, is saving face."

Sasha sniffed again, rose from the table, and marched from the room.

"I'm going to pack," she said as she went.

Fielding rose to follow her and Angela to follow Fielding. "It'll have to be now or never," Fielding whispered back to Angela. "You'd better go and take post."

A minute or two later, Angela was installed in a small booth behind the fake mirror. Although the air was very close in there, for some time at least she did not notice this, so absorbed she was by the scene in Sasha's bedroom.

When Angela had arrived in the booth, Sasha was already busy packing a small grey Revelation suitcase, while Fielding stood nearby and appeared to be arguing with her. Angela could not hear what Fielding said, but it was clear that he was trying to be calm and persuasive; his manner was not in the least aggressive, his countenance had a quiet sorrow which its deformities rendered more sorrowful. At first Sasha hardly troubled to answer him; but when her packing was almost finished, she turned to him and seemed to pay him closer attention.

Fielding now went into a long monologue. Though his manner was still calm, every now and again he made strange and intense gestures, one of which made Angela shiver in her closet : it was as though Fielding had mimed his own evisceration; he splayed his fingers over his heart, then over his belly, then in the region of his groin. As soon as he did this, Sasha's whole demeanour changed; she was no longer merely listening to him, she was suddenly possessed. Her eyes narrowed, her body tightened; and after a few more words from Fielding, she gave a brief, eager nod, and started to move very quickly and precisely about the room, stopping here or there to trace lines and circles on the floor with her finger, rather as if she were arranging a stage or set for a preliminary rehearsal and must mark out the boards with chalk to assist the actors in remembering their movements and their stations.

Meanwhile Fielding, fully clothed as he was, had gone to lie on the bed. After he had been there about a minute, Sasha transferred her efforts to the walls; on these too she traced imaginary figures, but figures very different from the ones on the floor. Whereas those had been pure geometrical forms, the designs which she indicated against the walls, while not entirely random, were variable and fluid. They were in fact, as Angela at length realised, the outlines of human bodies—though in one case Sasha reverted to her geometrical style with what appeared to be two long rectangles arranged to form an upright T.

A real nutter, Angela thought; a judgment which was confirmed when Sasha suddenly knelt down in front of the invisible T, hitting her forehead sharply on the floor and raising her rump high in the air as she did so. Perhaps she likes it like that, from behind, thought Angela; but already Sasha was on her feet and rummaging through her suitcase, from which she produced a bottle of Eau de Cologne and a small towel. She then walked briskly to the bed.

Angela's motive in watching Fielding and Sasha was not to obtain overt sexual excitement, which these days she thought to be impossible, but to associate herself with a sexual occasion (thus gratifying a life-long habit which persisted despite the disappearance of desire) and also to feed an almost intellectual curiosity. She expected, that is, to be amused, interested, informed, perhaps to be made mildly and theoretically envious of pleasures no longer available to her. What she had not expected was to be in any way stirred; and she was therefore surprised and discommoded by the sheer yearning . . . not lust, not immediate desire, but for all that a bodily yearning . . . which came over her as she witnessed the events that now followed. It was not that she was sexually excited but that she overwhelmingly wished to be; her body ached in vain to melt with the old abandon, to twitch with the remembered spasms.

What happened, hardly three yards from where she stood, was this. Sasha came to Fielding, moistened her towel from her bottle, and bathed his forehead. Then she put by the bottle and the towel, lifted her skirt, muttered fiercely, tucked the skirt into her belt, and began to lower her tights, still muttering fiercely and pushing her crutch forward as though presenting it for Fielding's closer inspection. When her tights reached her ankles, she stepped out of them and straddled slightly, said something directly to Fielding, then stretched both arms up above her head. For a few seconds she stood beautifully poised, as though about to sweep down into a ballerina's curtsy at the finish of a dance; but when her hands descended they did not spread wide for a curtsy, they came rending through the upper part of her dress, bringing it down in tatters to her waist and exposing two pointed and naked breasts, both of which were flecked with blood where her nails had passed over them.

Christ, thought Angela, and noticed old scars on Sasha's breasts and chest : if she does this very often, she won't have any tits left. Or any dresses either. What in God's name will she do next?

What Sasha did next was to leave the bed and go from place to place on the floor. At each place where she had traced a circle, she stopped, clawed her fingers through her hair and down her bare torso, and then appeared to address one of the invisible figures she had outlined on the wall. To judge from her face she was whining and howling, but very low, for Angela could still hear no sound at all. At last she went and stood before the space in which she had drawn the big T; she looked at the blank wall with horror, rent her hair once again, then ran back to the bed, where she stooped over Fielding, weeping and shuddering, and enfolded his inert body with her arms and shoulders. She stayed there a long time, during which Angela began to understand.

She understood still more when Sasha began, very slowly and with no help from Fielding, to remove Fielding's clothes, a difficult task which she performed with surprising neatness and dignity. So that's it, Angela thought : she wants to think that he's. . . . No, she couldn't. But oh yes, she could. That big T, sketched by her finger on the wall, that was the clue : a T, the Roman means of execution, which hadn't been a †, as most people supposed, but a large wooden T; it was like that in some of the old pictures. And when the body came down from the T, who tended it? His mother? Or the other Mary, Mary Magdalene? Both; at least, both were there in the old pictures. The Magdalene, thought Angela, had tried to tempt Him and failed; but she still loved Him and followed Him and was there at His execution; and when the body came down, she surely helped anoint it . . . which is just what that crazy girl is doing now. For Sasha had placed the towel over Fielding's crutch and was steadily rubbing the rest of him with Eau de Cologne from the bottle. Fielding lay absolutely still, eyes closed. Dead. But I am the body and the life; there's something stirring under that towel. God, thought Angela, why is this so troubling? Why do I tremble so and sweat?

Sasha now bowed herself reverently away from the anointed body of Fielding, then turned to face the wall. Once more she addressed the figures that only she saw there; but this time she implored rather than howled. Once more she turned to go back to the bed; but this time she did not run back to it, she walked. Walked slowly, paused once to say something to someone, smiled, and slowly walked on. And on the third day. . . . Open the tomb, take off the towel, and Fielding is risen indeed. No more lamentation, thought Angela; rejoice, Sasha, rejoice; rejoice now, as you kneel up over him in that torn and rucked up dress; wipe away the tears from your face and the blood from your bosom, yes, and use the tears and the blood . . . yes, like that . . . to anoint his quickening body, until it stands wet and gleaming, streaked with salt and gore. And now sink on to him, Sasha, and as you impale yourself give a great cry of triumph, and then plunge on down, Sasha, down, down and down.

"Good," said Jules to Fielding, "very good."

He stacked the sheets of script which he had been reading and put them away in a folder.

"You carry on like that," he said, "and there'll be no problems. I take it that Sasha is still under control?"

"Yes. She still tries to drag the proles in where they're not wanted but she's far less insistent. Nevertheless, it's a strain, Jules."

"You're being well rewarded . . . Foxy arrives back tomorrow. Will you come to the airport with me to meet him?"

"What time?"

"Twelve-thirty."

"Sorry, Jules. I've got an appointment."

"Change it. Foxy likes people to meet him."

"This appointment," said Fielding, "is quite unalterable."

Fielding waited under the cypress trees to keep his tryst.

So Foxy arrives today, Fielding thought: he's arriving at this very minute. I'll get hold of him this evening. No; this afternoon . . . as soon as he's finished his reunion with Gretel. He'll be at his most tractable then, poor booby. I've got everything I've wanted so far from these people, so why not this?

If only *this* came off as he hoped, there would be peace and quiet and comfort while he worked on Conrad, and no more truck with Harriet. But did he want to ditch her completely? She had been very loyal and kind. No; he wouldn't desert her altogether; he would just stay away from her when he wanted to . . . which would be for about ten months in every twelve. How would she take it? But that problem was for later, when his time was up in Corfu. Just now what he must remember was that in a fortnight or so Harriet would assume that his 'tour' was over and start pressing again to come and join him. That was the trouble with women: they were so relentless, they never let a man off. Take Sasha . . . no, he would not think about Sasha now. Now he was waiting for another woman . . . and here she was, coming towards him up the path.

Fielding stepped out of the shade of the cypress trees and went to meet her. Up the path she came: Angela Tuck, riding in her coffin. The Church of England chaplain fussed along behind it, and behind him walked Lykiadopoulos and Max de Freville.

The cortège halted by a newly dug grave, and Max came up to Fielding.

"This is a private funeral," he said.

"That's why I didn't come to the service."

"You've come here."

"She was a very old friend."

"You killed her."

"No. It was all her idea."

"You should never have agreed."

"Please, gentlemen," said Lykiadopoulos. "This is not a scene out of 'Amlet."

So Fielding stood his ground and the priest raised his book.

"Man that is born of woman. . . ."

Poor old cow. What on earth had happened to her? Heart attack, the doctors had said. The absurd thing was that Fielding hadn't even heard about it until late the following day. For after Sasha and he had finished on that evening up at Max's villa, Sasha had still insisted on their leaving. Max, with characteristic efficiency, had procured a taxi for them within five minutes, and Fielding had not wished to make further embarrassment by asking for Angela before they left. So he had just said to Max, 'Say good-bye to Angie for me', and Max had nodded and said, 'She's probably gone to bed . . . she goes very early these days,' and that had been that.

Then, the next afternoon, he had heard the news on the telephone. From Lykiadopoulos.

'The doctor says it was a heart attack, Mr. Gray. We found her unconscious, Max and I, and we carried her to her bed, and the doctor came and told us she was dead. The authorities are quite satisfied . . . after all, she's been ill for some time—but then again, they don't know exactly where we found her, and they might think it—rather curious . . . if they did. Do *you* know where we found her, Mr. Gray?'

'I've a very shrewd idea.'

'Yes; Max thought you might have. But none of us wants any scandal, so if the authorities should happen to call on you, you of course know nothing at all. You left the dinner table with Miss Grimes, you both packed your cases, and you went.'

"Suffer us not, at our last hour. . . ."

Angela's last hour had been passed behind that mirror.
Heart attack. Over-excitement, Fielding supposed. Round
about the time that Sasha had started to scream in her orgasm
it must all have proved too much for poor Angie, and down she
fell stone dead. A good way to go. But was it that way? Or had
there been a long agony of gradual suffocation and hideous
cramps? He would never know. She had been found unconscious and had later been pronounced to be dead. That was
all . . . and that was enough. It was not Fielding's business to
pry into what went on through the looking glass. He had kept
his bargain on this side of it, and however much Max might
blame him, his conscience was quite clear.

"We therefore commit her body to the ground. . . ."

Good-bye, Angie; Angie, good-bye. No trumpets for *you*
on the other side, I fear, but doubtless some of your dead lovers
will turn out to meet you. There must be a regiment of them
there by now. My own father among them . . . though God
knows what sort of welcome he'll give you. Because you did
for him, Angela, you did for him all right, twenty-five years
ago, that summer back in Broughton Staithe. My God, how
sexy you were then; no wonder he dropped dead with fucking
you, and serve the bastard right. And now it seems that you've
gone in much the same way. Funny, that. Oh, Angela, I wish
I'd fucked you more often myself. Only that once in Hydra . . .
Christ, your honey thighs in those stockings, your wet crotch
on my belly, I could almost come just thinking of it. My God,
how you'd laugh if you knew : me standing over your coffin
with a cock as stiff as you are.

Somewhat invigorated by the funeral, Fielding had a large and
late luncheon and then rang up Foxy Galahead's suite to ask
if he could drop by for a 'little talk'. Foxy said Gretel couldn't
bear to leave him just yet, but he'd be glad to see Fielding in an
hour.

And he looked it.

"Jules says you've got Miss Sasha eating out of your hand,"
he greeted Fielding. "That's my boy."

"If only it can last. But we'll come to that later."

Foxy, alerted by something in Fielding's voice which Fielding had hoped wasn't there, gave him a quick, sharp glance.

"Later?" Foxy said. And then, smiling broadly, "So where did you want to begin?"

In medias res, Fielding thought.

"Has it ever occurred to you," Fielding asked, "to have a good dialogue writer permanently attached to Pandarus and Clytemnestra? I mean . . . if you did employ such a man, on a retainer basis, you could call him in whenever you wanted a script to be patched up . . . as you wanted this *Odyssey* of ours patched up . . . for a much lower fee than you have to pay a writer on a temporary contract. And you'd be saving yourselves a great deal of trouble as well as money."

"Would we now?" Foxy said amiably. "And suppose this man wasn't right for a particular job when he was needed? Suppose he could re-dialogue some things quite okay, but we just happened to want some extra cracks for Jack Lemmon, let's say, and this writer couldn't write cracks?"

"Of course you'd have to choose someone pretty versatile."

"Like Fielding Gray, I suppose," said the grinning Foxy.

"Well, why not?"

"Yes. Why not? Other companies have done something like it. What sort of terms would you propose?"

He's making it too easy for me, Fielding thought.

"I should have reckoned," said Fielding, "that a lump sum... paid into a Swiss bank . . . of $50,000 would be a fair retainer for the next ten years. I would then guarantee to be on call for up to six months in any one year, and would only ask a relatively small fee, say $1000 a week, for working while wanted."

The best of both worlds, he thought. All this and lots of time for Conrad too.

"Six months at $1000 a week," said Foxy, "is about $25,000. In ten years you'd have made $250,000. $300,000 with the retainer. Isn't that rather a lot for a part-time dialogue-writer?"

"It would only be as much as that if you called me in for

the maximum period, which I take to be unlikely. But just suppose you did. You'd be getting a total of five years' solid work for $60,000 a year. That's a much lower fee than you're paying me at this minute."

"We need you at this minute. We might never need you again."

"Then all you'd have lost would be your initial investment of $50,000 . . . my retainer. Peanuts."

"Then why do you want them?"

"Not peanuts to me, Foxy. Peanuts to Pandarus and Clytemnestra."

"They're not all that rich, you know. Why do you think I spend so much time finding backers for them?"

"Because they need backers to mount a multi-million dollar picture. But not to pay out a mere fifty thousand to me. They'd do it without thinking twice . . . if you suggested it."

As to that, Fielding wasn't really sure. Was Foxy's pull truly as strong as Max had implied the other night? Never mind : the compliment would help his cause.

"Yes," said Foxy, "I think they'd go along with me. Like you say, they wouldn't think twice . . . which means, baby, that I have to think twice for them. Otherwise I shall screw them up—and find myself walking the plank. You savvy?"

"I savvy, Foxy. So you think twice . . . and then what do you say to my proposition?"

"I say you've made a good try, but no go. It's the fifty thousand that sticks in my arse. Money for work when wanted, yes . . . if it's work we think you can do. But an investment of fifty thousand in your future . . . no." Foxy paused. "You're not all that good, Fielding Gray," he said, smiling affectionately as he spoke. "This *Odyssey* thing suits you, but you're not all that good, and you'll probably get worse, and for all I know you may fall under a bus. There's always others glad of a job. We don't have to retain you . . . not even for peanuts."

Now for it, Fielding thought.

"So that's your decision after thinking twice?"

"That's it, baby."

"Then I'd appreciate it if you'd think three times."

"Why should I do that, baby?"

Foxy smiled more affectionately than ever.

"Sasha Grimes, Foxy. We don't want to upset her. Our money comes from Og-Finck every week for just as long as she says so. Right?"

"Right, baby."

"Well, it's me," said Fielding, "that's keeping her sweet."

"So Jules tells me, baby boy."

"And believe me, Foxy, it's hard work. Now, if I got all depressed and didn't feel up to that work any more . . . and stopped keeping her sweet . . . or even did something that turned her sour. . . ."

Foxy shrugged and went right on smiling.

"Okay, Fielding babes. So you squeeze the lemon, and you turn her sour. Then the money stops . . . and your job with it."

"And your film with it."

"So you've cut off your nose to spite your face." Foxy looked at Fielding's ruined face. "Sorry, baby," he said.

"That's all right. You see, Foxy, I've got other work to go to. Not as well paid as this but far more satisfying. So satisfying, in fact,"—now for the big bluff—"that I'd just as soon go and do it straight away . . . *unless,* Foxy, there's something extra to keep me here . . . like that fifty thousand retainer we were talking of."

Foxy smiled on and said nothing.

"For the rest," Fielding continued, "I shouldn't be heartbroken if this film folded tomorrow. But it would be different with you, I think. You'd have a lot of explaining to do . . . to Pandarus in London and Clytemnestra in New York. You'd have screwed them up good and proper, Foxy . . . and you'd find yourself walking the plank."

"What a cute little cookie you are," Foxy said. "You mean, you'd see all these people we've got here in Corfu done out of a job . . . a job they're relying on for months to come . . . unless I pay you $50,000 to keep on humping Sasha Grimes?"

"Let's not get crude, Foxy. Let's say what I've been saying . . . that if you can't see your way to retaining me under my very reasonable terms, I might just lose heart and start neglecting Sasha. Or I might get so nervous that I'd have a row with her. And then, of course, the consequences for most of us could be very unfortunate."

"All right, baby," said Foxy, "let's say that. And let's add that I appreciate your warning."

"Enough to act on it?"

"Sure, baby, sure. You say that you may get to feeling insecure and then do the wrong thing by Sasha. So I aim to keep you secure, right? What you want is I should take care of your future . . . so now I do just that. Then no more insecurity and no more trouble. Right?"

"Right. Thanks, Foxy."

Fielding gave a grin of genuine gratitude.

"But you'll understand," said Foxy, "that I have to talk to some people first. I have to get agreement."

"But you'll get it?"

"Yeah, I'll get it. They'll listen to me, Fielding baby. Give me three days?"

"A week if you need it, Foxy."

Be generous in victory.

"That's mighty fine of you, Fielding," Foxy said, and slapped Fielding on both shoulders. "I really do appreciate that."

It had all been too easy from the start. Much too easy, Fielding now thought. Was Foxy up to anything? But then . . . what could he be up to? Nothing hostile, Fielding was sure. Because if Foxy tried to pull the rug from under him, he'd bring Sasha down at the same time, and Foxy simply could not risk trouble with her. He might try to stall and cheat over Fielding's $50,000 for a bit; but he could never go into a positive attack without attacking Sasha too.

Fielding's telephone rang. He sighed, picked up the receiver, listened to Sasha, and then told her he'd be along to her room in ten minutes. She had had a new idea for the script . . . and a new idea for later on that night. The long day wasn't by any means over yet. Dear God, Fielding thought : if Foxy knew all that I go through, he couldn't grudge me $50,000.

About the time that Sasha was talking to Fielding on the telephone, Foxy Galahead was talking to Max, Jules and Lykiadopoulos out at Max's villa.

"So we're all agreed," Foxy said. "All of us here have put a lot of effort or a lot of money into this film, and we don't propose to let it be wrecked by Mr. Fielding Gray."

"He could be bluffing," Jules said.

"We can't risk that," said Max.

"Surely," said Lykiadopoulos, "even if Miss Grimes did report unfavourably to the Trust, they wouldn't want to throw away all the money they've already invested. That's what they'd be doing if they stopped remitting now."

"The Trust wouldn't want to bitch us up," said Foxy, "but the Student Committee would. With them it's politics, not money. No, gentlemen : we have to keep Sasha Grimes happy, and that means looking after Fielding Gray."

"You mean, pay him what he asks?" Jules said. "This retainer, as he calls it."

"It's one way, certainly."

"A bad way," said Max. "We couldn't trust him even when he'd been paid."

"Never trust a blackmailer," said Lykiadopoulos, "believe me. Besides, it is bad morals to pay blackmail. And very annoying."

"'And very expensive," Foxy said. "Though mind you, Pandarus or Clytemnestra could find the money."

"No money," said Max, thinking of Angela dead in the cemetery, "no money for Fielding Gray."

"Then what else do you suggest?"

Max thought of Angela. He had never been in love with her, but she had been his companion for over ten years. He had never made love to her, but they had often slept together just for fellowship. Now she was there no longer. Ill though she might have been, she would have stayed with him a while yet . . . if it hadn't been for Fielding Gray.

"Suppose," said Max slowly, "suppose we were to get him arrested. Imprisoned for the next few weeks."

Three faces looked at him blankly.

"Listen," said Max, "and I will make it all very plain."

"So you think it won't work?" Sasha said mournfully.

"No, love," said Fielding, "not in this film."

Fielding was having quite a job to persuade Sasha that her new idea for the script (though fundamentally brilliant, Sasha darling) would not do in the context of *The Odyssey*. Sasha wanted Penelope, on being reunited with Odysseus, to burst into a passionate speech about women's rights and how she did not propose to be his chattel just because he had at last condescended to come home. With considerable patience, Fielding had urged first that this would be out of character, and secondly that it would ruin the overall balance of the film. Why should it? Sasha asked. Because, Fielding told her, a sensational and socially aware Penelope would distract both popular and critical attention from the quiet perfection of Nausicaa. This, thank God, seemed to have done the trick, though Sasha was still sputtering on a bit for the look of the thing.

"All right. If you're sure," she said, and finally sputtered out.

So that was task one safely performed. Now for task two.

"And what was your *other* idea?" Fielding asked.

"Aaah," she said.

"But surely," Jules was saying at Max's place, "to get rid of Gray will do more harm than good. Sasha will resent it and then turn on us."

"Only," said Max, "if she thinks we have got rid of him deliberately. But if he were arrested for something entirely outside our scope . . . and if we appeared to sympathise with him and to be making every effort to get him released . . . then she would be both grateful and tractable."

"Good thinking," Foxy said.

L

"But for what," said Lykiadopoulos, "is Mr. Gray to be arrested?"

*"In 1962," Max said, "Fielding Gray conducted an investigation in Greece and Cyprus for BBC Television. He came to me for some hints . . . I was living on Hydra at the time . . . so I helped him and followed his progress. He was gathering information about the Grivas campaign in Cyprus, and he managed to put his hand on some stuff which was potentially very damaging, not only to Grivas himself, but also to Greek national prestige, and, incidentally, to the American secret service."

"What had *they* got to do with Cyprus?" Foxy asked.

"These days they have something to do with almost everything. . . . Now, as it turned out, Gray failed to establish proper proof . . . those concerned saw to that . . . so he was unable to broadcast what he knew on the BBC. But he did know it, and he still does, and all interested parties must have remained aware of this ever since."

"They'll be keeping on eye on him?"

"No," said Max. "They dealt with him very nastily last time he stuck his nose in, and they'll reckon to have cured him of his curiosity for good. As indeed they did. Fielding Gray will never trouble them again if he can help it."

"Then what's in this for us?"

"Suppose," said Max, "that they thought he *was* sniffing about again."

"But he isn't."

"But suppose they thought he was. Suppose they thought that after eight years he'd decided to have another look for the proof he never found . . . or, rather more likely after what happened last time, to sell a big tip about it all to someone else. There'd be quite a market for a tip-off like that. A possible chance to injure Greek . . . and American . . . prestige. . . ."

"Better still," said Foxy, entering into the spirit of the thing :

*See *The Judas Boy* passim. S.R.

"suppose they thought he'd *already sold* the tip, and they wanted to find out where."

"Good thinking," said Max.

"Corrupt thinking," said Jules. "Not decent."

"He's threatening to wreck our film," said Lykiadopoulos. "He started it all. Do you wish to offer the other cheek?"

"I don't want to smash him to pieces."

"Nor do we," said Lykiadopoulos. "We just want him safely out of the way for a time. Now, Max, my friend. These people you call 'they.' Who are they?"

"People . . . who are concerned for Greek 'face', Lyki. For American 'face' too."

"Not exactly policemen?"

"They have an understanding with the police."

"I am a Christian man, Max," Lykiadopoulos said. "Last time 'they' dealt with Mr. Gray, they were very brutal, you have told us."

"Not physically. They thought of a better way."

"Good. I deprecate physical violence. And so now we interest . . . 'them' . . . in Mr. Gray once more. They are not watching him, you say, but they can be made to think that they should. You know 'their' address?"

"One of their addresses. You'd be very surprised by it."

"I don't wish even to know of it. But what exactly, my friend, are you going to write and tell them?"

"What Foxy suggested just now. That Fielding Gray has just sold . . . or has agreed to sell . . . the injurious story which he found out eight years ago . . ."

". . . Found out but never *proved*, you say . . ."

". . . But can substantiate just far enough to put their enemies on a very strong scent."

"That's it," Foxy said. "Then they'll be wild to find out just how much he's said and to whom. They'll want very badly to have a nice long talk with Fielding Gray."

"And how," said Lykiadopoulos, "do you propose to make

them believe you . . . these gentlemen at the so surprising address?"

"Very fair question," Max said. "I see it all going something like this. . . ."

"Oh Sasha," said Sasha, "you foul bitch. You filthy, disgusting . . . oh, Christ, it's so marvellous . . . dirty, loathsome bitch."

". . . So you see," said Max, " 'they' may not believe what we tell them, but they won't ignore it, because it is not impossible and they'll be able to check up on it with so very little trouble. They've nothing to lose by checking, except a few minutes of their time, and a very great deal to gain. Just a quick look . . . and then they can take it or leave it alone."

"They'll take it," chuckled Foxy. "When do we fix it for? Mr. Fielding Gray is graciously allowing me a week to drum up the money."

"So we fix it for this day week," said Max. "That will give me very good time to make sure that 'they' are ready. Any problems, gentlemen?"

"Yes," said Jules, glad of a chance to diminish Foxy's satisfaction, "who's going to write the rest of the script?"

But Foxy was ready for this.

"Get as much as you can out of him this next week," Foxy said, "and then you finish it."

"Oh hell, Foxy. It won't be the same."

"Look, Jules baby. He's not writing a new script, he's rewriting an old one. You must know by now pretty much how he goes about making the changes. You must be familiar with his cute little tricks . . . his . . . what d'ya call it?. . . ."

"Idiom?" suggested Lykiadopoulos.

"Yeah, yeah. His idiom. You've handled a lot of his stuff, baby, and now you start writing it yourself, see, and bingo."

"Yes. Bingo and little Sasha jumps on my back."

"Little Sasha, Jules baby, is going to be our friend. She thinks we're trying to get her lovely Fielding out of the clinkeroo, and so she loves us, little Sasha does, and helps us all she can to produce a script worthy of her martyred darling who is languishing in the hands of the wicked fascists."

"I think it's a damned shame," said Jules. "He's worked very hard on that script."

"If only," said Lykiadopoulos, "he had confined himself to that, we wouldn't be having this disagreeable conversation. Poor Mr. Gray. He's a classical scholar himself, he should have known better than to indulge his own *hybris*."

"*Hybris*?" said Foxy.

"Insolence," said Max.

"Head-in-air," said Lykiadopoulos, "for which the traditional punishment assigned by the gods is to slip on an unobserved banana skin."

"And tomorrow," chortled Foxy, "we start getting that banana skin ready."

PART FOUR

THE JOURNEY TO ACHERON

Exactly a week after Fielding had first solicited a 'retainer' contract, Foxy Galahead sent for him to come up to his suite.

"I'm sorry it's taken all this time," Foxy said from behind his desk, "but now I've got good news for you."

"Ah." •

"Clytemnestra and Pandarus have agreed to retain you," said Foxy, "and instructions have gone from New York to Zürich that $50,000 be paid into your account there. It will be credited to you by tomorrow at the latest."

"Thank you, Foxy. I'm sure you won't regret it."

"I'm sure I shan't, baby. A contract will be prepared in due course on the basis of our discussion last week, and meanwhile will you please sign this receipt?"

"Receipt?"

"For $50,000, baby. Such sums must be accounted for."

"But I don't actually . . . know . . . it's there. Not yet. I'm sorry to be difficult, Foxy. Could I telephone the bank, do you think?"

"Why not go there yourself?" Foxy said. "It'll only take a day or so, and they'll want to see you and talk to you, now all this money's coming in."

Well, and why not? His work was well in hand, despite recent pressures from Jules, and he could do with a rest from Sasha.

"Yes, you go see the bank in Zürich," Foxy said. "Take a long loving look at your statement and introduce yourself to the manager. Have yourself a holiday."

"Thanks, Foxy. I will."

Fielding waved at Foxy across the desk and started to go.

"Oh, and take this receipt form, will you, baby, and post it off as soon as you're happy. Then they can get cracking on the contract."

Fielding went back to Foxy's desk.

"Which shall I send it to?" he asked. "Clytemnestra or Pandarus?"

"Neither."

Foxy passed Fielding an envelope which bore an address typed in capitals: LAMPAS, WILLIAM-TELLRING, 31, ZURICH.

"Lampas?" Fielding said. "Lampas?"

"Clytemnestra subsidiary for handling things in Zürich. They arranged this money of yours, so the receipt goes back through them. You can drop it in yourself if you're passing."

Foxy now handed Fielding the receipt form. It too was typed, and it read:

Received of Lampas, Zürich, the sum of Fifty Thousand Dollars ($50,000) in respect of contractual obligations orally agreed.

Underneath this was an empty space for the date and Fielding's signature, and underneath this again was his name typed in capitals: FIELDING GRAY.

"Fair enough," Fielding said.

He put the receipt form in the envelope and the envelope in his breast pocket.

"Don't forget about it. These accountants like things cut and dried. . . . And just have a word with Jules before you leave. Tell him your trip's got my blessing. One must never," said Foxy, "neglect professional etiquette."

"When shall you be back?" said Sasha crossly.

"I can get a plane on from Athens this evening . . . spend the night in Zürich . . . do my business tomorrow morning . . . and be back here tomorrow night or the morning after."

"What business," said Sasha, "have you got in Zürich?"

Steady now. Sasha did not approve of dealings done through Swiss banks.

"A publisher there is bringing out one of my novels."

This seemed to satisfy her. Lucikly she was not in the mood for conducting cross-examinations.

"Oh Fielding, I'm going to miss you. Can we . . . before you go. . . . ?"

Always part friends.

"Yes," he said. "That would be nice."

In the reconstructed Stoa of Attalus in the Athenian Agora there is a statue of a boy playing a flute. This statue is about a third of the way down the Stoa from the northern end, and next to it there is a door. About the time that Sasha was lowering her tights to take her pleasure with Fielding, a tall man in his early middle age knocked on the door in the Stoa and was admitted into a small and windowless room which was furnished with several metal filing cabinets and a lot of battered statuary.

"Well, Restarick?" said the man who had admitted him, a man with a nose like a hockey-stick and a thin, down-turned mouth.

"Our man's leaving Corfu. Probably leaving Greece."

"For good?"

"I can't say," said Restarick. "But the police have agreed to pick him up at the airport here in Athens. They'll hand him over to us and our Greek colleagues. And if we find anything on him. . . ."

"It's my bet there'll be nothing. Why should he start again after all this time? I simply don't trust your information. An anonymous letter. . . ."

"Anonymous letters have a way of being true. Ask any tax collector."

"Well, we'll see."

"Yes, we shall see," said Restarick. "Because if we do find anything on him, the police will let us keep him for investigation."

"That could be tricky, Restarick. This man's quite a well known writer."

"Only in England."

"Even the English can still make a fuss."

"But it's us Americans the Greeks want to please. The régime needs money, Aloysius. And in any case, if Gray is up to anything, the Greeks will be as interested as we are."

"I still say there could be a nasty fuss if this man is detained for very long."

"Well, yes," said Restarick. "You could be right. So I have a little plan. The American School of Greek Studies."

"What about it?" said the man with the hockey-stick nose.

"You are employed by it." Restarick waved a hand at the stumps of statuary littered round the floor. "You can arrange for Gray to be offered its hospitality."

"Like hell I can."

"Not in Athens, of course. In one of those remote hostelries of yours . . . which are empty at this time of the year. Mr. Gray, let us say, is taken ill somewhere out in the country, he is given temporary shelter in your hostelry, and you then 'discover' who he is . . . an English novelist, with strong antiquarian interests, who is scripting a film about Odysseus. So what more natural than that the American School of Greek Studies should offer so sympathetic a guest all the care and comfort he needs until he is fully recovered? The world hears this and the world is happy."

"His friends hear this and come to call."

"And find that he is indeed ill. Very ill."

"And at once they ask why he hasn't been moved to a hospital."

"Don't nag. Details later. Trust me for that."

"I hope I shan't need to. Because I still think," said the man with the hockey-stick nose (about the time that Sasha was pulling her tights on again), "that we shan't find anything on Fielding Gray."

Jules saw Fielding off at the airport.

"I'm sorry you're going," Jules said.

"Not for long."

"Suppose I need to refer to the script? I mean, those bits I haven't seen yet."

"You've had all I've done so far except for a few pages. They're in the left-hand drawer of my desk."

"I still wish you weren't going."

"Hell, Jules, I've earned a break. It'll be two days at most."

Jules shrugged miserably.

"Well, good luck," he said.

They shook hands and Fielding went to the barrier.

Oh Christ, Jules thought, he's deserved everything he's going to get. Foxy and Max are quite right: he's a dangerous threat to the film . . . my film . . . and he's got to be dealt with. And yet . . . he did seem to love the film and he's worked like a slave at it. Worked at it, loved it . . . and threatened to destroy it. So you go to hell, Fielding Gray; but I hope you don't get fried there, and I'm going to miss you very much.

Could this really be true? thought Fielding in the plane to Athens. Was he really richer by $50,000? (To say nothing of a potentially lucrative contract for work over the next ten years . . . a contract under which they would surely employ him occasionally, in order to get value for the retainer.) Could it really be as easy as this?

But what could possibly be wrong? Foxy himself had sent him off to see that all was well, had given him a receipt to sign and post when he was satisfied. Nothing could be wrong . . . now. All this last week he had watched for signs that Foxy or Jules might be meditating some treacherous riposte, but everything about them had been entirely normal. True, Jules had seemed anxious to make him get on with the script rather quicker than usual, but Jules was subject to such fits of restlessness from time to time, and his demands had not been too difficult to meet. The only odd thing had been that Jules had never once indicated that he knew what Fielding was up to, though Foxy must surely have discussed it with him. But probably Jules disapproved . . . how could he not disapprove? . . . and preferred simply to keep silent on the topic. Anyway, why should Fielding worry? He could put up with a good deal of disapproval in exchange for $50,000.

Fielding's plane from Corfu landed at the domestic airport outside Athens shortly after half past three. He took a taxi straight to the international airport, from which his plane for Zürich would leave at five. He presented his ticket at the flight-desk, and received it back together with his boarding card and an exit card, which latter he at once filled in. He then moved towards the Departure Lounge, where he proposed to examine the bookstall and have some tea while waiting for his flight to be called.

Before he could enter the Departure Lounge, he must go through Passports and Customs at the barrier. The Passport man took his passport, his boarding card and his exit card, looked at them, stamped all three, put the exit card on a pile to one side, and flicked the passport and the boarding card back to Fielding. The Customs man just nodded. Fielding went down the stairs into the Departure Lounge and started to thumb through a paperback copy of *My Secret Life* which was prominently displayed on the bookstall.

Restarick and his friend with the nose like a hockey-stick watched Fielding as he went down the stairs.

"That over-night bag he's carrying . . . that's his only luggage," said the man with the hockey-stick nose.

"So I've noticed," said Restarick.

"So it hardly looks as if he means to leave Greece for good."

"But he *is* leaving, Aloysius. Or rather, he isn't. Just you watch. It will be very nice and quiet. No one will even notice what is happening. So when we produce him down in Vassae, we can tell any story we wish."

"Suppose we find nothing on him?"

"Then he will still be in good time for his plane. Now just watch. . . ."

At the bookstall, Fielding was approached by a very ordinary airport policeman, who saluted rather sloppily and explained in passable English that Fielding had forgotten to record his passport number on his exit card. Would he kindly now come and repair the omission? Fielding was pretty sure that he had filled in the card correctly, but if they said he hadn't. . . . After all, he knew himself to be a little light-headed. He hurriedly purchased *My Secret Life* for 200 drachmae, picked up his over-night bag, and started towards the stairs in order to remount them to the barrier. But the policeman shook his head, pointed politely to a door near the duty-free counter, and walked off, leaving Fielding, who was mildly puzzled but well accustomed to the quirks of Greek bureaucracy, to make his own way.

"There you are, Aloysius," said Restarick. "No fuss. He just walks placidly through that door of his own accord, and nobody blinks an eyelid."

Fielding walked through the door.

In Corfu, Max de Freville rang up the international airport at Athens. Several times he was put through to the wrong desk, but at last he was connected with Swissair and learned what he wanted to know.

"So what's happened?" Foxy said.

"He didn't take the plane to Zürich. Swissair say he checked in for the flight, but then someone returned his boarding card to the desk, about ten minutes before the flight was called, and said that Mr. Gray would not be going."

"So they've got him in Athens."

"It seems like it."

"Good," said Foxy. "What now?"

"We simply sit here and know nothing. As far as we're concerned, Fielding Gray set out from here to Zürich early this afternoon and is expected back tomorrow night or the morning after. When he fails to turn up we shrug our shoulders and wonder why he's been delayed. After another twenty-four hours, we start to get worried. You make enquiries on behalf of your company, and eventually you get on to the Greek police: your British employee, Mr. Fielding Gray, is missing . . . has there been an accident?"

"And has there?"

"The police promise to enquire. Some time later they ring you back and give you the official hand-out. They very much regret that Mr. Gray is being held for investigation. *My* script-writer, you scream: *what* investigation? The police are sorry, *kyrios,* but the matter is . . . confidential. You start yelling about consuls and lawyers. Please, *kyrios,* this will not improve matters: the police will inform you as soon as there is anything more you should know. Then you tell everyone here what is going on, and you comfort the outraged Sasha, and assure her that everything possible is being done to get her Fielding back from those fascist beasts."

"The trouble is," said Foxy, "that something *will* have to be done. Just for the look of it. If I do too little, Sasha will get savage; and if I do too much, they might actually let him out."

"We shall have to strike a very delicate balance," said Max. "Exactly how we manage it must depend on the official version of what's going on."

"They'll claim he's being held for investigation . . . so you said."

"That's what I'm expecting. But there are other formulae, and a wide range of official attitudes to go with them. When they've spoken their lines, Foxy, we can start scripting yours. . . ."

When Fielding had been gone for two days, Jules Jacobson went to his room to collect the sheets of script which Fielding had said were in his desk. Jules took them from the drawer and read them, and then poured himself a whisky from Fielding's bottle. He drank it down in one, looked sadly round the room, and then went downstairs, where he instructed the management to pack up all Fielding's belongings and put them in store until further notice.

Fielding was being driven out of Athens. Restarick was at the wheel, while Fielding was sitting in the back with a stocky man who had a dark skin and close-cut hair. This was the first time Fielding had seen this particular man, and he did not like the look of him. Greek, Fielding thought; or perhaps Greek-Cypriot. Aloud he said :

"Where are we going?"

"We are going to a place called Vassae," said Restarick.

"Where the temple is?"

"Not far from it."

"Why?"

"So that you can have a nice rest," said the man beside Fielding, "after which you will be able to explain yourself more satisfactorily than you have done so far."

"There is nothing to explain."

"There is an unsigned receipt for $50,000 to explain," said Restarick from the front.

"I've told you. I've been telling you for two days. That is for money which is being paid to me by the film company Clytemnestra."

"The receipt says it is being paid by Lampas of Zürich."

"A Swiss subsidiary of Clytemnestra."

"Which Clytemnestra has never heard of," said Restarick. "We have rung Clytemnestra in New York, and they know of no subsidiary called Lampas. And they know of no payment to you other than £1000 a week for your present engagement."

Fielding shifted sweatily from ham to ham.

"Then there's been a mistake. Did you try Mr. Foxe J. Galahead in Corfu?"

"We did. He knows of no payment either."

Fielding went cold.

"All he knows is that you asked his leave to go to Zürich for a day or so. Private business, he understood. He expected you back this morning at latest and was beginning to get worried. We were able to reassure him."

"What did you tell him?"

"That you were in good care. We asked him too about Lampas of Zürich. It meant nothing to him."

Fielding went colder.

M

"But he suggested," Restarick continued, "that perhaps this private business you mentioned to him was to do with a company called Lampas. Although he had not heard of it, it might nevertheless exist. The only trouble is, Mr. Gray, that the company does not exist. Nor does the address on that envelope. A little work with Swiss directories has made that very plain."

"For Christ's sake," Fielding said, "what the hell can it matter to you?"

"We have memories," said the man beside him. "We remember your escapade in 1962."

"The devil you do. And what's it got to do with all this?"

"Lampas," said Restarick. "A Greek word in origin."

"Meaning a beacon," said the man beside Fielding.

"Thank you, Savidis." Restarick started to accelerate along the highway to the Isthmus. "A beacon. Just the sort of silly symbolical name such organisations always adopt."

"Organisation?" said Fielding stupidly.

"Yes. Not a company, that appears in respectable directories, but an organisation of another kind. You should know."

And he did know. Lampas. The word had struck a faint, uneasy chord when he first saw it on the envelope, but Foxy's plausible words had reassured him at once. Now he remembered: Harriet, years ago, babbling away about some new movement which they ought to subscribe to, an anti-fascist, anti-neo-colonialist movement, Lampada, she thought it was called, she had the details in a letter from a friend upstairs; and himself, Fielding, snarling that he was sick of all this left-wing rubbish, that he wouldn't give a penny; then a minor row and Lampada forgotten by mutual consent. Until now. Lampada: accusative singular of Lampas, feminine, a beacon.

"Just the sort of organisation," Restarick said, "that would be interested in what you discovered in 1962."

"Balls."

"It wasn't balls. You know that."

"I could never prove it. You know *that*."

"But you could put anyone who was interested on the right

track, and you can bet your life where it would lead 'em. To new knowledge of American interference . . . past and then present, Mr. Gray . . . in Greece and the eastern Mediterranean. Just the job for Lampas."

"At a price of $50,000?"

"Lampas has come a long way these last few years. Russian money. Guilty liberal money. This sort of thing is very much in fashion among the trendy rich."

"But $50,000 . . . just for a lead?"

"A great deal, certainly. We'll come to that in a moment. But first, Mr. Gray, do please recognise the logical case against you. We receive an anonymous tip-off that Mr. Fielding Gray, who is in Greek waters for an ostensibly innocent purpose, is in fact up to his old tricks and may be carrying evidence to that effect. The next thing we know, you are trying to leave Greece . . . carrying an unsigned receipt for a large sum of money which we deduce that you are going off to collect."

"From a non-existent company," said Fielding wearily, "at a non-existent address."

"From an existing organisation, whose representative you are obviously going to meet. Somewhere, anywhere in Zürich or Switzerland. Only you know the rendezvous."

"Only you . . . so far," Savidis said.

"The receipt, already prepared, is clearly your warrant of *bona fides*," Restarick went on. "The fictitious address on the envelope is probably some coded instruction for the person you are to meet. So off you go to meet him, to deliver your information and collect your fee . . ."

". . . But never even got there," said Fielding crossly. "So where does that leave us?"

"Sitting in this car," said Restarick, "wondering what you would have said if you *had* got there. And how much you have already said here in Greece. Because the receipt, already prepared, proves that you had already agreed a price with somebody . . . in Corfu, we presume. You wouldn't have told him everything, as he wasn't paying you out himself, but in order to get him to agree such a very large price, you must have dished out a very tasty appetiser. What was it, Mr. Gray? And to whom did you serve it?"

Fielding shrugged hopelessly.

"We shall ask again," said Savidis.

"Indeed we shall. You see, plainly the man in question is highly regarded by Lampas. He must be, so to speak, their resident expert here in Greece. The resident expert, responsible to chiefs who are based in Switzerland or elsewhere. He assesses the quality of information on offer, he sends those like yourself, who offer it, to Switzerland to deliver it, and he authorises— or at least suggests—the payment of very important sums. So he himself must be very important to Lampas . . . and to us, Mr. Gray."

"He is a fiction of your own making."

"Who is he, Mr. Gray? And how much did you tell him before he sent you off? In Vassae we shall have plenty of time to find out."

"It seems," said Foxy Galahead, "that he never went to Zürich but had some kind of nervous breakdown instead."

Foxy was talking to Jules and Sasha in his suite. Sasha was drinking fresh lemon juice and Jules was gloomily drinking gin. Every now and then Sasha looked with disapproval at Jules's gin, though in fact it had cost rather less than her own lemon juice.

"Someone rang up," Foxy said, "and told me he was Aloysius Sheath of the American School of Greek Studies. He was down at one of the School's hostelries, he said, at a place called Vassae, he said . . . does either of you know where that is? . . ."

". . . Ancient site," muttered Jules, "in the western Peloponnese."

". . . And he'd found someone wandering round a temple or something who afterwards turned out to be Fielding Gray. Fielding was in a terrible state, according to this Mr. Sheath, and hardly knew who he was. He talked a lot of rubbish about lump payments and banks and holding companies . . . can either of you make sense of *that*? . . ."

". . . He never spoke of money to me," said Sasha.

"Jules baby?"

Jules just shook his head and wished that Sasha weren't there, so that Foxy could stop putting on an act and tell him what had really happened.

". . . But eventually," Foxy was saying, "Fielding talked about Corfu and what he'd been doing here, so Mr. Sheath got my name out of him and was able to call me up. He says that finally Fielding went on a terrible crying jag, sobbing his heart out about Greek hexameters and compressed prose equivalents and oh, Homer, Homer, and was he worthy . . ."

". . . Oh, poor Fielding," Sasha said.

". . . So this Aloysius Sheath gave him a lot of sleeping tablets and sent for the doctor. The doctor said keep him quiet and don't move him and send for a specialist. So Mr. Sheath and his friends are taking care of Fielding in this hostelry, and they've sent for the psychiatrist who attends the American School in Athens. Very sensible, I'd say."

"I'd like to go there and see him," Sasha said.

"I'd wait here, baby, until they know exactly what's to be done. Mr. Sheath will call me again as soon as he's learned what the psychiatrist has to say."

"You'll tell me at once, Foxy?"

"Of course, Sasha baby."

"Then I think, if you'll excuse me, I'll go and lie down."

Foxy saw Sasha solicitously to the door.

"Now what is all this?" said Jules when Foxy came back.

"Just like I told you. A man rang up calling himself Aloysius Sheath and gave me that spiel about Vassae and nervous breakdowns."

"It can't have been like that."

"I don't know how it was, Jules baby, but that is obviously how . . . they . . . wish us to think that it was. This is what Max calls the official hand-out. You see, *they* don't know that we want them to keep him, so they think they've got to find a respectable excuse."

"They certainly have . . . if the American School backs it."

"The American School backs it, baby. I called them to check. Yes, they have a man called Aloysius Sheath, yes, he's down at their hostelry at Vassae, and yes, he's been on to them with some tale about a stray Britisher he's taken in."

"But if they're doing it this way," said Jules, "they'll have trouble on their hands before long. Sasha Grimes, for one, is going to be knocking on their door at Vassae."

"No trouble," Foxy said. "There are lots of good reasons why a psycho patient might not be allowed to see company."

"But sooner or later . . ."

". . . Sooner or later, Jules, they'll realise that he's no use to them, and then they'll let him go anyway. I don't think he'll show his face back here . . ."

". . . But he might tell Sasha or someone what had happened. That he'd been framed."

"And Sasha or someone might think, 'What the hell, he's had a nervous breakdown.' "

"Too many 'mights', Foxy."

"Very true baby. So now we use every second we've got, and we get to finish this mother-fucking film on the double."

Aloysius Sheath, with the nose like a hockey-stick, took Fielding for a walk round the temple of Apollo the Saviour at Vassae. Savidis, with the close-cut hair, came along too, walking always just behind them.

"The odd thing about this temple," said Aloysius Sheath, "is that it was erected in the loneliest part of the country. Pausanias says it was paid for by the people of Phigalia in gratitude to Apollo for their deliverance from the plague. But Phigalia was a long way from here . . ."

". . . And now," said Savidis, "there's nothing left of it. The only thing round here is this temple."

The grey columns sprouted from the grey rock. To the south a shallow mountain valley, broken by spurs, receded towards a backdrop of angular and intermittent peaks. To the north the same valley became a huge, swirling rift, which debouched on to a plain many hundreds of feet below. Grey sky and grey scrub and grey rock. Not a man, not an animal in sight anywhere. Not a house either . . . except the House of Apollo the Saviour.

"Four thousand feet up, we are," Savidis said.

"And yet outside Athens there is not a better preserved temple in Greece. Of course," said Aloysius Sheath, "we've helped a lot with that. They're very grateful. Now then. . . . You'll notice that it has six columns front and back, and fifteen on either side instead of the usual twelve. There are thirty-seven of them still standing here, but twenty-three panels of frieze have been carted away by . . . guess whom . . . the British. . . ."

Later on they walked back along the narrow, stony track that led up the valley to the hostelry. This was built between two spurs, sheltered from winds both north and south, and hidden from the road which ran past the temple.

"Very snug," said Aloysius. "We'll do very well here for a time. Very snug and very discreet."

"My friends in Corfu will find me."

But which of them were still his friends?

"My dear fellow," said Aloysius, who spoke a very anglicised American, "they already know where you are. I was the one who telephoned to tell them. They were very anxious about you, but I was able to reassure them. No one will come up here until we give the word."

"What did you tell them?"

"That you were ill with overwork and needed rest."

"They believed it?"

"Why shouldn't they? Responsible members of the American School of Greek Studies do not go round disseminating lies about distinguished English novelists."

"Except that *you* do."

"But you are ill with overwork. You took on too much when you took on this business with Lampas. And now you must be cured of your illness."

"Yes," said Savidis, "by having the truth sweated out of you."

And now, at last, Fielding more or less understood the nature of the trap which had caught him. These people thought he was the real thing and no one would ever undeceive them. They would keep him here till he told what they thought he had to tell, and Foxy would be only too happy to let them keep him. No one at all would agitate or protest, because on the face of it there was nothing whatever to protest about : he was the sick guest of the American School of Classical Studies.

"What do your superiors at the American School think?" he asked Aloysius.

"That I am down here studying such carving as remains in the temple, and have given graceful assistance to a distressed English traveller."

"Oh God," said Fielding, "what am I to do?"

"Tell us what we want to know. If you do it nicely, *we* might even pay you a bit."

"I've nothing to tell that you don't know already. Can't you believe that?"

"No," said Savidis.

"You see, my dear chap," said Aloysius, "your record is against you. You have gone in for this kind of thing before; you know your way around in these circles. So when we find a piece of paper on you that says 'Lampas', we take it at face-value . . . especially as no one at all supports your own explanation."

"You can't get blood out of a stone."

"You're not a stone," Savidis said.

"Come along, both of you," said Aloysius, "it's time for tea."

The next evening Aloysius Sheath telephoned Foxy Galahead again. Foxy listened carefully, then sent for Sasha and Jules.

"Good news about Fielding," he told them. "On the whole, that is. Apparently the psychiatrist says that all he needs is rest and quiet. Vassae's a splendid place for that, so his good friends there will look after him."

"Sounds all right," muttered Jules.

"The only thing is," said Foxy, who was reporting absolutely truthfully, "they say no visitors for the next week. It's definitely overwork that has caused the trouble, and if one of us went to see him, he'd start asking about the film and the script, and get all upset again."

"He must want to know about it all," Sasha said.

"I told them to tell him we could manage. Tell him 'Jules is making out', I said."

"I am too," said Jules, looking more cheerful. "I've studied the way he went to work, and Sasha," he put in tactfully, "is giving me some useful tips. I shall be able to finish off that script."

"Surely," said Sasha, "he'll be back to do that himself."

"One can't be sure," said Foxy.

"Well," said Sasha, "I shall go to see him as soon as the week is up. Is that all right with you, Foxy?"

"You forget, baby," said Foxy, "it's no longer me that employs you. You go where and when you please."

" 'Jules is making out'," said Aloysius to Fielding. "That was the message."

"So you see," said Restarick, "they're quite happy without you. No one is ever indispensable."

Restarick was standing in front of a log fire in the hostelry, holding a glass of ouzo. Savidis was cooking the dinner in the next room, whither Aloysius, who fancied his culinary gifts, now went to assist. The hostelry, as Aloysius had said, was very snug and despite its remote situation was well supplied from Andritsaena, the nearest town. In other circumstances, thought Fielding, one could have been very happy here : even as it was, he was getting quite attached to the cosy domestic routine. He got up from his chair and helped himself to another drink.

"That's right," said Restarick, "I'm glad you're feeling at home."

"One makes the best of things."

"Of course. We hope you will do just that. We don't want
to be nasty," Restarick said. "All we want is for you to tell us
who you were in touch with and how much you had to reveal
in advance to get an offer of $50,000. As soon as you've told
us the truth about that . . . the truth, of course, Mr. Gray . . . we
shall let you go and give you $1500 for your time and trouble.
I cannot say fairer than that."

"No," Fielding agreed. "But I've been in touch with nobody
and revealed nothing. I cannot say truer than that."

"We think you can. And if you don't, we shall have to turn
nasty after all. Now, let me see. Physical violence? Torture?
No, of course not. Much too crude, and makes a bad impression with the public if it comes out later. But there are other
ways. You see, your friends know that you've had a bad nervous breakdown; so they wouldn't be at all surprised at some
further failure, mental or perhaps moral. For example, we
could arrange it all something like this. . . ."

As Restarick started to tell him how they could arrange it,
Fielding forgot about his drink and rapidly lost the excellent
appetite which he had been building up for his dinner.

A week later, Sasha Grimes took an aeroplane to Athens,
where she hired a car and set out for Vassae. She was looking
forward very much to seeing Fielding, whom she expected to
find almost recovered. At Foxy's sensible suggestion, she had
telephoned ahead to say that she was coming, and Aloysius
Sheath had sounded very pleased.

'We'll get a room ready,' he had said, having first given her
some helpful directions about the route.

Sasha reached Vassae towards evening, as Aloysius Sheath
had told her she would, and parked her car in the small park
near the temple of Apollo the Saviour. Then, following
Aloysius's instructions, she walked along the path up the valley,
skirted the first of the two spurs, and approached the hostelry,
which looked like an elaborate German hunting lodge. When
she knocked on the front door, a polite servant appeared, very

trim with his white jacket and close-cut hair, and took her suit-case from her.

"Mr. Sheath is in the sitting room," the servant said, and opened the door for her before carrying off her case.

"My dear Miss Grimes, an honour," said Aloysius Sheath. "I was privileged to see you as Katharina last year in London."

"My favourite part," said Sasha. "I am a shrew, you see."

"You don't look it. Have a drink."

"I'd rather see Fielding," Sasha said.

"Of course. Just a moment, Miss Grimes."

Aloysius went out and almost immediately afterwards Fielding came in. How nice of that nice man to leave us alone, Sasha thought. She went to Fielding and kissed him warmly on the lips. He looked well and very happy to see her.

"Fielding. . . ."

"Elena. . . ."

"Fielding?"

"Oh, Elena, I am glad you've come. We can leave tomorrow morning and go back to Corfu together. You've got a car, Elena?"

"*Fielding.*"

"Well, have you?"

"Yes."

"Good. It'll be all right now you're here. They've given you the room next to mine, so we can do it tonight. I've been looking forward to that. Do it tonight and leave for Corfu tomorrow? What do you say, Elena?"

Sasha was about to say a good deal, in her best shrewish style at that, but then she thought about Fielding's breakdown and smiled bravely instead.

"Good," said Fielding, "I thought you'd like the idea of that."

He looked at her happily, then nodded his head. His eyes glazed over, he peered about him and sat down in an armchair, slobbered and then fell asleep.

Sasha went to the door and opened it.

"Somebody, please," she called.

The white-coated servant came across the hall and into the sitting room, took one look at Fielding, lifted the recumbent body from the chair (he must be very strong, Sasha thought), and carried it out. Aloysius Sheath appeared in the doorway.

"Thank you, Savidis," he called over his shoulder. "You know what to do, of course?"

"He . . . sort of fainted," Sasha said.

"Coma," said Aloysius. "I hoped he was over that. I thought he was so much better . . . so did the nurse."

"Nurse?"

"The fellow in the white coat. Very experienced. Doctor Harocopos the psychiatrist sent him down from Athens to help. I was going to send him back tomorrow, but now . . ."

". . . Mr. Sheath. He . . . Fielding . . . thought I was someone else."

Aloysius shook his head.

"What can we do?" said Sasha.

"Harocopos said there might be relapses."

"You'll send for Doctor Harocopos?"

"If the nurse thinks it's necessary. Miss Grimes, I am sorry. We thought he was ready to see people. I don't quite know how to say this" . . . Aloysius wrinkled his hockey-stick nose all down the shaft and round up the hook . . . "but let's put it this way. The nurse understands this illness. The School in Athens will send any help we need. Meanwhile, it seems that . . . you can't do much good."

"You mean, I've already done harm?"

"Perhaps. It's our fault for letting you come. But there it is."

Sasha, full of compassion, uneasiness, and resentment (which she knew to be irrational) at being called 'Elena'; rather disgusted by the slobbering object that had been carried away by the nurse; rather impressed by the nurse himself and by Aloysius Sheath's good will; confident in the resources of the American School in Athens; agonised at the thought of sleeping under the same roof as Fielding yet not being able to go near him : Sasha, confused yet reassured, desiring Fielding yet loathing him, wanted only one thing : out.

"There is an hotel the other side of Andritsaena," she said, "which I passed on the way up. I'll spend the night there."

"You'll come back tomorrow?" said Aloysius kindly.

"No."

He nodded in sad approval.

"You don't think he should go to a . . . to a hospital, Mr. Sheath?"

"Not in Greece," said Aloysius with gentle emphasis, "not in Greece. I'm sorry you can't take a better report back to Corfu, Miss Grimes, but let's hope he'll improve before long."

When Fielding woke up, Restarick and Savidis were standing over his bed.

"What happened?" he said.

"You had a visitor," said Restarick. "Can you remember? Miss Sasha Grimes."

"Yes, Sasha. Where is Sasha?" said Fielding sitting up urgently.

"She didn't much care for your behaviour, and she's gone. You mistook her for someone else, you see. And then passed out."

"Oh Christ. What have I done?"

"You've done nothing," said Savidis. "We did it."

"We gave you a preparation," said Restarick, "which made you suggestible. In your tea. Then we told you that you were going to see an old friend. You were talking to Aloysius the other day about a starlet called Elena . . . and very amusing you were, Aloysius says . . . so we decided to tell you it would be her. Elena was coming to see you after tea, we said. Elena . . . Elena . . . Elena."

"And I fell for this?"

"You couldn't help it. You saw, as you were bound to, this Elena. We understand these things," Restarick said. "These days they play an important part in our profession."

Fielding gave a little moan and lay back.

"That's right," said Restarick, "you stay there and have a

good rest. But remember. If you don't tell us what we want to know, we shall very soon have to start the treatment of which I told you the other day. After what's happened this evening, I think you can understand that it will be effective. The stuff we used just now is harmless in small doses; but there are other things which are less so."

When Restarick and Savidis left him, Fielding lay and thought about 'the treatment'. Restarick had explained very carefully about this. They did not wish to use it, Restarick had said, because it would make for permanent mental damage; but since the world was now amply prepared for Fielding to exhibit signs of mental oddity when he emerged, they could probably get away with using it, and were ready to take the risk if they had to. They would start by trying a truth drug. Not much harm in that, but little good either, from Restarick's point of view, because someone who had been given a truth drug was just as likely to start spouting childhood secrets or to confess a fondness for shoplifting as to reveal what was actually required of him. Truth drugs were random in their operation : Restarick desired relevance and precision. So when, as was probable, the results of administering the truth drug proved unsatisfactory, they would try something else . . . a moral strategy rather than a pharmaceutical one, though it too involved some use of drugs. It could be described, perhaps, as a kind of spiritual blackmail, and as Fielding thought about it now he hugged himself in terror beneath the sheets.

How long before they would start? Clearly they were indeed reluctant to do so, or they would have begun long since. How long had he been at Vassae? Well over a week. Time was going on. . . . Harriet, he thought suddenly : yes, *Harriet*. She would think that by now he was back in Corfu from his 'tour' ('a month or so', he had said). When he failed to communicate with her by letter or by cable, she would do one of two things : either she would come straight out to Corfu to confront him . . . God knew, she had done that often enough in the past . . . or she would telephone the Corfu Palace first to find out what was going on. And when she did find out, as in either case she was bound to, when she heard that he was 'ill at Vassae', she would come there to gather him up. Harriet would not be put off if he thought she was someone else or called her once or twice by the wrong name. She would know he was in trouble, she would love him as she always had, she would stay with him, stand by him, and take him home. Oh Harriet, Harriet in Norfolk, hear my call *de profundis* and come to take me home.

Harriet behaved just as Fielding thought she would . . . up to a point. About a week after she received the last of the four hasty jottings which he purported to have written while on tour, she began to expect further word, to tell her that he was or soon would be back in Corfu. Further word of some kind at any rate. Since none came, she decided to telephone the Corfu Palace, and began by asking for Mr. Fielding Gray.

The concierge, with whom she was connected, knew exactly where Fielding was: he was convalescing from some illness at Vassae, and his belongings were being held for him in a store-room until there should be further instructions. But this was not what the concierge told Harriet. For he remembered that the *kyrios* Gray had been paying him regularly to be prepared to tell a simple lie to inquisitive ladies who might chance to telephone from England. True, the weekly payments had now lapsed, but the *kyrios* had been very generous, there was no reason to suppose that his wishes had changed, and here was a chance to perform an effortless act of kindness for which the *kyrios* would doubtless reward him should he return to the hotel.

The concierge therefore consulted the note he had made when the matter was originally discussed, and politely informed Harriet that Fielding was to be gone from the hotel for some four or five weeks and had not, as yet, sent back a forwarding address.

"But surely," Harriet wailed, "he's *already* been gone for four or five weeks."

The tone of Harriet's voice aroused the concierge's compassion . . . for Fielding and not for Harriet. So he simply repeated what he had told her and put down the receiver, congratulating himself on having done a good turn to a fellow male.

Oh dear, oh dear, thought Harriet in Broughton Staithe. He must have changed his plans. Why hasn't he told me? He said nothing in those beastly letters except how busy he was on his tour, and busy he doubtless was, but when he knew his plans were changing, why didn't he say? If he could tell the hotel in Corfu, he could have told me, three words by wire would have been enough, *why didn't he tell me* instead of leaving me to find out from some foolish concierge . . . who couldn't even give an address. How thoughtless, Harriet told herself, how careless, how very, very unkind. He doesn't care, he can't, whether I come or not, it's been like this a long time now, I should have woken up to it before, he doesn't want me to come, that's what it is, he doesn't want me there at all.

Always before, when she had thought this, she had simply packed and gone right after him. But this time she had no idea whatever where to go; and something about this particular piece of cruelty, so easily avoidable, so shabbily prolonged, had stricken all present will to act and poisoned all hope. Leave him be, wherever he is, she thought : there's nothing I can do now. Sooner or later, I suppose, he will come back to England . . . but after this, do I really want to see him any more?

In Corfu things carried on quite smoothly. Foxy went away and came back; Lykiadopoulos went to Milan on business and stayed there; Max de Freville went nowhere. Circe came out again from England to re-make her scenes with Odysseus, re-made them, and departed; and Sasha Grimes, who was rather subdued these days, cooperated with Jules over the script, doing everything as she thought Fielding would have wanted it done. She felt guilty about the way she had left him in Vassae and spoke of him often, wanting reassurance.

"There's nothing you can do for him," said Jules day after day, "except hope that he gets better. You know that."

Sasha, remembering the glazed eyes and the slobbering lips,

was compelled to agree. After all, Aloysius Sheath and the nurse were there to take care of Fielding; they did not need her at Vassae, and to be honest with herself she was very glad they didn't.

"Now," Jules was saying to her, "here is a list of the scenes I want to get finished before Christmas. They cover Odysseus's stay with the swineherd and the earlier episode with the Cyclops. I've pencilled in the camera directions on my script, but I want you to look 'em over for me before I go firm on them. Okay?"

It was an honour to be asked for such specialised advice, and well Sasha knew it. She spared a quick, sad thought for Fielding and settled to her work.

"As I thought," said Restarick to Fielding, "truth drugs have proved no good on you. You've told me nothing."

"I've nothing to tell, that's why."

"You had plenty to say, mind you. Stories about hitting your mother and God knows what. But nothing I wanted to hear."

"I can't tell you what I don't know."

Restarick sighed.

"I'm going away for a little while," he said. "Savidis and Aloysius will take care of you as usual. When I come back, we start the treatment proper."

Fielding shrank.

"Yes," said Restarick, seeing this. "Think about it while you have time. Small doses at first, you'll resist them of course, but you'll be given more and more, and eventually you'll be hooked. You know what happens to people who get hooked on heroin. They deteriorate. They gibber, and go grey, and stop washing. They do no work, even if they're offered it; they live, while they do live, only for their vice. Sad . . . but just what people might expect . . . or so they'll say when we turn you loose . . . of someone who's had a nervous breakdown. That was only the beginning, they'll say; that was when he started to crack up. Poor Fielding Gray."

"Please," said Fielding, "please don't do that to me."

N

"I must. I must frighten you into telling me what I *must* know, and in order to frighten you I must mean what I threaten. I do mean it, Mr. Gray. You choose; either you come clean or you turn dirty. Into a dirty, shambling junky . . . human refuse."

"Look," said Fielding, "I am a reasonable man and I am not brave. In the face of a threat like this, if I had anything that I could tell you, I should certainly yield. Can't you believe that?"

"Oh, I do. I believe that you will yield. The only question is when. For $50,000, which may still be waiting in Zürich, you obviously think it's worth resisting us till the very last moment. In the forlorn hope, I suppose, that something will turn up. Or perhaps you still think that we're bluffing?"

Fielding bowed his head.

"Well, nothing will turn up," Restarick said, "and as soon as I get back here you'll find out that we aren't bluffing. I'll be with you again just before Christmas, Mr. Gray; whether or not we shall make merry at that season must depend on you."

PART FIVE

THE WILL OF ZEUS

A few days before Christmas, Max de Freville's guests arrived at his villa. They were the Marquis Canteloupe, Minister of Commerce in the new Conservative Government, Somerset Lloyd-James, M.P. (Canteloupe's understrapper in the House of Commons), and Captain Detterling, M.P. and publisher, a distant cousin of Canteloupe.

"We'll have a nice quiet time this evening," Max told them as they sat drinking in one of the little arbours off his lawn. "Party night tomorrow."

"Good sort of party?" asked Canteloupe.

"Pandarus's Christmas piss-up."

"Pandarus?"

"The film company out here. Making *The Odyssey*."

"Good," said Detterling, "I'll be able to get hold of Fielding Gray."

"I don't think so," said Max, and told them about Fielding's nervous breakdown at Vassae.

"What's his trouble this time?" Canteloupe asked.

"Overwork," said Max.

"He's used to hard work," said Lloyd-James.

"This time he took on too much."

"You mean," said Detterling, "that he couldn't cope with writing for films?"

"More or less that."

"Well, I hope there's no permanent damage," said Detterling. "He's doing a book on Conrad for me and Gregory Stern. That's what I wanted to talk to him about. I'd better go and see him at Vassae."

"I wouldn't," said Max, "not until he's better."

He told them of the report which Sasha had brought back with her.

"Then I'll leave it till after Christmas," Detterling said. "He sounds a real mess. Has he been drinking?"

"He's always been drinking," said Lloyd-James, "but I thought I'd heard that this woman of his . . . Harriet something . . ."

". . . Ongley . . ." put in Detterling.

". . . I thought I'd heard that she kept him straight about his drinking."

"Harriet Ongley hasn't been here to keep him straight," said Max de Freville.

"You never know with boozers," Lord Canteloupe said, "but talking as an old soak myself, I find it very odd that he should have gone all the way to this Vassae place just to get himself sozzled. I mean to say, he could have done that here."

"No one said it *was* drink," Max reminded them. "The doctors say nervous breakdown."

"Whatever that may mean. Look at that fellow, Peter Morrison. They said he had a nervous breakdown, but all it was," said Canteloupe, "was a fit of pique because he didn't get a job when we came to power in June."

"He never expected one," said Detterling; "he couldn't have. He was out of the House for a good twelve years . . . right up till that by-election in sixty-eight."

"He expected something," insisted Canteloupe, "so when we gave him nothing he got into a tantrum, and they called it a nervous breakdown."

"He doesn't want anyone to know this," said Detterling, "but his elder son's got meningitis. That's what upset Peter."

"Oh," said Canteloupe bleakly. "Will the boy die?"

"Worse. He'll be potty for life. He'd just got a scholarship to Oxford."

"Oh," said Canteloupe again. "Let's go back to Fielding Gray."

"There's nothing to go back to," said Max. "He's had a mental breakdown, and some fellow from the American School of

Greek Studies found him in a bad way at Vassae. They're looking after him in a hostelry there. We'll be told when he's fit for visitors."

"I still don't understand," said Canteloupe, "why the devil he went to Vassae."

"Apparently he'd just wandered off there."

"He was always wandering off somewhere," said Somerset Lloyd-James.

"And so far," said Detterling, "he's always wandered back. But I do want to see him before I go home."

"Leave it a few days," said Max. "There'll be plenty of time to think about it after Christmas."

When Restarick arrived back at Vassae, he handed a small and stoutly wrapped parcel to Savidis.

"We'll be needing the things in there," said Restarick, "starting tomorrow. Unless he's changed his mind."

"He hasn't."

"No choice then. Where is he?"

"In his room. Playing chess with Aloysius."

Restarick went to Fielding's room and knocked on the door. Aloysius Sheath's voice told him to enter.

Fielding was lying on the bed, apparently asleep. Aloysius Sheath sat over a chess board on which the pieces were set ready for a game. Opposite Aloysius was an empty chair, at which he now pointed.

"He couldn't start," Aloysius said. "He lay down instead."

"Frightened, is he?"

"Sort of . . . numb. While you were away, he kept saying, 'I'd tell him everything . . . if only there were anything. Whatever he does, there's nothing new to say.' You don't suppose," suggested Aloysius, very low, "that he's telling the truth about that?"

"We can't give up now. Mr. Gray," said Restarick, shaking Fielding, "Mr. Gray."

Fielding stirred but did not open his eyes.

"I hear you," he mumbled. "So you're back?"

"Back to keep my word. We'll start tomorrow."

About the same time as Restarick was talking to Fielding,
Max de Freville and his friends arrived at the Corfu Palace
Hotel for the Pandarus Christmas piss-up.

Since Sasha Grimes had insisted that this should not be
elaborate or expensive, Foxy had concentrated on basic essen-
tials. He had provided an ample but plain buffet, two bottles
per head of cheap Thracian red wine for the entire company,
and a demotic band. The cheap Thracian wine was far stronger
than anyone had anticipated, and by the time Max and his
party got there it had wrought pretty fair havoc. Angus Carnavon had long since been carried off unconscious, and Margaret Lichfield was dancing frantically with Gretel.

"That lousy Lichfield wants my Gretel," Foxy greeted Max.
"Come to the bar."

On the way to the bar, they passed Sasha, who was dancing
in a refined but egalitarian way with the clapper-boy, and
Elena, who was sitting by the wall munching a huge plate of
cold fish.

"Come and meet the guests," said Foxy to Elena. "This here
is Dook Canteloupe, and Mr. Devonshire Lloyd-Thing, and
Colonel Dett. Dook, Devonshire, Colonel . . . this is li'l Elena,
luscious li'l Elena, lovely, luscious, prick-lifting li'l Elena,
lovely, luscious, lecherous . . ."

". . . For Christ's sake," said Elena, "give them food and
drink."

Food they declined, having prudently dined before coming,
but they accepted huge beakers of red wine. When Canteloupe
heard it was Thracian, he proposed a Thracian sconce.

"Sconce?" said Foxy.

"All down in one," said Canteloupe, and poured his whole
beaker into himself without even swallowing.

Foxy tried to do the same, but he gagged painfully half way
through and spouted a jet of wine into the air which came
down again on to Elena.

"You mother-fucking pig," said Elena, and put down her

fish with a clonk. "You ruined my dress."

"Elena baby . . . you come with me, and we'll take off that dress and dry it and—"

"—Balls," Elena said.

"Absent friends," said Canteloupe, raising another beaker. "Here's to that one-eyed bugger, Fielding Gray."

Canteloupe poured down his beaker and Elena gave him a quick look.

"You know Fielding Gray?"

"We all do," said Detterling.

"Never mind Fielding," said Foxy, "he's gone off his nut. Nice uncle Foxy-woxy buy li'l Elena a new dress . . . if li'l Elena come and take off the old one."

"I don't go for trips down memory lane," said Elena. "You get Gretel to take off her dress."

But Gretel was leaping through the exit arm in arm with Margaret Lichfield.

Meanwhile, Jules came over to talk with Max, and Somerset Lloyd-James went off to dance with a starlet. Detterling said he was going to have a little go in the Casino (which had now moved in from the Achilleion to the Corfu Palace) and Lord Canteloupe tackled his third beaker, listening vaguely to the conversation between Jules Jacobson and Max. Max had heard from his Greek pal Lykiadopoulos, and it seemed that Lykiadopoulos had got on to something in Italy which might suit Pandarus Films rather well after they were finished in Corfu.

"Can't talk properly in all this racket," Jules said. "Come up to my room for a bit."

"Back before long," said Max to Canteloupe. "Make yourself at home. They're a friendly bunch."

Max and Jules moved off together, and Canteloupe thought it would be nice to make himself at home with that jolly little girl who'd had all the wine spewed over her. Just at the moment, however, she still seemed to be having a pretty fierce conversation with the producer-chappie or whatever he was who'd done all the spewing. Leave them to it, Canteloupe thought : have another mug of this red infuriator first, and *then* we'll see. He moved off to the filling-point.

"Li'l Elena come with nuncle Foxy-woxy," Foxy was saying.

"What's in it for li'l Elena?" said Elena.

"I just said. A lovely new dress."

"Like a lovely new dress which costs five hundred quid," Elena said, "or a mink coat while we're about it."

"That's asking high, baby."

"Not for chewing your old cod, it's not."

"You listen to me, Elena baby. You're bugging me. I don't like greedy girls. You know what happens when people get greedy with Foxy? They come unstuck, baby, when they get too greedy with Foxy J. Galahead."

"Knackers."

"You don't believe me, baby? Then you think what happened to Fielding Gray. He got too greedy with Foxy, too greedy and too smart Master Fielding got . . . so now he's having a breakdown on the top of some fucking mountain."

"You mean . . . that was your work?"

Foxy sucked his wine.

"Sort of, baby. So you watch out, and you come and play pee-wee pies with uncle Foxy, or . . ."

". . . How did you do it, Foxy?" Elena said.

Foxy winked obscenely and belched, then sat down hard on the floor. Elena went over to Canteloupe, confiscated his beaker, and swept him on to the dance floor.

"Zow-eee," said Canteloupe, and put his right hand in the cleft of Elena's bottom.

"Dook Canteloupe . . . you're a friend of Fielding Gray's?"

"I know him a bit."

"This business at Vassae. There's something wrong."

"Thought it was odd when Max told me."

"I don't know the whys and the hows," Elena said, "but there's something in the oven that stinks. Fielding behaved like a swine to me, but I'm not letting him be done down like this. It just isn't decent."

Canteloupe stopped dancing, unhanded Elena's fesses, and looked at her carefully.

"What's not decent?" he asked.

"What they're doing to Fielding."

"How do you know?"

"Because of something I've just heard. Don't ask me any more, because I've got to live here till this lousy film's done. Just you go to Vassae and have a look for yourself."

"We thought of going after Christmas."

"Better go now," Elena said. "Now."

She hurried back to Foxy, who was now slumped against the bar.

"Come on," she said. "Let's go and play pee-wee pies."

"Great, baby." Foxy blundered up against her, spilling more wine on her dress. "Did I say anything just now?"

"Nothing much," Elena said.

"But you went away from me, baby."

"Just saying good-night to a friend. Come on, uncle Foxy-woxy, you come on with li'l Elena. . . ."

A good girl, that, thought Canteloupe. Nice botty. A warm, honest girl. She thinks Fielding Gray's a bastard, but some bigger bastard's shat on him a bit too hard, even for a bastard like Fielding Gray. 'Just you go to Vassae and have a look for yourself . . . now.'

Canteloupe rumbled off to the room which served as the Winter Casino, waved aside the doorman who asked for his ticket, and shipped Detterling off from the Chemmy table.

"But it's my bank next," said Detterling as Canteloupe led him out.

"Go to the telephone," said Canteloupe, "and see if the airport can fix us a private plane. To the airfield nearest Vassae . . . whatever it is."

"Kalamata, I'd say. Can't I run my bank first?"

"No," said Canteloupe, and sent Detterling reeling towards the concierge's desk.

Canteloupe then returned to the Pandarus piss-up and looked for Somerset Lloyd-James, who was prancing gawkily about with a fat girl whose navel was showing.

As the pair passed Canteloupe, he put both hands on Somerset's shoulders.

"Say good-night to Maisie," he said to Somerset.

"I'm called Beryl," the girl said.

"He knows what I mean."

"I'm damned if I do," said Somerset, his pimples glowing with resentment.

"We're going on a trip," said Canteloupe as he ushered Somerset off. "Fielding Gray's in trouble. I've been warned."

"Rubbish. You heard what Max said last night."

"And I heard what I've just heard now."

"Can't it wait till tomorrow? I was hoping to have one of these starlets. I've never had a starlet before."

"They're really only chorus girls."

"Then they'd be that much cheaper, wouldn't they? I can't imagine," Somerset said, "why you want to spoil the evening like this."

"Look," said Canteloupe. "Once upon a time we helped to sod up Fielding Gray, you and I. We had good reason, and I'm not ashamed of it, but we did sod him about something rotten, and now we've a chance to make it up. If my information is correct, that is."

"And if not?"

"We lose nothing except the price of a plane to Kalamata."

"*You* can pay for that," said Somerset lisping with annoyance, "ath you're tho keen. I'm thaving up for a thtarlet."

"Chorus girl," said Canteloupe. "Half of them have got clap. If you start bunking up with that lot, it's six to four on you'll be pissing fish-hooks within a week."

"That's not saying I want to spend good money on lunatic trips to Kalamata. Anyway, we couldn't possibly get there at this time of night."

"Yes, we can," said Detterling, who had just joined them. "We leave in thirty minutes flat. The pilot says there's room for four passengers, so Max can come too."

"Good," said Somerset, "that'll cut the cost."

"No," said Canteloupe, "no Max."

"Why on earth not?"

"Instinct. If my informant was right, there's something nasty going on. Why didn't Max tell us?"

"Perhaps he didn't know."

"Perhaps he didn't. But then again," said Canteloupe, "being Max, perhaps he did. So we go without him."

"But we can't just push off and say nothing."

"That's exactly what we must do," said Canteloupe. "Luckily Max has gone upstairs to talk business with that shonk called Jules something. When he comes down and doesn't see us, he'll think we've all got off with dirty girls from Pandarus, and he'll leave us to find our own way home. We'll be later than he thinks."

In the taxi on the way to the airport, Canteloupe told the others what Elena had said to him.

"But what in the world *can* be wrong?" said Detterling sceptically. "Why should anyone be . . . doing Fielding down . . . as this woman says?"

"Perhaps he's been up to his old tricks," said Somerset, "and underrated the opposition."

Now they were under way, Somerset was enjoying the expedition. Since he himself had no axe to grind (for once), he could simply go along and see the fun. He had always been amused by Fielding's antics and was glad of a chance to find out what was at the bottom of this one.

"Depend upon it," Somerset said, "he's been putting his hot little hand where he shouldn't, and somebody's got out a chopper."

"I only hope he can still use his typewriter," Detterling said. "Gregory and I are setting a lot of store on this book about Conrad."

But far better, Detterling reflected, that Fielding should be the victim of human malice (as now seemed to be the case) than that he should be suffering from a mental breakdown. With malice to combat one could at least see how one stood; with mental disorder there was no knowing where the thing began or ended.

"I rather hope," Detterling now said, "that your little girl was right, Canteloupe. Otherwise we're going to look frightfully silly, charging off like this."

"Better look silly now," said Canteloupe, "than soppy later."

The reason why Canteloupe had got everyone moving so quickly was that he was fiercely offended by the idea that anything untoward could happen to an Englishman (a gentleman at that, more or less) in a foreign country. He believed Elena because he had seen that she was amiable and honest; and believing her, he must assume that Fielding Gray was somehow being got at. Why or by whom was not clear, but one thing certainly was: it was all happening in some mucky little foreign state, and that it should be allowed to happen there showed a lack of respect for the English and for England. These days there was much too much of this kind of thing. Englishmen were being constantly abused and maltreated all over the globe, and no one lifted a finger, let alone despatched a gunboat. It just wouldn't do, thought Canteloupe, and here, thank God, was one instance at least in which the right man (himself) was on the spot when wanted.

"Remember, you two," Canteloupe said, "whatever's going on, we're English and we're on the side of Fielding Gray. We'll take no bloody nonsense from anyone . . . least of all from the natives."

Fielding turned sweatily in his bed. We start tomorrow, Restarick had said; tomorrow, which was now today. Three or four doses, Restarick had said, and you'll need it, you'll have to have it. And when we refuse it you'll talk. After that, of course, we'll set you free, but by then it'll be too late for you, you'll be hooked. So why, oh why, won't you tell us before we begin?

I've nothing to tell.

Oh dear, oh dear, oh dear, Restarick had said: then we start tomorrow.

Canteloupe and his chums reached Kalamata airport at four-thirty a.m. After a lot of telephoning Detterling procured them a taxi. "Vassae," said Canteloupe to the driver.

The driver shook his head.

"Near Andritsaena," said Detterling.

The driver spread his hands. Detterling took a touring map from his pocket and showed the driver the route. The driver laughed scornfully. Canteloupe took a large wad of money from his pocket and passed it under the driver's nose. The driver shrugged petulantly.

"He thinks it's too far," said Somerset. "Let me try."

Somerset took off his glasses and tapped the driver on the shoulder. As the driver turned, Somerset looked him in the eyes and grinned. The driver made a quick gesture with the fingers of one hand, turned back to the wheel, clicked off the inside light, and started up the car.

"What was all that about?" said Canteloupe.

"My irises are rather peculiar," said Somerset, replacing his glasses. "Simple people very often think that I have the Eye."

"Savidis knows how to give the injection," said Restarick. "It will be much easier for all of us if you don't struggle."

On the table lay a syringe, which Savidis now picked up.

"Take off your coat," said Savidis to Fielding, "and roll up your sleeve."

Aloysius Sheath came in.

"There are three men in dinner jackets," he said, "coming up the path. They can only be English."

Restarick went with Aloysius to the window. There in the bright morning were three black figures, walking in Indian file : an old man, tall and stooping but with a certain spring in his tread, was leading; a man of vaguely military style came second; and a shambling weed in spectacles brought up in the rear.

"Roll up your sleeve," said Savidis to Fielding.

"Put that thing down," said Restarick to Savidis, "and come with me to the front door." And to Aloysius : "You stay here with Mr. Gray."

When Savidis opened the front door, the old man in the dinner jacket nodded very politely.

"My name is Canteloupe," he said. "These gentlemen are Captain Detterling and Mr. Lloyd-James. We have come to see Major Fielding Gray."

Neither Savidis nor Restarick answered.

"This building does belong to the American School of Greek Studies?" Canteloupe said.

Savidis pointed to a plaque by the door which confirmed this.

"Well, we've had a devil of a job finding you, and now, if you please, we wish to speak with Major Gray."

"He is not well," said Restarick from behind Savidis.

"He will be none the worse for seeing three old friends."

"You don't understand . . ."

". . . That is why I am here. Kindly let me in." Savidis barred the door.

"I am a Minister of Her Britannic Majesty," said Canteloupe, "and these two gentlemen are members of the British Parliament. We demand to see Major Fielding Gray."

"Your writ does not run here," said Restarick.

"And we want none of your British arrogance," Savidis said.

Somerset took off his glasses, looked Savidis straight in the eye, and grinned. Savidis flinched and drew back.

"Peasants never change," said Canteloupe as he walked under the lintel. "You can educate them and dress them up and tell them they're free and equal . . . and the very first owl that screeches they're back on their knees, crossing themselves and snivelling. But you," he said to Restarick, "are not a peasant. You have not even that excuse for your obstinacy. What am I to say to you?"

"You can ask my pardon," said Restarick, "for trespassing on American property. And I shall grant it, on condition that you leave."

There was a scuffling noise from behind a door across the hall, and Fielding shot out, followed by a red-faced Aloysius.

"Oh Canteloupe," said Fielding breathily, "is it really you?"

"It is," said Canteloupe. "What the hell's going on?"

"They're keeping me here," sobbed Fielding. "They're giving me drugs and—"

"—Details later. You're not potty or anything?"

"I shall be if I don't get away."

"Then you can come with us. I ask your pardon," said Canteloupe to Restarick, "for trespassing on American property, and whether you grant it or not we shall now leave."

"Not with Gray."

"Yes, with Gray."

"He's ill, I tell you. Those drugs he's babbling about, he has to have them for his illness."

"Never mind all that." Canteloupe turned to Fielding. "Do you, or do you not, wish to come with us?"

"Yes," said Fielding, "for God's sake, yes."

"Then that is settled," Canteloupe said.

Restarick made a slight movement of menace in Fielding's direction.

"Don't be a cunt," Canteloupe said. "You cannot detain him by force without our bearing witness against you. You cannot detain us by force, because whoever you may be you dare not lay hands on a peer of the British Parliament and a Minister of the British Crown. I don't know what you were up to," said Canteloupe, "and I don't much care; but now I'm here, and that's an end of it. Major Gray is an Englishman and he's leaving with his English friends."

"He won't get far without his passport. You'll never find that without my help."

"If he travels with me," said the Marquis Canteloupe, "he won't need to worry about his passport." And to Fielding, "Come along, my dear fellow, I fancy we're no longer welcome here."

"Ridiculous foreigners," said Canteloupe as they all walked down the path. "All they need is to be *told*. The trouble is, no one's told them for so long that most people have forgotten how."

o

"It's considered wicked to tell them," Detterling said slyly. "It degrades them, you see."

"Degrades them? A superstitious Greek peasant and a couple of bent Yankees? Who the hell cares," said Canteloupe, "about degrading a shower of shit like that?"

"They were . . . very frightening," said Fielding.

"That's because there was no one there to put them in their place. Of course people can be frightening," Canteloupe said, "if you let them get out of hand. It's happening everywhere: students, coons, labourers, all getting out of hand because no one dares to *tell* them and put them in their place."

"They don't want to listen," said Somerset.

"They've never wanted to listen, but they always have if they were handled right. You just have to bounce them into it, that's what. Frighten them," said Canteloupe, "before they can frighten you."

"Superior fire-power," said Aloysius to Restarick. "You couldn't say no to an English Minister. Unfair opposition."

"If we'd had more time we might have managed. If we'd been warned. . . . Ah, well," said Restarick, "that's that. This round we lose." He picked the syringe off the table on which Savidis had left it half an hour before. "I wonder," he said, "if Gray would ever have realised that there was only a mild tranquilliser in this syringe. That was what really interested me, you know. Lampas we can deal with when and as they show their hand. What fascinated me was not so much what Gray might have had to tell us as the process of breaking him down . . . of reducing him to a gibbering wreck by entirely illusory means. Illusory threats," he mused, "are so much cheaper and less harmful and less incriminating than substantial ones. And just as effective. But there's one thing wrong with them."

"As we've just seen," Aloysius said.

"Yes. It only needs some coarse brute like Canteloupe to appear," said Restarick, "and the whole delicate structure crumbles at the sound of his voice."

"Well," said Canteloupe in the taxi back to Kalamata, "what now? Back to Corfu?"

"No," said Fielding, "or not for me." And he gave a broad account of all that had happened, as far as his own knowledge would serve, playing down his own treachery and playing up everyone else's.

"So it looks as if Max had a hand in it," said Somerset.

"If you remember," said Canteloupe with satisfaction, "I said something of the kind last night. In all the circumstances, we can hardly go back to his villa."

"We can't walk around in dinner jackets for the rest of our lives," said Detterling.

"Well now," said Canteloupe. "You know Max best, so you can go back to Corfu and collect our kit."

"And mine, please," said Fielding. "It's still in the Corfu Palace, I suppose."

"And then you can rejoin us," said Canteloupe, "and we can all go somewhere *nice* for Christmas before going on home. How about Monte? It can be very agreeable in December."

"I wath looking forward to a free holiday," Somerset whined.

"So were we all. But whichever way you look at it," Canteloupe said, "I think we should be wise to leave Greece without undue delay. We'll call in at the Embassy in Athens, to arrange about a passport for Gray and make sure there are no other little difficulties . . . and then we'll take an aeroplane for Nice. And I for one," he said, peering out of the window at the grey scrub and the grey rock, "shall not be sorry to be gone."

From his office behind the American Express in Corfu, the Pandarus accountant in the Red Indian get-up put through another routine weekly payment to Zürich for credit of Fielding Gray. That Fielding was absent, and had been for some time, he was well aware; but no one had told him to suspend Fielding's salary. Although this was probably an oversight, he wasn't going to enquire into the matter, because he was glad of his own five per cent every week, and what was more, he had rather liked Fielding.

'Let him have his dream money,' the accountant thought, 'and much good may it do him, wherever he may be.'

Some weeks after he left Vassae, Fielding had a letter from Jules Jacobson.

'. . . And so now we are nearly finished with the shooting, almost a month ahead of the original schedule. This means that all the more time and money will be available for cutting and tidying, and when that's been done I think I can promise a very passable picture.

'I missed you after your departure, in every way. However, I flatter myself that I got by rather well with completing the script, and Sasha was very clever at going over my stuff and adapting the style to match what you had already written for us. She was upset when she heard that your chums were removing you to England, because until then she'd always hoped you would come back to her in Corfu; but Max de Freville assured her it was all for the best, as your friends had your welfare much at heart. So Sasha settled back to work and was if anything more helpful than ever; I think she saw herself as performing a loyal duty, *in piam memoriam* to you, so to speak. But her piety did not extend to fidelity : she has consoled herself by an affair with the clapper-boy, and there is even talk of their being married some time soon.

'But to get back to our film . . . and when I say "our" I mean it. I have not forgotten the excellent work you put in before other ambitions intervened, and I have arranged that you shall have a full-screen credit. We are not ungrateful, you see. As for money—well, you probably know by now that Foxy, amid all his other preoccupations, forgot to cancel your salary payments. You were paid out for the full period of your contract. Foxy was furious when he found out, but eventually he agreed with me that all things considered justice of a kind had been done.

'So all's well that ends well, except that it might have ended so much better. You see, Fielding, after what you tried to do to Pandarus we can never employ you again. This is a great pity, as Lykiadopoulos has just returned, after a long absence in Italy, with news of a really splendid project of Cine-Milano's . . . in which, at Lyki's suggestion, they have invited Pandarus and Clytemnestra to cooperate. They are to film *The Golden Ass*; I am to direct. Preliminary work starts in six months' time (when I shall be finally finished with Odysseus) and next July or August I must begin preparing a script with the assistance of a suitable script-writer. We have all been telling each other that it would have been just the thing for you. Only now, of course, it is not for you. . . .'

Just the thing for me, Fielding thought, as he looked across the salt marshes to the sea. Six months to get well on with Conrad, and then a nice fat fee for scripting *The Golden Ass*. Only now, of course, it is not for me.

And yet . . . all things considered, as Jules had said . . . he had got much of what he wanted. He had got £10,000 in a Swiss bank, and he had, it appeared, got rid of Harriet. For the time at least. When he had reached London, after Christmas with Canteloupe at Monte, he had telephoned Broughton Staithe to announce that he would arrive there the evening after next. (He would have to live somewhere while deciding on his next move, and even to old friends of Tessie's Buttock's Hotel did not, these days, come cheap.) A rather small-voiced Harriet had said yes, everything would be ready for him; and so it had been . . . a fire in the grate, the water hot for his bath, and a nice stew cooking in the oven. But there had been no Harriet. The car was still in the garage and there was no message on the pad in the hall, so at first he had thought she must have gone out just for a few minutes (perhaps they were short of whisky and she had walked up the road to the off-licence): but the minutes had become hours and the hours days, and still there was no sign or word of Harriet. She's rumbled me at last, he thought when a week had passed by; she's rumbled me and she's left me and now there will be peace and quiet.

£10,000 (or rather £9500) tax free; no Harriet; peace and

quiet. But how was he to get the money to England? Dream gold, the Pandaras accountant had said, would turn to dross if carried over the English Channel. Should he go abroad then? After all, he could suit himself. But where to? There was no point in going anywhere unless there were people to wish it and resent it, unless there were people to weep at his departure and others to welcome his arrival. If no one cared where he went, there was no pleasure in going. Anyway, he wanted to be in England for a while; England, as Canteloupe was always saying, was the only decent country left. But England without Harriet? For at least Harriet had been something to fuck (however tedious the process) and somebody to swear at. At least Harriet had cared what he did. And Harriet had money. . . .

Well, perhaps she would be back and perhaps she wouldn't. Meanwhile, he had enough money of his own in England for the time being: after all, his first four weeks' salary from Pandarus had been sent to his English bank, and Gregory Stern was to pay a very fair advance for his book on Conrad. Conrad; work; there was his consolation. Work never let a man down . . . as long as he could still do it. Work suffereth long, and is kind; work vaunteth not itself, is not puffed up. Doth not behave itself unseemly. . . . He would sit down at Broughton and work. In loneliness? Yes, but also in tranquillity. In happiness? No, but in seemly acceptance of his lot. And there could have been many worse lots. The hours would pass quickly, he knew, the weeks would be gone almost before he noticed them, and always at his left hand the pile of written sheets would grow steadily thicker, witness and measure of his work.

So now he would walk on the salt marshes for a little and look at the crumbling gun-sites, and remember, as he always did, that first summer after the war. Then along the beach and across the golf course (oh Angela, Angela, striding over the turf); and then back to the empty house, to sit at his desk and make some notes on *Nostromo*, lifting his head from time to time to look at the never-resting sea.

PRINCIPAL CHARACTERS IN
ALMS FOR OBLIVION

The *Alms for Oblivion* sequence will consist of ten novels, of which eight so far have been published. They are, in chronological order: *Fielding Gray* (FG), set in 1945; *Sound the Retreat* (SR), 1945–6; *The Sabre Squadron* (SS), 1952; *The Rich Pay Late* (RPL), 1955–6; *Friends in Low Places* (FLP), 1959; *The Judas Boy* (JB), 1962; *Places Where They Sing* (PWTS), 1967; *Come Like Shadows* (CLS), 1970.

What follows is an alphabetical list of the more important characters, showing in which of the novels they have each appeared and briefly suggesting their roles.

Balliston, Hugh: an undergraduate of Lancaster College, Cambridge, in 1967 (PWTS).

Beatty, Miss: a secretary in the firm of Salinger & Holbrook (RPL). † 1956 (RPL).

Beck, Tony: a young Fellow of Lancaster College, well known as a literary critic (PWTS).

Beyfus, The Lord (life Peer): a social scientist, Fellow of Lancaster College (PWTS).

Blakeney, Balbo: a biochemist, Fellow of Lancaster College (PWTS).

Blessington, Ivan: school friend of Fielding Gray in 1945 (FG); later a regular officer in The 49th Earl Hamilton's Light Dragoons (Hamilton's Horse); ADC to his Divisional Commander in Germany in 1952 (SS); by 1955 an attaché at the British Embassy in Washington (RPL).

von Bremke, Herr Doktor Aeneas: a prominent mathematician at the University of Göttingen (SS).

Brockworthy, Lieutenant-Colonel: Commanding Officer of the 1st Battalion, the Wessex Fusiliers, at Berhampore in 1946 (SR).

Bunce, Basil: Squadron Sergeant-Major of the 10th Sabre

Squadron of Earl Hamilton's Light Dragoons at Göttingen in 1952 (SS), and on Santa Kytherea in 1955 (*ref.* FG).

Bungay, Piers: Subaltern officer of the 10th Sabre Squadron at Göttingen in 1952 (SS).

Buttock, Mrs. Tessie: owner of Buttock's Hotel in the Cromwell Road (RPL, FLP, JB, CLS), a convenient establishment much favoured by Tom Llewyllyn and Fielding Gray *q.v.*

Canteloupe, The Marchioness (Molly): wife of The Marquis Canteloupe (FLP, SR).

CANTELOUPE, The Most Honourable the Marquis: father of The Earl of Muscateer (SR); distant cousin of Captain Detterling *q.v.* and political associate of Somerset Lloyd-James *q.v.*; successful operator of his 'Stately Home' and in 1959 Parliamentary Secretary for the Development of British Recreational Resources (FLP); Minister of Public Relations and Popular Media in 1962 (JB): Shadow Minister of Commerce in 1967 (PWTS); Minister of Commerce in the Conservative Government of 1970 (CLS).

Carnavon, Angus: leading male star in the Pandarus/Clytemnestra Film Production of *The Odyssey* on Corfu in 1970 (CLS).

Chead, 'Corpy': Corporal-Major (*i.e.* Colour Sergeant) of the 10th Sabre Squadron at Göttingen (SS).

Clewes, The Reverend Oliver: Chaplain to Lancaster College (PWTS).

CONSTABLE, Robert Reculver (Major): demobilised with special priority in the summer of 1945 to take up appointment as Tutor of Lancaster College, Cambridge (FG); by 1955 Vice-Chancellor of the University of Salop, and *ex officio* member of the Board of *Strix* (RPL); elected Provost of Lancaster in 1959 (FLP); still Provost in 1962 (JB) and 1967 (PWTS).

Corrington, Mona: an anthropologist, Fellow of Girton College, Cambridge. Chum of Lord Beyfus *q.v.* (PWTS).

Cruxtable, Sergeant-Major: Company Sergeant-Major of Peter Morrison's Company at the O.T.S., Bangalore, in 1945–6 (SR); 'P.T. expert' at Canteloupe's physical fitness camp in the west country (FLP).

DETTERLING, Captain: distant cousin of Lord Canteloupe;

regular officer of The 49th Earl Hamilton's Light Dragoons (Hamilton's Horse) from 1937; in charge of recruiting for the Cavalry in 1945 (FG); instructor at the O.T.S., Bangalore, from late 1945 to summer 1946 (SR); by 1952 has retired from Hamilton's Horse and become a Member of Parliament (SS); still M.P. in 1955 and a political supporter of Peter Morrison *q.v.* (RPL); still M.P. in 1959, when he joins Gregory Stern *q.v.* as a partner in Stern's publishing house (FLP); still M.P. and publisher in 1962 (JB) and 1970 (CLS).

Dexterside, Ashley: friend and employee of Donald Salinger (RPL).

Dharaparam, H.H. The Maharajah of: an Indian Prince; Patron of the Cricket Club of the O.T.S., Bangalore (SR).

Dilkes, Henry: Secretary to the Institute of Political and Economic Studies and a member of the Board of *Strix* (RPL, FLP).

Dixon, Alastair: Member of Parliament for safe Conservative seat in the west country; about to retire in 1959 (FLP), thus creating a vacancy coveted both by Peter Morrison and Somerset Lloyd-James *q.v.*

Drew, Vanessa: *v.* Salinger, Donald.

Elena: 'starlet' in Pandarus/Clytemnestra production of *The Odyssey* on Corfu in 1970 (CLS).

Engineer, Margaret Rose: an Eurasian harlot who entertains Peter Morrison *q.v.* in Bangalore (SR).

de FREVILLE, Max: gambler and connoisseur of human affairs; runs big chemin-de-fer games in the London of the fifties (RPL), maintaining a private spy-ring for protection from possible welshers and also for the sheer amusement of it (FLP); later goes abroad to Venice, Hydra, Cyprus and Corfu, where he engages in various enterprises (FLP, JB, CLS), often in partnership with Lykiadopoulos *q.v.* and usually attended by Angela Tuck *q.v.* His Corfiot interests include a share in the 1970 Pandarus/Clytemnestra production of *The Odyssey* (CLS).

Frith, Hetta: girl friend of Hugh Balliston *q.v.* (PWTS). † 1967 (PWTS).

Galahead, Foxe J. (Foxy): Producer for Pandarus and

Clytemnestra Films of *The Odyssey* on Corfu in 1970 (CLS).

Gamp, Jonathan: a not so young man about town (RPL, FLP).

Gilzai Kahn, Captain: an Indian officer (Moslem) holding the King's Commission; an instructor at the O.T.S., Bangalore, 1945–6; resigns to become a political agitator (SR). † 1946 (SR).

Glastonbury, Major Giles: old friend of Detterling *q.v.* and regular officer of Hamilton's Horse; temporary Lieutenant-Colonel on Lord Wavell's staff in India 1945–6 (SR); officer commanding the 10th Sabre Squadron of Hamilton's Horse at Göttingen in 1952 (SS).

Grange, Lady Susan: marries Lord Philby (RPL).

Gray, John Aloysius (Jack): Fielding Gray's father (FG). † 1945.

Gray, Mrs.: Fielding Gray's mother (FG). † *c.* 1948.

GRAY, Major Fielding: senior schoolboy in 1945 (FG) with Peter Morrison and Somerset Lloyd-James *q.v.*; scholar elect of Lancaster College, but tangles with the authorities, is deprived of his scholarship before he can take it up (FG), and becomes a regular officer of Earl Hamilton's Light Dragoons; 2 i/c and then O.C. the 10th Sabre Squadron in Göttingen in 1952 (SS) and still commanding the Squadron on Santa Kytherea in 1955 (FG); badly mutilated in Cyprus in 1958 and leaves the Army to become critic and novelist with the help of Somerset Lloyd-James (FLP); achieves minor distinction, and in 1962 is sent out to Greece and Cyprus by Tom Llewyllyn *q.v.* to investigate Cypriot affairs, past and present, for BBC Television (JB); in Greece meets Harriet Ongley *q.v.*; by 1967 has won the Joseph Conrad Prize for Fiction (PWTS); goes to Corfu in 1970 to rewrite script for Pandarus/Clytemnestra's *The Odyssey* (CLS).

Grimes, Sasha: a talented young actress playing in Pandarus/Clytemnestra's *The Odyssey* on Corfu (CLS).

The Headmaster of Fielding Gray's school (FG): a man of conscience.

Helmutt, Jacquiz: historian; research student at Lancaster College in 1952 (SS); later Fellow of Lancaster (PWTS).

Holbrook, Jude: partner of Donald Salinger *q.v.* 1949–56 (RPL); 'freelance' in 1959 (FLP); reported by Burke Lawrence *q.v.* (CLS) as having gone to live in Hong Kong in the sixties.

Holbrook, Penelope: a model; wife of Jude Holbrook (RPL); by 1959, divorced from Jude and associated with Burke Lawrence (FLP); reported by Burke Lawrence (CLS) as still living in London and receiving alimony from Jude in Hong Kong.

Holeworthy, R. S. M.: Regimental Sergeant-Major of the Wessex Fusiliers at Göttingen in 1952 (SS).

Jacobson, Jules: old hand in the film world; Director of Pandarus/Clytemnestra's *The Odyssey* on Corfu in 1970 (CLS).

James, Cornet Julian: Cambridge friend of Daniel Mond *q.v.*; in 1952 a National Service officer of the 10th Sabre Squadron at Göttingen (SS).

Lamprey, Jack: subaltern officer of the 10th Sabre Squadron (SS).

La Soeur, Doctor: a confidential practitioner, physician to Fielding Gray (FG, RPL, CLS).

Lawrence, Burke: 'film director' and advertising man (RPL); from *c.* 1956 to 1959 teams up with Penelope Holbrook *q.v.* in murky 'agency' (FLP); *c.* 1960 leaves England for Canada, and later becomes P.R.O. to Clytemnestra Films (CLS).

Lewson, Mark: a con man (RPL, FLP). † 1959 (FLP).

Lewson, Felicity: born Contessina Felicula Maria Monteverdi; educated largely in England; wife of Mark Lewson (though several years his senior) and his assistant in his profession (RPL). † 1959 (FLP).

Lichfield, Margaret: star actress playing Penelope in the Pandarus/Clytemnestra production of *The Odyssey* on Corfu in 1970 (CLS).

LLEWYLLYN, Tom: a 'scholarship boy' of low Welsh origin but superior education; author, journalist and contributor to *Strix* (RPL); same but far more successful by 1959, when he marries Patricia Turbot *q.v.* (FLP); given important contract by BBC Television in 1962 to produce *Today is History*, and later that year appointed Namier Fellow of Lancaster College (JB); renewed as Namier Fellow in 1965 and still at Lancaster in 1967 (PWTS); later made a permanent Fellow of the College (CLS); employed by Pandarus and Clytemnestra Films as 'Literary and Historical Adviser' to their production of *The Odyssey* on Corfu in 1970 (CLS).

Llewyllyn, Tullia: always called and known as 'Baby'; Tom and Patricia's daughter, born in 1960 (JB, PWTS, CLS).

LLOYD-JAMES, Somerset: a senior schoolboy and friend of Fielding Gray in 1945 (FG); by 1955, Editor of *Strix*, an independent economic journal (RPL); still editor of *Strix* in 1959 (FLP) and now seeking a seat in Parliament; still editor of *Strix* in 1962 (JB), but now also a Member of Parliament and unofficial adviser to Lord Canteloupe *q.v.*; still M.P. and close associate of Canteloupe in 1967 (PWTS), and by 1970 Canteloupe's official understrapper in the House of Commons (CLS).

Lykiadopoulos, Stratis: a Greek gentleman, or not far off it; professional gambler and man of affairs (FLP) who has a brief liaison with Mark Lewson; friend and partner of Max de Freville *q.v.* (FLP), with whom he has business interests in Cyprus (JB) and later in Corfu (CLS).

Maisie: a whore (RPL, FLP, JB) frequented with enthusiasm by Fielding Gray, Lord Canteloupe and Somerset Lloyd-James; apparently still going strong as late as 1967 (*ref.* PWTS) and even 1970 (ref. CLS).

Mayerston: a revolutionary (PWTS).

Mond, Daniel: a mathematician; research student of Lancaster College (SS) sent to Göttingen University in 1952 to follow up his line of research, which unexpectedly turns out to have a military potential; later Fellow of Lancaster and teacher of pure mathematics (PWTS).

Morrison, Helen: Peter Morrison's wife (RPL, FLP).

MORRISON, Peter: senior schoolboy with Fielding Gray and Somerset Lloyd-James *q.v.* in 1945 (FG); an officer cadet at the O.T.S., Bangalore, from late 1945 to summer 1946 (SR) and then commissioned as a Second Lieutenant in the Wessex Fusiliers, whom he joins at Berhampore; by 1952 has inherited substantial estates in East Anglia and by 1955 is a Member of Parliament (RPL) where he leads 'the Young England Group'; but in 1956 applies for Chiltern Hundreds (RPL); tries and fails to return to Parliament in 1959 (FLP); reported by Lord Canteloupe (CLS) as having finally got a seat again after a by-election in 1968 and as having retained it at the General Election in 1970.

Morrison, 'Squire': Peter's father (FG), owner of a fancied race-horse (Tiberius). † c. 1950.

Mortleman, Alister: an officer cadet at the O.T.S., Bangalore, 1945–6, later commissioned into the Wessex Fusiliers (SR).

Motley, Mick: Lieutenant of the R.A.M.C., attached to the Wessex Fusiliers at Göttingen in 1952 (SS).

Murphy, 'Wanker': an officer cadet at the O.T.S., Bangalore, 1945–6; later commissioned as Captain in the Education Corps, then promoted to be Major and Galloper to the Viceroy of India (SR). † 1946 (SR).

Muscateer, Earl of: son of Lord and Lady Canteloupe q.v.; an officer cadet at the O.T.S., Bangalore, 1945–6 (SR). † 1946 (SR).

Nicos: a Greek boy who picks up Fielding Gray (JB).

Ogden, The Reverend Andrew: Dean of the Chapel of Lancaster College (PWTS).

Ongley, Mrs. Harriet: rich American widow; Fielding Gray's mistress and benefactress from 1962 onwards (JB, PWTS, CLS).

Pappenheim, Herr: German ex-officer of World War II; in 1952 about to rejoin new West German Army as a senior staff officer (SS).

Percival, Leonard: cloak-and-dagger man; in 1952 nominally a Lieutenant of the Wessex Fusiliers at Göttingen (SS), but by 1962 working strictly in plain clothes (JB); friend of Max de Freville, with whom he occasionally exchanges information to their mutual amusement (JB).

Percival, Rupert: a small-town lawyer in the west country (FLP), prominent among local Conservatives and a friend of Alastair Dixon q.v.; Leonard Percival's uncle (JB).

Philby, The Lord: proprietor of Strix (RPL, FLP) which he has inherited along with his title from his father, 'old' Philby.

Pough (pronounced Pew), The Honourable Grantchester FitzMargrave: Senior Fellow of Lancaster College, Professor Emeritus of Oriental Geography, at one time celebrated as a mountaineer; a dietary fadist (PWTS).

Restarick, Earle: American cloak-and-dagger man; in 1952 apparently a student at Göttingen University (SS) but in fact taking an unwholesome interest in the mathematical researches of Daniel Mond *q.v.*; later active in Cyprus (JB) and in Greece (CLS).

Roland, Christopher: a special school friend of Fielding Gray (FG). † 1945 (FG).

Salinger, Donald: senior partner of Salinger & Holbrook, a printing firm (RPL); in 1956 marries Vanessa Drew (RPL); is deserted by Jude Holbrook *q.v.* in the summer of 1956 (RPL) but in 1959 is still printing (FLP), and still married to Vanessa.

Schottgatt, Doctor Emile: of Montana University, Head of the 'Creative Authentication Committee' of the Oglander-Finckelstein Trust, which visits Corfu in 1970 (CLS) to assess the merits of the Pandarus/Clytemnestra production of *The Odyssey*.

Schroeder, Alfie: a reporter employed by the Billingsgate Press (RPL, FLP, SS); by 1967 promoted to columnist (PWTS).

Sheath, Aloysius: a scholar on the staff of the American School of Greek Studies in Athens, but also assistant to Earle Restarick *q.v.* (JB, CLS).

Stern, Gregory: publisher (RPL), later in partnership with Captain Detterling *q.v.* (FLP); publishes Tom Llewyllyn and Fielding Gray *q.v.* (RPL, FLP, JB, PWTS, CLS); married to Isobel Turbot (FLP).

Strange, Barry: an officer cadet at the O.T.S., Bangalore, 1945–6, later commissioned into the Wessex Fusiliers, with whom he has strong family connections (SR).

Tuck: a tea-planter in India; marries Angela, the daughter of a disgraced officer, and brings her back to England in 1945 (FG); later disappears, but turns up as an official of the Control Commission in Germany in 1952 (SS). † 1956 (RPL).

TUCK, Mrs. Angela: daughter of a Colonel in the Indian Army Pay Corps, with whom she lives in Southern India (*ref.* JB, FLP) until early 1945, when her father is dismissed the Service for malversation; being then *in extremis* marries Tuck the tea-planter, and returns with him to England in the summer of 1945 (FG); briefly mistress to the adolescent Somerset Lloyd-

James *q.v.*, and to 'Jack' Gray (Fielding's father); despite this a trusted friend of Fielding's mother (FG); by 1955 is long separated from Tuck and now mistress to Jude Holbrook (RPL); in 1956 inherits small fortune from the intestate Tuck, from whom she has never been actually divorced *pace* her bibulous and misleading soliloquies on the subject in the text (RPL); in 1959 living in Menton and occasional companion of Max de Freville *q.v.* (FLP); later Max's constant companion (JB, CLS). † 1970 (CLS).

Turbot, The Right Honourable Sir Edwin, P. C., Kt: politician; in 1946 ex-Minister of wartime coalition accompanying all-party delegation of M.P.s to India (SR); by 1959 long since a Minister once more, and 'Grand Vizier' of the Conservative Party (FLP); father of Patricia, who marries Tom Llewyllyn (FLP), and of Isobel, who marries Gregory Stern (FLP); by 1962 reported as badly deteriorating and as having passed some of his fortune over to his daughters (JB). † by 1967 (PWTS), having left more money to daughters.

Turbot, Isobel: *v.* Turbot, Sir Edwin, and Stern, Gregory.

Turbot, Patricia: *v.* Turbot, Sir Edwin, and Lleweyllyn, Tom. Also *v.* Llewyllyn, Tullia. Has brief walk-out with Hugh Balliston *q.v.* (PWTS) and is disobliging to Tom about money (JB, PWTS, CLS).

Weir, Carton: Member of Parliament and political associate of Peter Morrison (RPL); later official aide to Lord Canteloupe (FLP, JB).

Winstanley, Ivor: a distinguished Latinist, Fellow of Lancaster College (PWTS).

Zaccharias: an officer cadet at the O.T.S., Bangalore, 1945–6; commissioned into a dowdy regiment of the line (SR).